Dedication

To my mother who shared with me her love of books.

Prologue

"Is this Hell?" Olivia asked.

"No, this is purgatory."

Purgatory gave the illusion of suspension with a tease of freedom.

"As a demon, shouldn't you be in Hell?"

"We cling to the dream of returning one day."

"How are you planning to do that?"

"Why do you think you're here?"

****

The colored sticks floated just above her bed. Fascinated, she watched them rise almost as tall as the light overhead. Once she got used to balancing them, she focused harder, and they slowly began to spin. That's when Gran walked in.

"Olivia!"

Olivia jumped, severing the connection. The crayons fell to the ground, hitting the wooden floor like raindrops. She really hoped none of them broke. They were an unexpected treat.

Olivia bowed her head and stared at the floor like she was supposed to do in prayer. She never closed her eyes when Gran said the words because of the flashes in the dark; purples, reds, and the soft glow of green that looked like her own eyes in the mirror. But the brightest ones were the yellow ones. Olivia learned if she kept her eyes open, she would know what was real and what

1

was only lurking in the corner on the other side.

Olivia sat very still, trying not to tremble. She was surprised at how loud Gran could scream. The only time she came close was when Gran caught her staring too long into the fire they built last year for Winter Solstice. She was mesmerized by the dancing colors tangled in the flames. They spun and spun until they became something else. Were they monsters, or were they friends? Olivia would never know because just as she started toward them, Gran jerked her back, almost pulling off her coat.

Olivia shut out the memory and concentrated on the rhythmical tick-tock of the clock in the hall. It was soothing compared to the silence surrounding her. It was deafening, almost as loud as Gran. Olivia resisted clamping her hands over her ears. Gran had told her not to do that. It called attention to herself. Even if she could hear or see things no one else could see, Olivia was supposed to act like everyone else.

Despite her best efforts, Olivia felt the energy she used to spin the crayons creeping down her neck. It was like a candle she lit and forgot to blow out. She pulled her knees up to her chin, trying to keep it inside, but it was seeping out, making the air feel heavy. Olivia doubted Gran could feel it, not yet anyway, but the crayons were growing restless in the corner. If she didn't stop them, they would lift off again.

Olivia visualized a candle. She pursed her lips and imagined she was blowing out candles on a birthday cake. The scene reminded her of the pink frosting she watched Gran make and how Gran let her spread it on her chocolate cake.

It worked. The crayons stayed on the ground where

they belonged.

Ginny Larsin felt the hair on her arms slowly start to rise. "Olivia Esme Osborne."

Olivia knew Gran was serious when she included all of her names.

"That's not what crayons are for," Ginny scolded, relieved the prick of energy was gone before she had to say more.

"I like looking at the colors and mixing them together. Do you think my father's eyes are yellow?" Olivia asked, hoping to distract her, but all it did was make Gran upset again.

Gran inhaled loudly. She called it a 'cleansing' breath. It meant Olivia had asked the wrong question.

"Why would you say that?" Ginny wanted to know.

"You told me my mother had blue eyes. I have green. Yellow and blue make green. It's science," Olivia tried to explain.

Ginny's eyes narrowed. Her granddaughter was too clever for an eight-year-old, and the line between science and magic was thin.

"Prayers sound like spells," Olivia said meekly.

Ginny clamped down on her thoughts. *Was Olivia reading her mind?*

Olivia squirmed at the silence. It felt like a vacuum this time. She concentrated on the multiplication tables she was learning in school. It kept her out of Gran's head and Gran out of hers. If Gran could even get in there. Gran would be angry if she learned the spinning crayons was what got her invited to the birthday party.

Olivia had looked forward to the party for weeks. When she got there, it was just like she imagined birthday parties were supposed to be. There were balloons and more presents than Olivia had ever seen. There were kids from school and some that weren't.

Amber insisted she show the trick to the other kids. Only then it was with the little silver jacks and the red bouncy ball. Olivia made them float just above the floor in Amber's room. For once, Olivia didn't care that Amber had a mommy and a daddy. Things Olivia didn't have didn't matter that day. Everything was grand until the magician showed up. Olivia knew he wasn't magic. She also didn't like how he looked at Amber and the other girls. He looked at her too, but only once. Olivia wondered if her eyes turned funny because he never looked her way again. He didn't even notice when she watched him slip into the bathroom.

He said he needed to wash his hands, but he lied. He went inside so he could unlock the window. He planned to come back later to do bad things to Amber, but only after he hurt her mommy and daddy. Olivia told Amber's mommy, but to her surprise, she called Gran.

Olivia waited under a tree while the other kids went inside, watching Gran talk to Amber's parents. Gran tried to tell them she didn't use words like that in front of her granddaughter. Gran told them Olivia didn't even know what those words meant. She told them Olivia had no idea what mommies and daddies did in private, but they didn't care. They just wanted Gran to take her away. Olivia didn't get any birthday cake or ice cream. On the way home, Gran bought her the new crayons she had been asking for instead. The ones she had were all broken and not from coloring.

"Livie? Are you listening to me?"

The use of her pet name meant Gran was softening. Her mad was going away–seeping into the air. It would be easy to raise the crayons again, but Olivia didn't dare.

"Yes, ma'am," Olivia assured her with a nod and direct eye contact. It told her Olivia was listening to her and not to something else.

"Where did you learn that trick?" Ginny wanted to know. Levitation was an advanced skill. It was beyond her level of expertise. Of course, there was always the possibility that Livie might not be doing it. The thought didn't make Ginny feel any better.

"Alice," Olivia admitted.

Ginny bent down so she was at eye level with her granddaughter. Ginny cursed herself for ever telling Olivia the story of her school friend who was killed in front of their house.

"Livie, you can't blame everything on Alice." Because of her gifts, Olivia was susceptible to spirits. Boundaries were something Olivia would have to learn.

"Not even the lights?" Olivia asked meekly.

They blinked again last night when Olivia was in the bath. Rather than answer the question, Ginny pulled Olivia in for a hug. With no real friends, was it surprising Olivia had an imaginary one? Instead of worrying about the money she didn't have for an electrician, Ginny thought about the plant on the window-sill in the kitchen. The sage belonged to Ginny's mother and her mother before her. She could use it to cleanse the house. Maybe the electrician didn't find anything wrong because the problem wasn't electrical.

"You may not realize it, but everything I do is to

keep you safe."

"Like the crayons? And at the party?" Olivia asked dutifully. Asking questions told Gran she was listening.

Ginny felt terrible all over again. The birthday disaster was over a week ago. She had hoped Olivia had moved past it. She should have known better.

"Amber's parents sounded mad, but they weren't. Not really. They were just scared," Olivia explained.

Ginny learned there was a break-in—as predicted. Ginny couldn't help but wonder who Amber's parents were more scared of now, the magician or Olivia.

"They were afraid of me, not him," Olivia said. "Are you afraid—"

Ginny shushed her. "Of course not. Go outside and play." She couldn't have Olivia reading her thoughts.

No matter what Gran said, Olivia couldn't help but think she was in trouble. But she guessed the backyard was better than locking her inside a closet. That's what her friend Gayle's mother did. She wasn't allowed to play with Gayle anymore. Not after she told Gran what went on at Gayle's house. Burning the plant on the window-sill wouldn't work, but if Olivia told Gran, it would upset her all over again. Gran had enough to worry about, so Olivia kept quiet.

Later that night, the dark came, and with it, the whispers.

"Forget about the trick. Gran won't always be around to tell you what to do."

Chapter One

Rogan Poe was supposed to be sleeping, but away from Olivia. He was too keyed up to sleep. Poe spent his time counting the minutes until he could return. He headed for the ICU with only minutes to spare before the end of visiting hours. The preordained times meant nothing to him. He wasn't there to pay a visit but to stand watch over Olivia while the rest of the hospital slept.

At least Barry Bartholomew had warned him the archbishop would be there. Barry was running on even less sleep, and the ICU was always in need of a cross-bearer. When Poe arrived Nicefero Saldaña Mendoza was the only one occupying the waiting room outside the doors of the locked unit.

"Does he know?" Mendoza asked.

It wasn't a greeting, but it made Poe stop. Something he hadn't planned on doing.

Poe turned around to give Mendoza his due, surprised to see the elderly man dressed in the simple frock of a priest and not the regalia fit for his title as archbishop. Poe wondered if it had to do with a penance of some kind. "Know what?" Poe asked.

"Our arrangement?"

That's what he was worried about? Poe bit back the sarcastic remark. "I haven't told him," Poe said, "*yet.*"

The word hung between them like the threat it was. As a police lieutenant, Barry was nothing but thorough. He dug deep into Poe's background. With more than a decade of contract work, Poe had only ever returned to one place more than once. Barry needed to know what lured Rogan Poe back to San Antonio. Olivia was the obvious answer, followed by the burning question of Poe's finances. Travel nursing was a lucrative career but still not enough to pay for the pricey assisted living facility that housed his beloved grandmother. The Church paid those bills with a simple swipe of the archbishop's signature. Poe needed Barry to understand the arrangement sooner rather than later. Trust was on the line and Barry would never grant it as long as he believed the money came from Olivia's mother.

"You still have a job to do," Mendoza reminded him.

"That is why I'm here, isn't it? What did you call me, the answer to an unsolvable problem?" Poe goaded him.

"Deus ex machina," the archbishop translated. The words were Latin, a theatrical term, a hold-over from Mendoza's first passion in life.

Olivia Osborne was the unsolvable problem the archbishop wouldn't say out loud.

"You just don't like how I'm solving the problem. You could have done the same and yet you didn't." The archbishop made the mistake of confessing that he met Olivia as a child. "I will not repeat your mistakes of the past to sit idly by and watch," Poe told him.

The look on Mendoza's face told Poe no one had dared to question him for a long time. The title of archbishop was bestowed by the Pope.

"Olivia Osborne must choose her own path," Mendoza said. It sounded like a decree.

"And I don't believe she can choose what she does not understand," Poe argued.

"This is an ancient battle between good and evil," Mendoza reminded him.

"Enemies and allies, isn't that what it always comes down to?" Poe asked. "I would rather have her as an ally than an enemy."

Mendoza didn't waver. "I would rather be on the side of the angels."

Poe smiled. Now Mendoza sounded like an archbishop. "Then you've already decided."

Poe stepped closer to stare down at the aged man. "I think you've forgotten your history—all demons were angels once."

Mendoza blanched at the suggestion. "And you're a hunter, not a shepherd."

Poe smiled and continued on his way.

Beyond the heavy doors of the locked unit, there was an uneasy air, pierced by beeps and hums of machines. Poe tried not to look inside the glass boxes, home to patients standing on the edge of the abyss. There was more death here than life.

Poe made his way to Olivia's room without interruption. No one was there threatening to throw him out or complain about his presence. Barry was the only one with the power to decide who could stay and who could go. Olivia was the olive branch between them. Barry and Poe had a strange relationship forged of necessity. Neither man trusted the other, but circumstances beyond their control forced an alliance. They were the only ones left holding Olivia's life together.

The two didn't have to like each other. They just had to be there *for her*. The former police lieutenant and the nurse/demon hunter were an unlikely pair. A week ago, Barry Bartholomew thought Rogan Poe was a serial killer. Last night, they made their first decision together. Neither of them wanted Olivia to wake up alone.

Poe entered her room in nurse mode. The soft blush on her cheeks told him that her blood loss from delivery had finally been replaced. He checked the corner and found the extra IV bags were gone. The machines monitoring her every breath registered stable vital signs. Poe paid particular attention to her blood pressure. Gone were the seizure-inducing heights from before. Her pressures were back where they should be. A quick inspection of the bags still draining into her arm told Poe the blood pressure-reducing medication had been cut in half.

Satisfied, Poe scooted the chair closer to the bed, noting the fresh blanket on the back of it. Maybe it was a token from the nurses. He appreciated the effort. Poe settled in and stretched his long legs. He was used to working the night shift. Poe could manage the hours ahead of him. He slipped his hand through the guardrail and placed it over Olivia's. Barry said that when she drifted, physical touch would bring her back.

Poe watched the rhythmical rise and fall of her chest and projected tranquil images, not knowing if they were received or left dangling in the ethereal realm. Between the preeclampsia and the postpartum hemorrhage, Olivia had almost traded her life for that of her daughters. A chemically induced coma was a little more than an ethereal drift, a safety precaution to allow her swollen brain time to heal. Not even the medicine men could tell him how long that might take. Until then, Olivia was vulnerable to influences from the other side. Someone had to watch over her, and like it or not, that was him.

As expected, Barry had protested the arrangement. He was Olivia's *Watcher*, an ancient assignment born after the great flood waters receded in the time of a man called Noah. Given the steep learning curve the former policeman was already navigating, Poe would have preferred to wait to tell him that with the birth of Olivia's daughters, Barry's role of watcher passed to little Genevieve and Gwendolyn. Poe needed Barry to do his part so he could do his. Olivia was on a perilous journey, and like it or not, Poe was the only one who could help her, and even he wasn't sure about that.

Olivia's fate was bound by both medicine and magic. The doctors had done their part. The artificially induced coma had undoubtedly saved her life but it placed Olivia on a path full of otherworldly influences all competing for her attention. Knowing that, Poe could not sit idly by and let her travel alone. While the doctors had done their part, the magic was up to Poe. He was the only one who could. He may have been raised by a witch, but that did not make him one. He also wasn't an empath, only in extraordinary circumstances. Since he and Olivia had shared thoughts, Poe hoped he could find a way to reach her now. His road to finding Olivia was as risky as the journey she was on now. Still, Poe was bound by the vow he made to her. The archbishop was correct. Poe traded his cloak as a demon hunter in favor of a shepherd.

"My allegiance is to you and to those you love. A life for a life. A soul for a soul."

Poe repeated the last words he said to her before she was wheeled away.

It was not about faith. It was about balance.

Poe reached for her hand. "Know that you are not alone," he whispered. He leaned back and opened his mind, searching for hers.

****

"You still with me, Agent Branch?"

The response from the man in the bed was a series of non-committal grunts.

"How much did you give him?" Bradford Dillon wanted to know.

"Look, that knee is a mess. They wanted him loaded until we get the right ortho guy here." More than one surgeon had passed on the opportunity. "I'm presuming you would prefer he not require a cane for the rest of his life," the doctor stated.

"Are you sure it's not an oxy problem?" Dillon countered. The addiction took hold after the second surgery when Silas Branch's hopes of the NFL blew out on the playing field along with his knee. The drug use could have impacted him if he used the law degree he had earned, but it didn't bother the Bureau. The feds knew but preferred to look the other way. Silas Branch could make them look good. If not, they always knew which strings to pull. Dillon couldn't help but wonder if the wife knew.

The interrogation gave the young doctor pause. He was still getting used to taking orders from non-medical personnel. Dillon made him think of a shark. Always circling, always looking to take someone down. "There's no indication he's still using, but it could be throwing his tolerance off. My orders were to keep him doped up so he won't start asking questions. I heard he has a pregnant wife at home," the doctor reminded him.

"Not anymore," Bradford Dillon quipped.

The doctor didn't know what that meant, but it didn't sound good. He needed to give Dillon something, or he would keep pressing for more. A few more hours, and his shift would be over. With any luck, the ortho guy would be here, and he could put this whole assignment behind him. The money had been too good to pass up, but the extensive non-disclosure agreement on top of his existing one with the agency should have given him pause.

The doctor pulled out his penlight and waved it across his patient. The room was so dark it was the only way he could do his job. Constant perpetual darkness wasn't helping the patient's level of consciousness. The doctor mimicked the motions of another assessment.

"It's not the drugs," he announced. "Agent Branch is deep in REM sleep. Not surprising. He's had a rough day or two. The body will take what it needs. Let him dream of home and his wife if that's what he needs to do."

"Ease up on the drugs," Dillon snapped. He activated the screen mounted to the wall and skipped ahead to the part he wanted. He had memorized it all—every screen grab that was sure to get the attention of the non-believers. Dillon hit play as the blonde woman's hand shot forward, stopping the guards coming her way. Agent Branch was caught in the middle. They all stopped when the Billy clubs the guards carried fell from their hands and clattered to the ground. Their faces went slack with confusion, all except the woman's. She uttered one word that sounded like a hiss. Dillon enhanced the view of her eyes. They were a brilliant green, piercing even, like those of a serpent.

Dillon hit the pause button, freeze-framing the eyes. They were the window to the soul. "Maybe that's what he's seeing," Dillon theorized. "Still think it's a dream, doctor? It looks like a fucking nightmare to me." Dillon needed the medicine man to wake up and get with the program. Dillon gave him a hard stare, expecting an answer.

The doctor's mouth was open, as slack as the guards in the video. It took him a moment to find his voice. "She said *prohibere*."

"It's Latin, at least that's what the translator told me. You have something to add?" Dillon inquired.

"It means stop."

Dillon smiled, confirming the doctor had definitely taken the wrong assignment. "I heard that too, but I don't take orders from her."

Dillon pulled the phone out of his pocket, signaling the doctor's services were no longer required. With the door closed, Dillon rewatched the scene, eager to show the drugged-up agent. The graininess was gone, but not the shock value. Dillon hoped that never went away.

Chapter Two

Her destination was a rambling old three-story house on one of the few cobblestone streets left in Old Town, Alexandria. The rocks were a bitch to walk on in heels, something Olivia never wore. They were too high, and the skirt too short for Olivia's taste, but Nora insisted. Since the shoes and the skirt were Nora's, Olivia couldn't find a way to say no. Besides, her closet was woefully understocked. She lived in scrubs, t-shirts, and jeans.

Nora texted to say she was running late just as Olivia found parking. Nora's timing was impeccable, especially considering Olivia was already here. That was probably the point. Nora had been bugging Olivia for weeks to get out of her apartment. Mission accomplished. Now, all Olivia had to do was open the door.

It wasn't like she was a stranger. Two of the four occupants were nurses Olivia saw every day. The party was a housewarming. Frustrated by their inability to sell, the owners had opted to rent, and four friends pooled their money and jumped at the chance to live in a place none of them could have afforded on their own.

The house was close enough to the Potomac for Olivia to hear the rhythmical lapping of water. The house was in the heart of the touristy part of Alexandria, full of quaint houses like the one in front of her. One block over were trendy bars and restaurants with the convenience of a Metro station within walking distance. Before that, this area was a known haunt of George Washington himself. The houses built closest to the water generally belonged to retired sea captains. They repurposed the wood from their dismantled ships, bringing something from their old life to anchor them to their new one on land.

The abundance of history brought another set of problems, none of which Olivia hoped would bother her tonight. The only spirits she wanted to entertain were the ones found in the bottles she cradled in the crock of her arm. With any luck, the white noise created by the crowd inside would drown out any lingering events. Her presence here should go unnoticed by those who came before, be it on land or sea. Olivia paused at the door and did a quick 'toe dip' into the waters of the past. As suspected, the well was dry. There was too much living energy inside for the dormant ones to rise to the surface for a meet and greet with her.

Glad for the reprieve, Olivia gathered her defenses and prepared for a different encounter, the emotional onslaught of the living. She didn't have a chance to knock before the door flung open on its own. Olivia heaved a sigh of relief that it was just a couple searching for some alone time.

She weaved her way through the narrow entryway, glad to see a few familiar faces, even if one of them was Stupid Jeff. He could start an IV with his eyes closed, but Olivia avoided asking him for help. It meant she wouldn't get rid of him for the rest of her shift.

As expected, Jeff wasted no time saddling up to her. He trailed behind as she added the two bottles of wine she brought to the growing collection.

"Wow, Doctor Osborne," Jeff said, openly admiring her.

His leer reminded Olivia of the makeup she was wearing and shoes that weren't hers. At least, she passed on the fake lashes Nora suggested. One flash of her green eyes and they were the only thing anyone would remember. She did apply the cherry red lipstick. Even Olivia had to admit she didn't recognize the woman staring back at her in the mirror. It was a departure from her usual just rolled-out-of-bed look for work. Another plus was she didn't get carded at the liquor store.

"Don't call me that," Olivia snapped. It wasn't official, at least not technically. Classes were dismissed, but she was still in the middle of her dissertation.

"Agent Osborne, then."

"Don't call me that either." It was impossible to keep her impending Ph.D. under wraps. She had been a student as long as anyone had known her, but her application to the FBI was a closely guarded secret. Since she had successfully passed her first round of interviews, Nora must have let the cat out of the bag.

Despite her lack of a law enforcement background, Olivia knew her credentials, impending or otherwise, bought her some traction. Academically she was rock solid, but she knew the powers that be doubted her. Like it or not, her gender put her at an immediate disadvantage. No matter what anyone said, the Bureau was still a "boys' club". She was also attractive and physically non-threatening. Gran taught her it wasn't about size but the strength she held inside. Olivia doubted the Feds got that memo. Still, they wouldn't be the first to underestimate her.

"Can I at least comment on your legs? You really should show them off more often," Jeff suggested, although his eyes hadn't left her cleavage since his first pass.

Typically, Olivia hid her breasts beneath loose scrub tops, but stuffed into the camisole and shrug set Nora had talked her into buying, they were on full display. This was starting to feel like a setup. But not with Jeff. Everyone at work knew to avoid him. He had successfully slept with almost everyone on the night shift, including Nora. Jeff was a fisherman. If he kept casting his lure, eventually, he would snag someone–just not her. By this time, they both knew it.

Jeff offered her a plastic cup of wine, but Olivia grabbed herself an unopened beer before he could slip the cup into her hand. Nora wanted her to get out, have fun, and try new things. The fruity girl beer seemed as good as any place to start.

Olivia was on her second by the time Nora arrived. She was surprised Olivia was still there. "It's a miracle," Olivia assured her. "Between the idle conversations, requests for my phone number and stares at my breasts."

"Told you the girls would look good in that top," Nora teased. She knew her friend was empathic, whether Olivia acknowledged it or not. The alcohol must have numbed Olivia's senses. A less populated area would lessen the assault on her synapses.

"Let's see if we can find you something more stimulating." Nora pressed another beer into Olivia's hand.

Nora grabbed one for herself before ushering them up two flights of stairs to the room in the loft. It belonged to Kendra and was where the "cool" guests gathered. The windows provided a nice view of the Potomac as the balcony spilled out toward the restaurants dotting King Street, along with the heavenly smells that came with them.

Olivia and Kendra also worked together, but the invite to tonight's event came from Nora. Kendra was jealous of anyone who might garner more attention than she did. At work, that included Olivia. Given there was a young intern downstairs, Olivia was surprised to find Kendra upstairs. That was before Olivia spied the man in the far corner.

He sat on the ground, his back against the balcony railing. The long legs stretched out in front of him kept the four women surrounding him at bay. They appeared to be in some deep discussion. Not far away was something that looked like a radio, but tuning into the sound, Olivia didn't hear music, just random beeps. Her eyes were drawn back to the man. She took a tentative step forward, her interest piqued for the first time that night.

"Doesn't all your investigation into murder scare you?" Kendra asked.

She sounded breathless. Olivia was sure the question came with a bat of her fake lashes. It was a legitimate question despite the delivery. Olivia crept closer, eager to hear his answer.

"Not really," he said, taking a pull on the beer bottle cradled between his legs.

Olivia wondered if he had any idea how suggestive the move looked and then quickly decided he didn't. His blue eyes were shining, but they had nothing to do with the cleavage Kendra was flaunting. He was interested in the hunt.

"Olivia."

The faraway sound of her name startled her.

"See something you like?"

Olivia jerked, but it was just Nora behind her.

"Told you I would find you something interesting," Nora said.

Olivia turned her focus back to Kendra.

"Doesn't it bother you? People getting killed all the time? With the crime rate, it could happen to any of us."

"Most people know their killer," Olivia suddenly spoke. All eyes turned on her, the man with the beer included. He tipped his bottle her way and flashed a crooked grin.

"So, how am I supposed to know which one of you it will be?" Kendra asked when the stalemate Olivia caused dragged on too long. "You're going to have to be more specific. Give me a top three."

Kendra might have punctuated the question with a giggle, but Olivia knew she was annoyed the conversation had been interrupted.

"The best way to avoid murder is don't do drugs," the man answered.

A snort came from the corner where the smell of pot was the heaviest.

"And don't associate with people who do drugs," the man said louder, with a laugh of his own.

"And don't date a psychopath," Olivia bantered back.

There was laughter all around, but not from

Kendra. She vacated her space in the circle and pulled Nora into a corner. The next thing Olivia knew, Nora's arm was linked through hers, and they were picking their way across the cobbled street.

Olivia wondered what happened, then decided she didn't care. Odd sounds pierced the background like a storm was coming.

"You know you're a real buzz kill, right?" Nora asked her. "And I say that in the kindest possible way."

"It's not people who are evil. It's what's inside of them," the words tumbled from Olivia's mouth.

"That's what I'm talking about," Nora said. "You need to get out of the house more. And probably out of your head."

"Should I be driving?" Olivia asked as they continued down the street. Her legs felt heavy.

"Definitely not. I'll bring you back after," Nora assured her. "We're going to get pancakes. You'll be good as new, with some sugar and caffeine in your system."

The all-night diner on the GW Parkway was hopping despite the hour. They ended up waiting even longer because Nora insisted on a booth. Olivia fought off sleep by watching the neon sign outside. It was pulsating, rhythmical like a heart.

"Finally," Nora moaned as she slid into her seat and put her feet up.

The thuds Olivia heard must have been Nora's shoes hitting the floor.

"My feet are killing me."

Olivia almost believed her until she saw the guy from the party slip inside. He was alone, but it didn't take long for him to find her.

"I might have let it slip where we were going," Nora whispered.

Olivia opened her mouth to say something. She was going to ask who the guy was, but Nora interrupted her.

"It was all him. You can thank me later."

Olivia lost her focus, her eyes catching the light outside. It was blinking now, growing brighter. "How did you get here?" Olivia mumbled.

The man slid into the booth next to Olivia.

"Hi, I'm Jason, remember me?"

"Jason?"

****

Poe wasn't sure what woke him, the blinding lights or the piercing sound of a code blue. He pushed himself to his feet and quickly determined it wasn't Olivia who was coding. Her vital signs were stable, but her heart rate and respiration were elevated. There was movement below her eyelids. Maybe she was responding to the sound of the alarm and the thudding of feet running past her room.

Poe peered past the privacy curtain and noticed the hallway was bathed in warm light, like a brown-out. Maybe that was why it seemed so bright in here. Poe recalled purposefully dimming the lights to signify night. Delirium was common among ICU patients, fueled by disturbed sleep-wake cycles and the constant exposure to artificial light. Poe was still trying to reconcile what had woken him when the alarm stopped as abruptly as it started.

The commotion in the hall seemed to be ease when one of the nurses who had run past poked his head into Olivia's room.

"What?" Poe asked first. Had the staff just realized

he was here and thought now might be a good time to ask him to leave?

His nametag said Jace, and he didn't look old enough to shave, let alone graduate from nursing school.

"Did the lights go out in here?" Jace asked.

It wasn't the question Poe expected, but it was a good one. It prompted him to consider it must have been the blinding light that woke him–*before the alarm.* "The lights may have flashed, but they never went out," Poe said carefully, as an alternate theory started to take shape.

Olivia's nurse showed up, the same one Poe had tangled with last night. She pushed past Poe and Jace to beeline to Olivia's ventilator. "We need to check everyone's battery reserve and access to the backup generator."

"Is it just this floor?" Jace wanted to know.

"As far as I know," the nurse responded, but the look on her face said she was distracted.

Jace shrugged. "Probably should let maintenance know this is the only room where the lights didn't go out."

When they were gone, Poe dimmed the lights again, lower this time than before. He leaned over Olivia's bed, waiting and watching for what he didn't know. There was no movement beneath the lids.

"Was that you?"

The buzzing from his pocket distracted him. Poe reached for his phone. It was Sarah Larsin's response to his accusation that she was behind Silas Branch's disappearance.

Ironic, Olivia's husband or his whereabouts hadn't

crossed Poe's mind since. Still, something compelled Sarah to respond.

—*I hope you found him.*—

Considering the response, Poe decided it must be honest.

It left him with an unexpected dilemma. If Olivia's mother wasn't behind Silas's disappearance, then who was?

Chapter Three

Patrick Monahan boarded the plane in Las Vegas with blurry eyes and a growing knot in his stomach. He was truly a man at a crossroads. He was turning his back on the institution he had served for twenty years. While no one had told him not to go, Patrick knew his superiors would never approve of what he was about to do. He was headed to San Antonio to deliver news he refused to talk about over the phone to a man he felt like he knew but had never met. Everything he was doing was for Silas Branch, a man who had once been his best friend. While Patrick prayed Silas was alive, he couldn't help but fear the consequences if he was.

When the flight attendant came around, Patrick requested a Bloody Mary and recalled the events that led him to this moment.

Patrick tossed two steaks on the smoldering embers before plopping back into the chair and opening a beer.

"So, it's just the two of us?" Silas asked.

Patrick was glad for the question. Talk of Melinda would fill the void and delay discussion of why Silas was really here.

"You like being the third wheel?" Patrick joked. It was a running commentary between them.

Silas shrugged. "Don't go there with me. I'm not the one who's ready to settle down."

"Who says I am?" Patrick pondered.

"Your place smells fruity and there are dish gloves in your sink. She probably even has her own drawer," Silas teased him.

"Don't profile me," Patrick scolded.

"I just call them as I see them." Silas took another swig of his beer. It might be his first, but it wouldn't be his last. The night would end with bourbon, either at his place or somewhere else. Silas knew people who kept a bottle on hand for such impromptu visits.

"You don't think about it?" Patrick probed, even though he knew the answer. *"Settling down, building a family?"*

Silas shook his head. *"Don't count on it."* There had been a lot of women in his life. Silas saw a lot more in his future. He had yet to find one he could imagine keeping around for very long.

"You're like Ahab chasing the elusive white whale," Patrick observed. Silas wanted them to be beautiful and brilliant.

"I won't apologize." Or compromise. Silas was forced to alter his career plans. He refused to do it with his personal life too. *"There are a lot of beautiful women, but the trouble is I've started to notice the really smart ones don't like me very much,"* Silas grinned.

"You mean they won't put up with your shit?" Patrick translated. Silas was a workaholic. *"It's an age thing, Silas."* At least so far, Silas kept it age-appropriate. It was probably the intelligence factor. It took a certain amount of life experience to pique Silas' interest for long. *"You are on the downhill side of thirty-five. It's only going to get harder the older you get. Women expect you to share. Somewhere beyond the*

bedroom."

Silas waved him off. "That's why it's just about sex. That part is easy. I'm not much of a sharer."

Patrick believed Silas was being difficult, as well as uncompromising. By chasing something so elusive, Silas guaranteed himself a free pass for his behavior. While hunting for something akin to a unicorn, he would never have to dig deep enough to acknowledge his shortcomings.

Silas drained the bottle in his hand, waiting for the real discussion to begin. Melinda's absence told Silas what he already knew. "Why don't you just say what you need to say so we can move on? You're going to be my boss. I'm guessing you invited me over as a consolation prize," Silas stated.

"It's nothing personal, you know that, right? You have a stellar career ahead of you," Patrick assured him. Silas Branch was a man accustomed to getting what he wanted in life. Other than not catching a football thrown by some Superbowl-winning quarterback, Patrick doubted there wasn't much Silas hadn't achieved. The career-ending knee injury of his senior year wasn't even his fault. That honor belonged to some overzealous cornerback from USC. Silas' father had talked him out of chasing the football dream at the cost of injuring himself further.

Patrick was glad Silas followed the advice, even though he had dreamed of nothing except playing sports since the age of six. After graduating from Notre Dame, Silas took some time to lick his wounds before bouncing back and going to law school. It was the discipline and challenge that intrigued Silas, not the practice. He was methodical and tenacious, the same traits that made him a good field agent and precisely what Patrick needed.

"I know I don't play well with others," Silas *admitted.*

"Not much of a team player," Patrick *repeated the preferred vernacular. He and Silas had been friends long enough that Patrick knew he could speak the truth. Silas might be suave outside the office, but he needed to glean that same finesse with other law enforcement entities. Silas was old-school FBI, but times had changed. The FBI might still be an elite organization, but they were no longer the accepted "good guys". Silas had trouble sharing the inter-jurisdictional sandbox.*

"You deserve the director's spot," Silas *admitted. Patrick's service was unblemished. He had also proven he would keep his mouth shut when told.*

"I want you to stay with me at the BAU and lead a team," Patrick *told him. "But I wanted to run it by you first."*

"Of course," Silas *assured him.*

"Good, because I already have a big ask of you," Patrick *warned.*

"Pressure from above already?"

"Time is of the essence on this one."

Patrick talked while they ate.

The subject was Remington Pope, known as Rhemy to his friends at the country club and senator to those he served alongside at the Virginia State House. Not long ago, Pope had hoped the good citizens of Virginia would be calling him governor. Too bad for Pope, those well-laid plans hit a snag when his twelve-year-old stepson, Elijah Stoddard, was the only one at home when his six-year-old brother ended up dead.

Patrick knew Silas had heard the story—everyone had.

"I thought it was ruled an accident of some kind," Silas speculated.

"In truth, the investigation is 'ongoing'," Patrick used the colloquial term that said no one wanted to talk about the details of the case. Like other tragedies, this one was quickly replaced by another. Even if it hadn't been, someone would have still buried this one. There were powerful forces at work that determined which cases and which details weren't for public consumption. This was one of those on many levels. The least of which Rhemy Pope still had powerful friends who wanted to see him as governor.

"Upon further investigation, the death doesn't appear to be an accident," Patrick revealed.

"Please tell me there was someone else in the house," Silas begged.

Patrick stayed silent and continued to sip his beer.

Silas pushed his plate away. The steak had lost its appeal. "Are you telling me the twelve-year-old brother did it?"

The story was even more disturbing than that. "According to Elijah, his little brother ran into the knife."

Silas felt his gut clench. "How many times?"

"Seventeen."

Silas shook his head. "You know I don't do kids."

Patrick knew that. Just like he knew Silas didn't do relationships. But this was different.

"I need you on this," Patrick pleaded. "Elijah's mother insists he didn't do it. Not on his own."

"As a mother, what do you expect?" Silas dragged a hand over his face. "This kid needs way more than an FBI agent."

"This case was sent to the Behavior Analysis Unit for a reason," Patrick reminded him.

"Then the kid needs a psychologist, or a psychiatrist," Silas told him. "I'm neither of those things. There're not enough initials at the end of my name."

"There's more," Patrick confessed.

Silas inhaled loudly. Of course, there was.

"Julia, Elijah's mother, insists her son is possessed," Patrick said.

Silas pushed back from the table. "This is the first case they give you?" He paced around the patio in search of the ice chest.

Patrick took the bottle Silas offered, even though he wasn't halfway through the one in his hand. "They knew I would know who to call," Patrick confessed.

"My first thought would be a priest." Silas couldn't believe he had suggested such a thing. He twisted the cap off his new beer and took a quick sip. "Are you even Catholic?"

"It doesn't matter. The Popes are–no pun intended. I know how these things work. The Church won't get involved until the kid has been evaluated by a professional such as the kind you first suggested."

Silas took another drink. If this story got any weirder, this would be his last beer before switching to something else.

"Discretion is obviously paramount. The family doesn't want the story to end up on the evening news or, worse, social media. The senator has friends at the

Bureau. Long story short, we have a consultant who's agreed to come in. One I've worked with personally. I'd like you to go with her. A priest will listen to what she has to say. Her evaluation of the boy could mean the difference in how Elijah Stoddard spends the rest of his life."

Silas took another swing and traded the beer for his phone. After lining up a place to go after this, Silas turned back to Patrick. "How do you know this consultant?"

"I worked with her before, when she used to be an agent," Patrick admitted.

"Do I know her?"

Patrick joined the Bureau before Silas, but they crossed paths early in Silas' career when they both worked special weapons and tactics together. Silas was a good fit with the high-octane testosterone types. It had also been a launching pad for a move to the BAU.

"She has a Ph.D. in forensic psychology. She also knows a priest or two," Patrick added.

"Why's she not working for the BAU?" It was a legitimate question.

"That would have been her choice, but things didn't work out," Patrick said carefully, waiting for Silas to fill in the blanks. It was a subject they didn't talk about, a rip in the fabric of their service together.

Silas' phone buzzed. He texted a short reply and slipped the phone in his pocket. With his plans made, Silas' attention returned to the matters at hand.

"It's Dr. Olivia Osborne," Patrick said, giving a name to a woman Silas had heard about but had never met. "I get the strong feeling the Bureau would like her back, but reintroducing her is going to take some

adjustment."

"You think?" Silas shook his head. "How could they do that, after what happened?"

"You weren't there," Patrick reminded him. Silas was tucked away in some high-priced FBI-chosen rehab to kick the oxy addiction he developed in college. The events of that night prompted Patrick to look at another unit and to seek something outside work. Things were never the same again.

"I heard she washed out." Silas would have said more, but the look on Patrick's face stopped him. His friend was right. He wasn't there. He didn't see it. For a time, Silas wondered if the outcome would have been different if he had been.

The mood of the night was ruined. Silas guzzled the rest of his beer. He had somewhere else he could go. The woman on the other end of his phone didn't want to talk about things he didn't want to remember. Theirs wasn't a talking kind of relationship.

"Dr. Osborne didn't wash out," Patrick corrected him. That was the story the Bureau wanted people to believe. It was better than the real one. The veteran commander on scene gave an order, explicitly against the advice of the expert they sent him. The decision cost the commander his life. The agency buried him as a hero and asked the doctor who predicted the bloody outcome to leave.

Silas nodded his head. "I get it now. You want me to what, baby-sit the spooky chick," he surmised.

"Dr. Osborne was the smartest person in the room that night," Patrick emphasized. He knew how much Silas had trusted and admired their dead leader. "Trust me when I tell you, she is absolutely, one hundred

percent, the person we need for this case. And under no circumstance let her hear you call her chick."

"I'm seriously reconsidering being your friend," Silas said with a last pull on his beer. "Is she smarter than me?"

Patrick was relieved to see Silas crack a smile. "Even you."

"So, then tell me. Why did the Bureau ask her to leave?"

"They didn't like the answers she gave them," Patrick repeated what he had been told when asked to handle this new situation.

Thinking back on it, Patrick wondered if it was because he was there the night things went to hell that he was now being asked to do this. There had been a negotiation that night too, after the dead were hauled away. The cost had been Dr. Osborne's departure from the FBI in exchange for the tape recording she had on her phone. She had to translate the Latin before she left. Patrick and another agent had been asked to sign an NDA to remain with the Bureau.

"What I really think is, people are afraid of things they don't understand."

Chapter Four

Barry Bartholomew sat at the high-top table, sipping coffee he didn't taste. A week ago, he was a veteran police lieutenant living in a thirteen-story condo with a stunning view who went for his regular morning jog. When he left that day, he never expected he would return jobless, homeless, and a surrogate father to two tiny girls. Barry felt an overwhelming sense of inadequacy. Life was still filled with life-and-death situations, even without the badge and gun. Barry might have managed some sleep, but the nightmare was still there when he woke up. The text message waiting for him said as much. Was today the day another part of Olivia's world would crash and burn?

Barry was huddled around his cup when Sergeant Will Ibarra slid into the chair across from him. "You look like shit," Will said. Barry would be uncomfortable with anything close to sympathy.

Barry raised his middle finger in response.

The gesture told Will his friend was still in there somewhere. Will cast a glance around before getting down to business. He could almost forget they were in a hospital. The lobby looked more like a hotel, and the little café beat the hospital cafeteria where they met last time.

"I was hoping to run into that Poe guy," Will said, knowing the mention of Rogan Poe was sure to get a different reaction than whatever was currently in Barry's head. He needed to keep Barry talking so he would see which way to steer the conversation. Will wasn't sure whether to start with bad news or worse news.

"He's upstairs with Olivia. I had to come in early to catch the neonatologist," Barry explained. It was a fancy name for the baby doctor. He was drowning in a new reality filled with words he couldn't pronounce and acronyms he didn't understand, but he was getting there.

"How are the girls?" Will asked.

Barry managed a quick smile. The tiny humans stirred emotions in him that he never knew existed, just as their mother did. "Still not intubated. That's good news for the NICU. It means they are breathing on their own. A good sign for twenty-eight-week-old twins," Barry explained.

Will saw the light in Barry's eyes as he spoke. He hoped his friend could hold on to that spark of joy. "That was the one thing Kim wanted to know. I'll be sure and tell her," Will said. Kim was the niece of Will's partner, Jessica.

"Kim asked if she could come over and help out at Olivia's. I'm pretty sure I blew her off," Barry admitted. "I don't have the first clue what babies need."

Will knew Kim and Jessica had been planning a baby shower for Olivia, but their other planning partner was MIA. Will needed to breach the subject with Barry, but was reluctant.

"Can you let Kim know if the offer still stands, I'll take it." Kim might be a teenage girl, but she had a baby of her own and Kim knew the kinds of things

Olivia would need. More than that, Barry knew Kim wanted to be there for Olivia, because, like him, Olivia had saved her life.

Nothing explained Barry's place in life more than the words he had just uttered. The Barry Bartholomew Will knew never asked for help.

Barry fished around in his pocket and pulled out a set of keys. He pried one off and tossed it to Will. "That will get Kim inside the house. Might as well make some copies. To be honest, I couldn't tell you if I set the alarm today or not. The password to Olivia's security system is the same as her phone," Barry explained.

"Someone should talk to her about security." Will tried to make a joke.

Barry once had the same thought. Olivia used the same six digits 11-23-75 for all her protective devices. "It's Jason Austin's birthday," Barry answered, a question Will did not ask.

Will had never met Jason Austin or his brother, Mark. The latter had been Barry's former partner. Mark Austin's death was a solemn reminder of what led Will to this place. No further reflection was needed.

Given Barry's request for assistance, Will eased into something he could do to help. "We need to talk about Kevin Branch. He's blowing up Olivia's phone wanting to know why she's not answering his texts or emails."

Barry rubbed his eyes. "Did he say what it's about?" All Barry knew was that Silas' younger brother data mined for Olivia.

"Information on a nurse," Will said, leaving the thread hanging for Barry to pick up.

"It was Kevin who got background on Rogan Poe," Barry said. "I'm guessing it's probably not him."

"Have you made peace with him?" Will wanted to know. Barry had trust issues with Rogan Poe. The only reason Barry granted Poe access to Olivia was out of necessity.

Barry shrugged. He didn't want to drag Will into his problems with Poe. Barry moved on instead.

"Lily didn't show up for work," Barry revealed. He had arrived at the NICU early hoping to catch her. One of the nurses told him it had been a slow night, so maybe Lily wasn't needed. She had already worked an extra shift to be there when the babies were born. It was a plausible excuse, except Lily never came home last night. It was easy to keep tabs on her since she was Olivia's next-door neighbor.

"And she's not responding to my texts," Barry confessed.

Will only nodded. The statement didn't require a response. Barry had lost a lot in the last week. Lily had been the bright spot on Barry's horizon. Will couldn't help but feel for Barry but in the end, it was probably for the best. A simple conversation with a nighttime security guard had debunked Lily's version of the safety measures for the NICU. Lily's story was a half-truth, which in Barry and Will's line of work equaled to a lie. There were no coincidences in their world and Lily going radio silent only confirmed Will's worst suspicions.

"I asked Brennon to join the meeting," Barry revealed.

The meeting was the hospital administration's response to a security issue that occurred the night of

Genevieve and Gwendolyn's birth. Hospitals had many codes. The most common was a code blue, meaning an adult medical emergency, usually a cardiac or respiratory arrest. A code pink signaled a possible infant abduction. One sounded not long after Olivia's daughters arrived in the NICU. Fortunately, the code turned out to be a false alarm, but the fact it happened with no plausible explanation put everyone on high alert. Brennon Kaine's presence was sure to get everyone's attention.

Will was glad for the assist. Brennon Kaine was an unexpected addition to Barry's life. Kane was the high-priced New York attorney representing the still missing *Good Samaritan Killer*. The illustrious Mr. Kaine was also who Olivia called to get Barry out of jail before he could be arrested for the death of Amanda Greene. Dr. Greene's leap from a thirteen-story balcony ended more than just her life. She was the reason Barry no longer had his job or his condo.

"Anything else you need from me?" Will offered.

"I'm assuming you know about Patrick Monahan's visit," Barry ventured.

Will shook his head. He had never met BAU Director Monahan but Will did receive an early morning text message the same as Barry. Silas's former boss, and friend, was on his way into town. They were meeting at Olivia's house at Monahan's request. Monahan was the one who suggested Will be there. Without saying it, Will theorized it was for moral support. The last report from Vegas was Silas Branch was still missing. Will doubted Monahan's visit was good news.

"I want you there," Barry confessed.

"Of course."

"You look like you have something else to say," Barry probed.

Will nodded. "I do, but you're probably not going to like it."

****

Poe hadn't slept since the first round of blinking lights. When he wasn't watching Olivia, Poe was thumbing through his phone, reading emails. His employer had approved his request for emergency time off. They knew he had an aged grandmother, and Poe was happy to let them connect those dots, even though his beloved Mémé was fine enough to email him.

Well into her eighties, Cloteel Bouvier's fingers were too gnarled for texting, but adequate for a full-sized keyboard. Moving to the assisted living home forced her to learn the magic of electronic communication and the benefits of email. It helped her keep up with her grandson's crazy travel and work schedule. It also kept Cloteel in touch with her collective of friends. They came in all ages with the common thread of magic intersecting their lives. The history his grandmother shared with other gifteds was rich and Poe was eager to introduce that world to Olivia and her daughters. Mémé's email reminded him of how precarious the future was without Olivia.

Two orderly-looking types dressed in scrubs parted the privacy curtain and squeezed inside the room, shocking Poe back to the present.

"We're here for Olivia Branch."

Poe faded into the corner at the same time Renaye, Olivia's day shift nurse, appeared to help prepare her patient for a trip to radiology. It wasn't a simple process with the ventilator and a reason why the transport team included a nurse.

The coma was induced preemptively to preserve Olivia's brain against her escalating blood pressure and repeated seizures. An initial MRI was performed as a baseline. Since then, daily EEGs were used to monitor brain function since the test could be done at the bedside. All had been well until last night. The room seemed very vacant with Olivia gone. She was the centerpiece.

"Please tell me you've been home since I last saw you," Renaye broke the ice. Today was supposed to be her day off, but she picked up the extra shift without being asked. She was the only one in the unit with postpartum experience. Fortunately, they didn't get many new mothers in the ICU.

"I learned in report there was a spike in Olivia's vitals last night," Renaye quickly explained. The night shift nurse was worried it could be another seizure, but with everything going on last night, Renaye wanted to hear it from Poe. "Care to elaborate?"

"I nodded off," Poe admitted.

Renaye didn't believe him. He had taken the night shift for a reason. He was stalling and it wasn't because he didn't know. Renaye admired his devotion. She couldn't help but wonder what role Rogan Poe played in her patient's life. The cop was the only one with access to the babies, but he denied being the father. Neither was Poe. He didn't even make the list of approved visitors. He only made the cut after the cop and a lawyer got involved. Poe reminded Renaye of a sentry, watching, hovering even. He was emotionally invested in whatever drama was unfolding here.

"I know who she is," Renaye confessed. "I'm betting you're the one who put the crystals on the windowsill. The cop doesn't seem like the type. Neither does the archbishop who dresses like a priest."

Her words finally got his attention. Renaye thought she saw his eyes flash as they slowly trailed over her. It wasn't a suggestive look, but one that bore through her, looking for something. The feeling was so fleeting, Renaye wondered if she imagined it.

"She could have been responding to the noise," Renaye suggested, seeking to fill the void that had opened up between them. *Or it could have been another seizure.* Maybe she was forcing round pieces into square holes, seeking any other explanation but that one. This patient had gotten to her. Two tiny babies needed their mother, and it looked like so did Rogan Poe.

Chapter Five

Olivia removed the earbuds she no longer needed. "Do you have something to say, Agent Branch?" she asked. The recording had been silent for a while, the earbuds a diversionary tactic. They delayed any attempt at conversation. He had been looking at her throughout the drive. She, on the other hand, had been doing her best to avoid him. It was better than talking when she didn't have the first damn clue what to say.

His question was simple. "What are you listening to?"

"The 911 call Elijah Stoddard made the night his brother died."

Silas noted she used the word died in place of murder. "What did you hear that you didn't like?"

Olivia shook her head. "Not sure. Maybe it's what I didn't hear."

Now Silas was the one with no idea what to say. He wished he had known they were doing this today—then he could have listened too.

"So, how did you get this detail?" Olivia attempted small talk. It wasn't one of her strong points.

"I was asked—just like you."

Olivia nodded as her eyes bore into him like she could see his thoughts. God, he hoped not. "I've worked with Patrick before," Silas offered.

"He trusts you. You didn't have a say in this. You

really should rethink that friendship. If this thing works out, you could find yourself stuck with me." Olivia gave Silas a thin smile and put the earbuds back in place. She made a show of turning on the recorder but didn't. She needed the silence.

Olivia didn't know how she felt about being back. She was trying not to feel anything at all. All she had ever wanted to do was work for the BAU. It was why she joined the Bureau in the first place. This case was tailored specifically for her. It was about ancient belief systems and faith.

****

"What are you looking for that we haven't found already?" The question came from Nathan Aberdeen.

His fellow officers called him Abby. Maybe that's why he was pissed off, but with fifteen years on the force, Olivia doubted it. More than likely, Aberdeen was bothered by the fact she wore a suit and looked like a fancy lawyer.

When she didn't answer immediately, Detective Aberdeen blocked her way into the interview room. Olivia was alone in the hallway with him. She had gone on ahead while Agent Branch was delayed at the desk. He had to turn in his weapon. Something she didn't have. That's how Olivia found herself alone with the DC cop who arrested Elijah Stoddard.

With the forced stop, Aberdeen wedged himself into her personal space. Olivia had to look up at him, even in her heels. Up close, she noted the flare of his nostrils, reverting to some ancient animalistic ritual. What did he see her as? A trespasser on his turf? Or some object to be toyed with? Olivia had met his type before. In another setting, one with loud music, low *lights, and copious amounts of alcohol, the latter would be his choice.*

The laminate Olivia flashed with the word "consultant" paired with "doctor" earned her a steely stare. Aberdeen had heard the 911 call. He had walked the crime scene. He was putting it together. Olivia felt another eruption brewing, but just like that, it evaporated as she felt the presence from behind. Olivia knew then her old friend Patrick had cast Agent Branch in the role of a handler, but Agent Branch saw himself as something more—a bodyguard of sorts. Maybe he was picking up on the testosterone-filled vibes from Aberdeen.

Cop instincts finally kicked in, and Aberdeen noticed they were no longer alone. "No one told me the Feds were coming–with a shrink." In one swift movement, Aberdeen retreated from her space and feigned a smile, no doubt in an attempt to elicit support from the other alpha male on the scene. "So, what are you looking for, Doctor Osborne? A pass for this kid?"

"Not that kind of doctor," Olivia assured him with a flick of her lashes. She noted the puff of his chest had deflated with Agent Branch's arrival. Her face registered nothing despite what she felt. It was one of her abilities, a skill honed, not gifted. Olivia was good at hiding her emotions—until she couldn't. "I'm doing what all good investigators do. I'm seeking answers."

Aberdeen balked, some of the bravado returning. "Answers? I'd be happy with a little understanding."

"Answers come before understanding," Olivia countered.

"Who says?"

Aberdeen's demeanor told her he was feeling

confident again—exactly what she wanted. "Merriam Webster," Olivia said smoothly. She reveled in the flash of anger she saw erupt in his eyes.

"Detective Aberdeen." Silas used the title, but there was no mistaking the snap in his voice. "If you would be so kind to get the door for Dr. Osborne." It didn't sound like a suggestion.

Olivia turned back, waiting for Silas before she went through.

"I'll join you in a minute," Silas assured her.

Silas waited until the door clicked between them before he moved into Aberdeen's space, forcing the detective to look up at him. "It's my understanding you're here as a courtesy. This is her show and I'm with her. Don't make me have to ask you to leave."

Olivia entered the standard interview room with the obligatory table and chairs and one-way glass. Aberdeen was on the outside. Inside, she and Silas sat on one side of the table with Elijah Stoddard and his therapist on the other side. The boy's attorney hovered in the corner. This was a conversation, not an official interrogation. Elijah wasn't under arrest. He was on a psychiatric hold for individuals experiencing a mental health crisis.

Olivia noticed right away that appearances were deceiving. Elijah looked like an average twelve-year-old boy until she got a look at his eyes. They were aged, not the eyes of a child. They were stony but not with anger, more like sadness or hardened due to a long-term burden. The aging process began before he ever arrived at this place. Olivia was relieved to see he didn't appear to be drugged, but she did note the dark circles under his eyes. He wasn't sleeping. Maybe they should give him something for when the darkness came. That was where his fear lived.

Olivia took Elijah back to the events that brought him here. The Pope family was staying at a corporate apartment in the District for a four-day-long political event his stepfather was attending. One of the senator's staff was supposed to watch over the boys, but she hadn't arrived by the time they needed to leave. Elijah's stepfather insisted to his wife the boys would be safe alone for a brief time. Unknown at the time, the staffer was involved in an accident on her way into the city. The staffer would never make it to the corporate apartment.

"Tell me in your own words what happened," Olivia coaxed.

Elijah spoke freely. "I told them not to leave me alone with him."

"Why?" Olivia had heard the statement before. She wanted to know if the boy would tell her the same.

"My little brother was a demon."

Olivia had also heard this part. Silas, on the other hand, had not. To his credit, his expression remained neutral.

"Why did you think your brother was a demon?" Silas asked.

This was the first time Elijah looked away from her. "He talked funny. I couldn't understand him because he wasn't speaking English. He sounded the way the priest does at special mass."

Olivia studied Elijah. She had read his six-year-old brother, Benji, had a speech impediment. His mother acknowledged she sometimes couldn't understand what he was saying. Interestingly, he hadn't always had it.

"Tell me something Benji said. Something you could understand," Olivia requested.

"That if I did this, I'd end up talking to someone like you," Elijah responded.

Olivia slowed her breathing and tried not to be distracted by Agent Branch. He had just leaned back, away from the table. She wondered if he was rethinking this assignment.

Someone like her could mean a doctor. At least, that's what she told herself, but not what she asked. Instead, Olivia got straight to the point. "Describe the demon," she asked Elijah.

Elijah glanced at his therapist. Out of the countless questions he had been asked since he arrived at this place, this wasn't one of them.

Olivia had researched Elijah's doctor as well. He was young, and while juveniles were his specialty, he was out of his depth with one. He had been requested, like everyone else, because the senator knew and trusted him. Rhemy Pope was protecting his family by keeping his circle small.

Elijah hesitated, squirming in his chair. "It doesn't always look the same."

"What do you mean?" Olivia probed. "What does it look like?"

"Other people. Not just Benji."

"People that you know?" Olivia wondered.

Elijah didn't have to think about this one. "My third-grade teacher, Miss Judy. Father Mike from our old parish, and Mr. Price. He's a friend of my stepfather's," Elijah told her.

Olivia nodded, taking a moment. "Anything else you noticed about it?"

"It doesn't have horns, if that's what you think."

The therapist shifted at the statement. So did the lawyer. Elijah leaned forward in his chair, studying her face but not threatening her like Aberdeen did. "It has green eyes. They shine like yours do when you get excited. Kind of like now."

Agent Branch was looking at her now too but Olivia didn't show him her eyes. They weren't important. "Why did you tell the 911 operator you performed CPR on Benji?" Olivia asked. She purposefully said the name to illicit sympathy. So far, it hadn't worked. Elijah shrugged, a much older motion for one so young, accompanied by a vacant stare.

Olivia stared harder, all her missing pieces falling into place. It was the thing she told Agent Branch she hadn't heard.

"That's what they wanted me to do," Elijah finally confessed. "I told them he was already dead. It was the truth."

"I believe you." During the 911 call, Olivia heard Elijah count two rounds of thirty compressions. "Why do you think Benji said you would end up talking to someone like me?"

The response was immediate. "It wanted to see if you would come when you were called."

Olivia gathered her purse from the floor by her feet. "I think we're done for today. Thank you, Elijah, for speaking with me."

Detective Aberdeen remained silent as she passed. Silas didn't speak until they were alone. Olivia was eagerly waiting for him to start the car and get back on the road to DC. Traffic would be a bitch this time of day, but he sat there, keys in the ignition, going

Lullaby

nowhere. Finally, when he couldn't keep it to himself anymore, Silas turned to her.

"Pardon my French, but what the fuck was that?"

"You're going to have to be a little more specific, Agent Branch," Olivia encouraged. He needed time to gather his thoughts, but she could tell by the look on his face he wasn't happy with any of them. He was a methodical man. He not only wanted a logical explanation, he needed one.

"How did you know he didn't do CPR?" Silas asked.

Olivia sighed, a heavy blanket of exhaustion settling over her. Talking to the boy had drained her resources. She would need to direct Agent Branch to the nearest drive-through for a jolt of caffeine, or she would drift off to sleep in the car.

"Something didn't sound right in the call. He sounded rhythmical, which is how it sounds when you recite instructions. I've heard clinical instructors sound the same way. But that's not how you sound if you're really trying to save someone's life. Life-saving is exhausting, yet Elijah was never short of breath. Then I remembered the crime scene photo—the only one I saw of the death scene. To receive CPR, Beenji would need to be on his back. Not face down on the floor. Elijah only went through the motions. He repeated what he was told. I'm sure he's been doing that his whole life. It's learned behavior—a defense mechanism."

Olivia finally looked over to find Agent Branch still staring at her. He had been doing it all day, but this look was different.

"Defense from what?" Silas asked.

"The chaos of the world around him."

49

Silas paused to contemplate her response before moving on. *"You got all that out of the phone call and one crime scene photo?"*

"I used to be a nurse. I know what it takes to do CPR." Olivia threw in the part about her past vocation because she wanted to forget the last time she tried to save someone's life. It came with visions of a basement filled with blood. *"I've also been a twelve-year-old child. When we're younger, we can't stop talking, but as we age and mature, we grow a filter. We adapt and learn how to play the adults around us. It didn't take me long to learn what my Gran wanted to hear and what she didn't."*

"Is Elijah still doing it? Playing the adults?" Silas wanted to know.

"No. I don't think he is. I believe his survival instinct has kicked in because he knows he's in trouble."

Silas nodded, digesting the information. *"You mentioned that you were bothered by something you didn't hear. I get it now; it was about the CPR. That means you did hear the part about the boy seeing a demon. You care to explain why that doesn't bother you?"*

Olivia was too tired to smile this time. *"You still don't know why they called me, do you?"*

"Not a fucking clue," Silas admitted.

"I hunt the monsters in the dark."

Chapter Six

"How many hits did that thing get?" Dillon asked, looking at the grainy video he had watched countless times.

The technician neglected to assign a number. He had heard this Dillon guy was a real pain in the ass. Anything with more than a few zeros was probably too many. He might be wearing a suit, but everything about him screamed military. "It was three in the morning. No one was monitoring the fifth floor of the parking garage at that time," the IT tech assured him. "We accessed the building surveillance system and wiped the incident."

Dillon recognized the redirection for what it was and decided he could let the number go *for now*. Still, he had questions. "If it was three in the morning in an empty garage, then how did this end up streaming on the internet?"

"Trollers. They're bored pre-teens hacking into random security cameras. This garage is a frequent go-to spot for a quick blow job," the tech explained. "Luckily, the hacker doesn't have a large on-line audience. We wiped it from his feed and the cloud."

"Were those your instructions?" Dillon asked.

The question caught the technician off guard. "Excuse me, sir?"

"I requested it be contained, not confiscated," Dillon clarified.

The tech was confused. He was an online hitman, scooping up secrets men like Dillon didn't want for public consumption.

"Monitor the hacker and control the flow of information. He might be useful, but I'm not ready to open the floodgates just yet. Now, go undo whatever you did."

Dillon waited until the tech left before turning on Leo Dennis, the local FBI agent. "What's the cover story for why your agent was there?" Dillon wanted to know.

"He was there for the same reason as the hacker," Agent Dennis answered as previously instructed. It was a dig at a fellow agent, but a bit of truth made the lies more believable. With a history of booze and women, Mason Deveroux would forever be known as a man who made questionable decisions. The last one got him killed.

Satisfied with the answer, Dillon moved on. "What about the body?"

"Landed in the bushes next to the parking garage," Dennis replied.

Dennis didn't like Dillon's use of the term *body* instead of victim. He also doubted Dillon was FBI. Something was wrong with this operation, but Dennis wasn't one to ask questions. The fewer questions, the better was an unspoken rule not just in Vegas, but in the Bureau. Whatever *this* was, it was important enough to pull him off the blowout at Deveroux's house in favor of babysitting the *body*. The only upside to the reassignment was that Agent Branch probably wasn't missing. Dennis just hoped his outcome was better than Deveroux's.

"How did it go with the coroner?" As a general rule, Dillon detested working with medical personnel outside his purview. They were too nosey and didn't fall in line as easily as others. The medicine men were used to being the ones in charge. Dillon tended to avoid using them whenever possible.

"I gave him the assigned cover story. The FBI is eager to take care of their own. Besides, Halloween is a big night here. The coroner was glad to let someone else take this one off his hands," Dennis replied.

The coroner, like the hacker, would be useful at another time.

"What about Deveroux's vehicle?" Dillon would have left it to be impounded by the local Vegas police if not for the phone inside. There was a video on that as well.

"Prints match the girl from Texas. Blood smears match the owner," Dennis reported.

"Thank you for your service, Agent Dennis— you're dismissed," Dillon said.

Another man, who had remained out of sight, slid into the empty seat across from Dillon. "I'm not gonna lie, I was as surprised about the video feed as the IT guy. I would think you would want it squashed."

"I'm playing the long game, Douglas. He who controls the narrative controls the story," Dillon reminded him.

"What about the BAU Director?" Douglas asked.

"Once Agent Dennis was pulled off the case, he went on his way. He's already left Vegas. He's staring down retirement, so I don't expect any interference," Dillon explained. "Besides, even if he was suspicious, who would he tell?"

"Speaking of, how is the good doctor?"

"Still in the ICU." Dillon would never admit it, but they were lucky they weren't dealing with her. There would be time enough for that later. Maybe a brush with death would make her more willing to accept their offer.

"And the little ones?"

"Holding their own. The samples you requested are on the way," Dillon said. He left out the part about only one sample and the compromised nurse.

"So, what about your golden boy?" the shadow man asked.

"He'll get the new knee he needs, as soon as I learn what he saw at Deveroux's house and why the last call on his cell phone was to Sarah Larsin. Afterward, he can go."

Douglas knew the last part was not the truth. Silas Branch would never be free.

****

Barry didn't text Poe to say he was coming. He was still wrestling with Will's suggestion Poe join them for their meeting with Patrick Monahan. The jolt of finding Olivia gone stopped Barry in his tracks.

"It wasn't a seizure," Poe rushed to assure him.

"Then why did they take her for the MRI?"

"I just got a call from Radiology," Renaye said, slipping in behind Barry undetected. "They wanted to know what happened to her restraints."

Renaye knew she should have noticed, but she had been distracted—by her patient, by the arrival of the transport team, and if she was truthful, by Poe. "Don't try and blame it on Norma, either," Renaye warned. The night shift nurse liked working in the ICU because her patients were either sedated or restrained, usually both.

Barry's hands moved to his hips, signaling he was siding with Renaye.

"Her wrists were starting to chafe," Poe said.

Renaye shook her head. "Not possible with the amount of sedation she's on."

"You have no idea what's possible," Poe countered. A high percentage of gifteds worked in healthcare—the desire to heal was strong—yet when he scanned Renaye earlier, he sensed no obvious gifts.

Poe looked to Barry for support. "It's subtle, like a prisoner trying to break free."

Barry had seen his share of suspects who thought they were Houdini and could wiggle out of handcuffs. None of them were successful, but that didn't stop them from trying. Resistance was instinctive.

"It's a sign she needs to come off the sedation," Poe reaffirmed.

"Or that she's still having seizures," Renaye argued. "The induced coma saved her life."

"Medically, yes, but it has served its purpose," Poe retaliated. "It's time she came back."

"That's not your call," Renaye argued. "As a nurse, I shouldn't have to remind you that the only way she's breathing right now is through that tube down her throat. Removing her restraints is risky business." Manipulation of the tube by a patient or some external force could damage the airway, causing bleeding, aspiration of fluid into the lungs, and even death.

"I loosened them. I didn't remove them," Poe clarified.

The confidence in his voice angered Renaye

further. "It's reckless and dangerous. You're playing with her life."

"No more dangerous than where she is," Poe snapped back. "The cost is the same."

Poe was out of control, forcing Barry to intervene.

Barry turned on Renaye. "We need a minute."

With a scathing look toward Poe, Renaye snatched back the privacy curtain and disappeared into the hall. Barry followed her as far as the sliding glass door. His back to Poe, Barry took a moment to gather his thoughts, one hand on the door, the other in his pocket, fidgeting with coins Brennon Kaine gave him. Brennon didn't say what they were for, only that Poe would know.

"Tell me why I should trust you."

"The doctor would have ordered an MRI eventually," Poe explained. "I just gave Olivia a chance to free herself," Poe stressed. "It's not uncommon for comatose patients to experience an altered reality. I know what Olivia's other reality is like. You don't want her there," Poe cautioned.

Barry had witnessed Olivia's return from just such a place. The first time was when he rescued her from a murder victim's car. She came out disoriented and frightened. She described a dark place with a purple sky and shadows that stalked her. The second time, she was alone in a cellar full of snakes. Olivia walked out of there a different person.

Barry turned back to face Poe. "I'm listening."

Relieved Barry was staying, rather than following Renaye, Poe began. "Something happened last night. Two different times the whole unit went dark—all but this room. Hospital maintenance spent half the night up here looking for an explanation they are never going to find. I'm convinced Olivia is trying to bring herself back. It will be harder if she's sedated."

Doubt lingered in Barry's eyes. Poe didn't fault him. Barry wasn't born *gifted*. His role as Olivia's *Watcher* was a calling, not a birthright. Barry would cling to his own world until Poe could explain otherwise. Poe needed Barry to trust him enough to cross the bridge into his new reality. Finding common ground was his best hope for an alliance. "I told Mémé your story about the barn, and how Olivia started the fire," Poe began. "According to Mémé, Olivia tapped the energy around her and used it for her own purpose. That sounds a whole lot like what happened in here."

"She did that because we were in danger," Barry told Poe. "Are you telling me Olivia's in danger?"

Poe needed to skirt the issue for now because he needed Barry to keep listening. "I got a peek into where she is," Poe admitted. "I was on the outside looking in, but I could hear murmurs in tongues I didn't understand."

"Was it Latin?" Barry had heard Olivia speak it before. First in the barn and the other day at Poe's apartment.

Poe shook his head. "No. I speak Latin, French and some Hebrew. I didn't understand, because it's deader than Latin. Something very powerful over there interested in Olivia, and I don't want her to hang around to find out what that is. I'm pretty sure she doesn't want that either."

By now, Barry's fists were clenched inside his pockets. "You felt this from her?" How did Brennon and Will trust this man they never met? Was it because

Olivia trusted Poe? Barry was the holdout and that too had to do with Olivia, but it was Barry's feelings, not hers. He felt confident he could protect her and the babies—*if* they stayed in this world. As for the other one, the world that Poe knew, and the one beckoning Olivia right now, Barry was clueless. He could not protect what he could not understand.

"The other day, after I shared with Olivia my memory of our first meeting, she never severed our connection. We don't have to speak to communicate," Poe explained, as his eyes strayed to the empty space in the room. "If I don't help Olivia come back, she'll find her own way. Last night it was the lights. Today it could be the ventilators."

Barry shifted his gaze outside the glass door. They were surrounded by vulnerable patients who were only alive because of the electronic devices keeping them that way. "You realize how crazy that sounds, right?" Barry asked.

"Not any crazier than you telling me Olivia started a fire and used a dead snake to kill some really bad people," Poe reminded him. "A life force is powerful. Taking it can raise the dead," Poe cautioned. "Olivia has many gifts. Once unlocked, they can't be put back," Poe warned.

While Barry struggled, Poe wrestled with his own doubts. As a gifted, Poe knew Olivia's biggest threat was the one he couldn't see. As Olivia's former watcher, Barry was focused on the visible one. Poe may have pledged his servitude willingly, but he was ill-prepared to fulfill it. Olivia would always have something or someone stalking her. Maybe it was never meant to be a one-man job.

"Olivia called you a demon hunter." Barry watched as Poe's stoic mask slipped. Rogan Poe didn't like hearing those words.

"Hunter implies I kill things," Poe corrected him. "The roles we play, just as the gifts we receive, all have ancient roots. The words were more barbaric, as were the times. They burned people like Olivia at the stake. In today's world, I protect the vulnerable and provide a safe crossing for those departing."

Just like a suspect, Poe was downplaying his role. Barry might not be a product of Poe's world, but Poe had educated him. "You told me in the chapel Olivia is the way she is because she has a witch for a mother and a possessed man for a father. I think that was your way of skirting the issue that her father is a demon. I don't have to be gifted to know that makes Olivia part demon."

"It sounds like you're asking me if I'm hunting Olivia," Poe clarified.

"Yea, I guess I am," Barry confirmed.

"I'm not hunting her. I knelt at her bedside and offered myself as a guide and a protector," Poe reminded him.

"Why?" Barry asked. It was a simple question and the most important decision of his life.

Poe searched for words, for feelings he couldn't express. "Because she needs me." It was a simple answer to a complicated question. Poe hoped it was enough.

After learning there were other gifted ones, Olivia was relentless in her search for more. Rogan Poe was the one she found. *Olivia hunted Poe because she said she needed him.* There was no one Barry trusted more than Olivia.

"Then tell me what these are for," Barry said, passing Poe the coins. "There are two little girls who need their mother."

"*For He will order His angels to guard you wherever you go,*" Poe recited the verse. "It's a lullaby of sorts, from the book of *Psalms*. Where did you get these?"

"Brennon Kane. Olivia has known him a long time. I've learned from recent experience, he's not a bad guy to have around," Barry admitted. Kane swooped in at Olivia's request to keep him out of jail. "Kaine is also the reason the staff is no longer trying to throw you out of here," Barry added.

Poe nodded his appreciation—that could only have happened with Barry's permission. This had just become an alliance.

"Lullabies aren't just sweet songs sung to babies. They are a way to pass down traditions. In Jewish folklore, the word *lullaby* means *Lilith abi* which translates to *Lilith, be gone.*"

Poe dropped the coins back into Barry's hand. "According to lore, *Lilith* is a demon. These charms offer protection against Lilith. There's four for each baby. Affix them to the outside of their cribs." Poe's face was grave. "Does this Brennon Kaine know about the code pink?"

"He and Sergeant Ibarra are meeting with hospital administration as we speak," Barry told him.

"I warned Olivia there would be threats to her offspring. Not all those with gifts want the secrets we keep to become known. There are those who prefer the shadows. They wear their anonymity like a cloak.

Olivia is the product of a fable. Because she carries demon blood, there will be those in the collective who won't trust her, or her offspring. The non-gifted have their own shadow dwellers. They fear change, but more importantly, they fear what they cannot control." Poe watched the news settle over Barry. If word of the *Gifted* ones spread, there would be a gathering of shadow dwellers on both sides.

"This Mr. Kaine must know what Olivia is," Poe ventured. She was good at collecting followers. The skill would serve her well.

"That's why I've asked him to stay with her while you come with me. It's time you learn what there is to know about Silas Branch."

Chapter Seven

"How do we know he's not dead?" Poe asked.

"We found his phone and the keys to his rental car. Silas is the only thing missing," Patrick Monahan repeated.

"Whoever took him needs something only he can give," Barry suggested what Patrick wouldn't. The BAU Director wanted someone else to put the pieces together. Maybe it was plausible deniability, maybe it was personal.

"What would that be?" Poe wanted to know. As far as he was concerned, the people who took Silas Branch were the same ones the director worked for. Patrick, whether he wanted to admit it or not, didn't trust the Bureau either. Otherwise, they would be meeting in the local FBI field office.

Poe could see Patrick beginning to waver under his stare. *Good.* "There's more," Poe prompted him.

Barry remained silent despite the escalation in Poe's voice. Poe was kicking down doors and flipping over all the rocks, looking in places no one else wanted to look. It was exactly what Olivia would have done if she were here. It was scary how much they were alike.

"I think they want to know what Silas knows about the whereabouts of Agent Deveroux. His car is gone but so far no body parts in what's left of his house. Deveroux is the reason Silas went to Vegas in the first place," Patrick reminded them.

"A house fire can cover up a lot of things," Will theorized. "If it was bad, as you say, not finding body parts wouldn't be surprising." Will had worked with the fire marshal service enough in Atascosa County to know more than he ever wanted to know about fire and the damage it could do. "Whoever took Silas left his phone behind so no one could track him," Will theorized.

"Silas also went looking for Sarah Larsin," Barry added.

"She has nothing to do with this," Poe assured him.

"How can you be so sure?" Barry asked. Olivia's mother was one subject they hadn't covered.

"I threatened her," Poe confessed.

Barry didn't hide his surprise. "Why would she listen to you?"

"If Sarah Larsin had Agent Branch, she would have told me to go fuck myself. Sarah's not the problem." Poe shifted his gaze toward Patrick. "The problem is the same as it always is."

Poe looked like he had something else to say, but Patrick beat him to it. "He's right. The Bureau knows it's not her," Patrick confirmed.

"You'll are in cahoots?" Barry sounded annoyed.

"Let's just say it is an ever-shifting alliance," Patrick countered. "This time her story checks out."

Poe was ready to move on. "So, what is happening in Vegas?"

"I was working with one of the local agents, the one Silas contacted when he got into town. That agent has been reassigned and there's radio silence on Deveroux," Patrick admitted.

"Well, there you have it," Poe proclaimed. He was tired of bullshit and was ready to get down to business. He should be at the hospital with Olivia, not here playing do-si-do with the government man. "Two agents missing, the helpful local agent is reassigned, and the BAU director is what? Did they ask you to leave or tell you?"

Patrick studied Rogan Poe glad he wasn't chasing someone like him. Poe knew more than he should. Like, Olivia. Barry introduced him as a nurse and a friend of Olivia's. Poe, whoever or whatever he was, was more than that. "Whoever is behind this, isn't from the Bureau," Patrick said.

"You sure about that?" Barry beat Poe to the punch this time. Barry didn't trust the FBI and obviously, neither did Patrick—or he wouldn't be here.

Poe gave Barry a side glance. "More shadow dwellers."

"Agency," Will suggested.

"Mr. Director, why don't you just tell us why you're here? Is it because you needed to tell someone? Relieve your conscience, maybe?" Poe pushed himself from the chair he had been occupying. He had resisted pacing the room like a caged animal. He was trying not to intimidate the FBI man, but maybe that was exactly what needed to happen.

To his credit, Patrick held his ground. "I came here because Silas Branch has been my friend for almost fifteen years. I care what happens to him and to Olivia," Patrick confessed.

"All roads lead to Olivia." Poe didn't even make it a question. "From what I understand, she had a pretty rough go of it at the Bureau. They hired her for the jobs no one wanted and then didn't listen to her. When the shit hit the fan, they hung her out to dry. The FBI knew what Olivia was all along because she's not the first they've encountered." Poe's pacing led him back to Patrick. The FBI man remained in place, but he looked like he was braced for impact.

Barry looked to Patrick for answers, but he had gone mute, so Barry turned to Poe.

"You asked about my finances. They don't come from Sarah Larsin. They come from the archbishop, courtesy of the Church. There is no separation between church and state when there are secrets to hide. Archbishop Mendoza is the one that strongly suggested I return to San Antonio when Olivia decided to return after her Gran died. No matter how much Ginny Larsin confessed her fears, no one saved her. They listened and left her and Olivia on their own." Poe watched a shadow fall across Barry's face.

Poe looked back to Patrick. "There will forever be a dividing line in Olivia's life. Part of it will include what happens here today. Now tell me, how long has the FBI known about her?"

"Since Jason Austin, at least," Patrick admitted.

Poe remembered *Jason*–the guy from the party. For Jason to occupy a place in Olivia's memories meant he had once owned a piece of her heart.

"Those murders caught a lot of attention," Patrick said. He thought it was because the body count included the two cops who worked the scene. Now, he was reexamining everything he thought he knew about not only Silas but Olivia as well.

"Probably because the demon found what he was looking for," Barry theorized. "I've been looking into the cases that got Jason Austin killed."

Poe recognized there was more to Barry's investigation, but now wasn't the time for that discussion. "What kind of monster did the Bureau dangle in front of Olivia to convince her to come back?" Poe wanted to know.

"A twelve-year-old boy," Patrick confessed. "Elijah Stoddard, the stepson of a Virginia state senator. He killed his six-year-old brother. According to Silas, Elijah claimed his brother was possessed."

Poe wondered what Olivia told the parents, but mainly what she didn't.

"It would be nice to know where Elijah is now," Will said, beating Poe to the punch.

"The kid was placed in a facility that he should have gotten out of at eighteen," Patrick answered, wondering why he had never considered why things worked out the way they did. Maybe because he never needed a reason. *Until now.*

"There was always someone in the shadows watching the cases Olivia worked, pulling whatever strings it took to keep her around," Patrick mused. "I was cut out of everything as soon as Silas transferred to San Antonio, except when Larry Pittman's name came up a few months ago. After I got Olivia to agree to take another look at the case, I was cut out of that loop as well." Realization settled in as Patrick considered how the Bureau had used him just as they had Olivia.

"Was Silas Branch part of that arrangement?" Poe dared ask.

Patrick looked away, his silence telling Poe he had considered it.

"My guess is the same people pulling Olivia's

strings are now betting Silas is their best chance to keep her around," Poe theorized, doing nothing to hide the disgust on his face. "They are the ones responsible for Silas' disappearance. They are making him a deal."

The sound of Poe's phone broke the stalemate. He pulled it from his pocket and walked out of the room.

****

With Poe gone, Patrick heaved a sigh of relief. "I need a minute," he said and slipped out the front door to the porch.

Barry didn't move, not to follow Poe or Patrick.

"What's going on with you?" Will asked when the silence of the room grew deafening.

Barry shook his head, still not present. Poe's words echoed in his ears, ripping open old wounds, stirring feelings of resentment, and fanning the flames of others he had tried hard to bury.

"While I'm here, I thought I might try to get into Olivia's laptop. That way, I can not only answer Kevin Branch but get a look at what he thinks is so important," Will suggested when Barry didn't elaborate.

"The laptop's in her office," Barry said offhandedly, pointing Will down the hall. "The password is the same as everything else."

"I didn't say anything before, but what's happening with me at the Bureau, it's not routine. They're fast-tracking me specifically to work with Silas. I think it has to do with what went on at Sheriff Tennent's house. That was a dead man walking, and no one will ever convince me otherwise."

****

The snapping sound next to his head was loud

enough to slice through the throbbing in his leg.

"Agent Branch, I need you awake for this and then we can do something about that pain in your knee. From what I heard, you need a new one," Dillon Bradford said before he pushed play.

Silas focused on the screen in front of him instead of the pain. It was nighttime on the video. There was light, but it was artificial. It looked like a parking garage. The place was empty except for whoever was behind the camera. The feed had to be from a phone. It was too close to be a security camera. The figure on screen was a man in a blue suit and white shirt, minus a tie. Silas watched him move slowly across the empty lot. Something was wrong. He wasn't so much walking as shuffling, but he didn't appear drunk. The angle of his mouth was slack. He looked like a sleepwalker.

"Do you recognize this individual?" Dillon asked.

Silas searched for an identifying marker while watching the man bump against the cement barrier. The man's feet kept moving even though he was going nowhere. The movement reminded Silas of a mechanical toy stuck in motion. When the man ran out of juice, he bent at the waist and tumbled over the side. There was no surprise, no scream. The guy was dead already.

Silas managed to spit out a name. "Mason Deveroux." It was the buzz cut that gave it away. Memories flooded back in a rush. The last thing Silas could recall was going to Deveroux's house. Before he could find more words, another video appeared.

This location was familiar. Silas had been there. The man was different, but the shuffling walk was the same. The gait was off just as Frank from Forensics described. The man was dragging one foot. According to Frank, it was something a stroke victim or someone with a neurological condition would do.

Or someone dead. That had been Silas' description.

The screen went black and the man with the clicker turned around. "Look familiar?"

Silas squinted. He knew the man asking the questions too. Silas rifled through his memories searching for a name.

"The last one is of the dearly departed sheriff of Atascosa County. Rose Corey was kind enough to commemorate her work—both times. In your world I believe it's known as a signature. She signed her kill is the more colloquial term, I believe."

Dillon stepped in Silas' line of sight. He bent down closer so Silas could see him and not the screen. "But that's your world, not mine. Feel free to correct me."

Even in pain, Silas knew no one corrected this man. "What is your world?" Silas asked instead. It was how he would question a suspect, one who was also proud of their work.

"I track people too," Dillon told him.

Silas decided against another question. He was still searching for meaning in the answer the man had just given.

Dillon stepped away again so Silas could focus on the scene frozen on the screen. "Ms. Corey isn't shy. She's proud of her work. It means she has a purpose. She wants someone to know who did this, and I don't think it's us."

Silas had no response. This man was looking for something.

"Your wife met her. After that, Rose Corey slipped

away and right back to Sarah Larsin."

Silas couldn't find a response because it wasn't a lie.

"Will she help us, your wife? Ms. Larsin is another matter entirely."

"Of course, she can," Silas said. It was the only answer he could give.

"I didn't ask if she could, but if she *would*," Dillon emphasized.

The blank screen on the wall flickered to life, replacing the scene from the sheriff's house. It was more video, this time from a prison in Gainesville, Florida, and home to Larry Wayne Pittman.

Silas blinked at the image of Olivia. Her eyes were brilliant green. She tilted her head, her forehead streaked with concentration as she focused on the advancing guards. A hiss slipped past her lips. The words were Latin. The sound of the guard's batons clattered to the ground, startling Silas even though he knew it was coming. Mercifully, the screen went back to black this time.

"Tell me, Agent Branch, does your wife scare you?" Not waiting for an answer, Dillon leaned in closer as the words weren't meant to be heard by others. "What else can she do?" Dillon asked.

Silas recalled the last man who confronted Olivia. Marc Singer railed at her just like this man was doing. Her eyes flashed green and Silas felt the electric charge run down his arm now just as he did then. Olivia all but confessed to leaving Andre Roche to die at the hands of a demon. Singer attacked her again, days later, only that time Olivia didn't speak. Singer left without the answers he wanted. He died a few hours later of a brain aneurysm.

Silas tried to speak, but his voice cracked.

A younger man stepped from the shadows. He had a cup with a straw that he held while Silas drank. In the background, Dillion watched the interaction with interest.

A memory bubbled to the surface. Silas had met the man with the clicker before, after the *Good Samaritan* case. Silas and Olivia both put a bullet in Jamie Smythe the night he showed up at her house. When a federal agent discharged their weapon, it was customary for the Office of Professional Responsibility or OPR to open an investigation. The man with the clicker was the same one who interrogated him. He had been the one calling the shots then too.

"He remembers you," the man assured Dillon.

Dillon leaned in closer so Silas could get another good look.

"You're not from the OPR, are you?" Silas asked, his throat dry despite the water.

Bradford Dillon smiled down at Silas. "Who told you that?"

Chapter Eight

Inside the kitchen, away from the others, Poe was hit with a rush of memories. Even if the space no longer looked the same, it was a place he'd seen repeatedly in Olivia's mind. This is where she felt safe and warm as she watched her gran. Beneath the avalanche of recall, the underlying smell of cinnamon leaked into Olivia's memory. Poe knew if she carried the memory, it must mean something just like with Jason Austin. The name flashing across his phone screen prompted him to sweep the questions of Olivia's past aside in favor of the here and now.

"Yea," Poe answered.

"It's Renaye. I wanted you to know Olivia's MRI and EEG looked good. She's not back to the floor yet, but her doctor called with orders to begin weaning her medication at her next dose, which is in about an hour. Her neurologist will be by later to check on her. The lawyer is still here, but I thought you might want to be here when she wakes up."

Renaye's words hung between them as Poe struggled to take in what she had said. Yes, he wanted to be there. His face was the one Poe wanted Olivia to see first. "Thank you for calling." Poe used the most neutral tone he could manage.

There was an awkward silence, neither of them hanging up, even though the information had been shared and acknowledged.

Renaye broke first. "Sorry if I sounded harsh before. I was just worried about my patient."

"It's okay. I understand. I'm sure Olivia will appreciate everything you've done."

"The doctor hasn't shared this with anyone. I think he was waiting on the husband, if he ever shows up."

"Shared what?" Poe prompted her.

"After the babies came, when she started to hemorrhage, Olivia died on the table. Luckily, they got her back pretty quickly, but I thought you should know. I was fighting *for her*, not against you," Renaye explained.

In need of an escape, Poe slipped out of the kitchen and into the backyard.

****

Patrick passed the conference room and saw her with her eyes closed, her hands over her ears as if she wanted to escape from what she was hearing. The arch of her brow told Patrick she didn't like whatever it was. He would let her finish while he put his things down and grabbed another cup of coffee to add to the half pot he had already consumed. That's when he saw Silas outside his door. The coffee would have to wait.

Who's the chick in the room down the hall?"

Patrick laid his briefcase on the desk. It had been a gift from Melinda for his promotion. "I told you, you're gonna have to drop the chick reference," Patrick scolded while motioning for Silas to close the door. "Get your game face on. You and Dr. Osborne are going to meet with the boy today."

"Dr. Osborne." It took a moment for Silas to catch up. It had been a long weekend after leaving Patrick's

the other night. Despite his MO, Silas didn't make it home the first night. "Wait, the woman down the hall with the headphones is Dr. Osborne?"

"In the flesh,' Patrick confirmed. "She's due in LA later in the week, so we scheduled an interview as soon as possible to accommodate her. You'll accompany her to the juvenile psych facility where they're holding the boy. The arresting officer will be there as an observer only. You and Dr. Osborne, along with the boy's attorney and therapist, will be the only ones in the room. The therapist, with direction from Dr. Osborne, persuaded the parents not to attend. They agreed, but only after conferring with their parish priest. He concurred with Dr. Osborne that the boy would be much more willing to speak freely if they weren't there. Anything else you have to say about her?" Patrick asked, hands on his hips, waiting for Silas' assessment of Olivia more than the situation.

"You didn't say what she has been doing since leaving the Bureau."

"Is that important?" Patrick asked. Considering Silas's strong sense of justice, it probably was. Maybe that's why Patrick had elected not to tell him.

"I saw the designer handbag. She has good taste, but doesn't want to show it off. That's why it's on the floor by her feet. The suit might be understated, but it's also expensive and not something she would wear working here." Silas knew enough successful women to know how much those things cost. "She conveys professionalism, but not the government kind." It meant she wasn't flashy. "Whatever she's been doing since leaving here, is lucrative."

Patrick was impressed with the attention to detail.

But this was Silas, and Olivia did not go unnoticed. "She's a consultant—for high-priced defense attorneys."

Silas' eyes narrowed.

"She provides expert testimony for those seeking a not guilty by reason of insanity verdict. She's knocking it out of the park. I'm sure you can see why the Bureau wants her back."

"She would give that up to come back here?"

"For her, it's not about the money, not that she will be making agent pay." Patrick had just gotten a look at her consulting fee and was surprised a government agency was paying it. They weren't kidding when they said they wanted her back. "It's about justice."

"Getting murderers off?" Silas made it sound like something illegal.

"She believes in real evil. Not the man-made kind. She only takes cases like the one you're looking into today. It's why I told you she was the only one I trust to get to the bottom of this. It's also why she can afford all those things you mentioned. There's a high demand for what she does and there isn't anyone with, shall we say, her experience."

Instead of waiting for Patrick's watered-down version of Dr. Osborne's experience, Silas provided his own. "The kind of evil the Catholic Church would be interested in," Silas said, intoning the words slowly, watching Patrick's reaction.

Silas knew more than he pretended. Still, Patrick wasn't ready to debate where he got his information. Besides, Patrick was more interested in the glint he saw in his friend's eye. "Anything else?" Patrick asked, giving Silas the chance to confess.

Silas looked annoyed but knew what Patrick was asking. "You want me to state the obvious? She doesn't look like the doctorly type. Her looks are a definite plus for any defense team that hires her. She will have the jury's attention before she ever even opens her mouth."

"I don't want to have to say this, but..."

"You're going to do it anyway," Silas grumbled.

"I know she's just your type, but hear me when I say this—I need you to not go there with her. She's off limits."

****

"I appreciate you coming here."

Barry's intrusion shattered Patrick's memories. It was for the best. He should cut back on his trips down memory lane. "I didn't come here to betray my friend, but it feels like it." Patrick stared off at the empty street.

"I don't think that," Barry said the words Patrick needed to hear, no matter how self-serving. Barry's allegiance was to Olivia. He would do or say anything to get what he needed.

"Then what am I doing?" Patrick sounded desperate and unsure.

"You're sharing your concerns for people you care about," Barry replied. Poe had gotten into both of their heads about Silas. It was obvious Patrick was grappling with his own competing feelings. They were what drove Patrick here, but the window for sharing information was closing and guilt was settling in. Barry had to get to him before the walls of defense came crashing down. "You also said you were here because of Olivia. It's because of her I need you to tell me what Silas will do," Barry coaxed him.

Patrick knew what Barry was doing. Patrick had set his own trap. He should have gone further than the front porch. "What do you mean, what Silas will do?" It was a question Patrick didn't want to answer.

Barry led him as he would a suspect, reminding him of all the knowns of the equation before urging him to answer the question. "I think we're all in agreement that Silas was taken. If it wasn't by Ms. Larsin, then who? Who else would have something to gain?"

The look on Patrick's face was both defeat and release. Rogan Poe had already said it, but Barry wanted confirmation. "The same ones who dropped the breadcrumbs they knew Silas would follow."

The analogy was one Barry would wrestle with later. Right now, he needed Patrick to keep talking. "The FBI or some other three letter agency." Barry paused, allowing Patrick the opportunity to change the narrative. "If that's true then that means they have an agenda and I think we all know what that agenda involves." Barry gave another pause.

"It started with Atascosa County and I don't mean the fire in the barn or the sheriff. I mean the murder of Ferdinand Roche."

For Barry, the memory came back in a rush. *A blue folder.* The details inside involved a male impaled with a pitchfork and an inverted pentagram carved into the shoulder. His body anointed with red pepper and salt pointed to a ritualistic killing.

"The murder had already bubbled to the surface before we got wind of your Good Samaritan Killer," Patrick acknowledged. "The case caught the attention of Mason Deveroux first, but something else about it piqued the interest of others, that's why it got shoved to

Silas. Deveroux has been a useful idiot all along," Patrick surmised. "He spewed all sorts of allegations about witchcraft. Those in the shadows sat back and watched while he ruined his reputation at the same time they believed he was onto something. They just wanted him to forge the path and pave the way for them whenever they believed it was time to release the truth to the masses. Then along comes Rose Corey who can make corpses rise if the stories of Sheriff Tennent are to be believed."

"They are," Barry assured him. He had seen the photos Silas sent Olivia of the crime scene. Will had confirmed as much over the weekend during their beer run. Before that was the discussion Barry and Silas shared the night Silas freed him from jail. It was all about Deveroux's quest. How much of what Silas fed him that night was confession or bait? Barry was the only one who could corroborate what happened in the barn. For a moment, Barry felt the same spark of betrayal as Patrick. Barry had spilled secrets to Silas he wished he could take back.

Patrick shook his head. "Their timeline is fucked now and they're in acceleration mode. An incident like that can't be ignored. Rose Corey isn't like Olivia. She can't be passed off as simply having keen intuition or some other parlor trick. Ms. Corey's antics legitimize fear. Now those who watched Deveroux in silence will harness Ms. Corey's actions to push their own agenda. No one will be in the shadows anymore."

So, Poe was right. All roads did lead to Olivia. "Is there any truth to the suggestion Silas was sent to…" Barry couldn't bring himself to say the words so Patrick did it for him.

"Be with Olivia?"

"They both worked for you. Were you the one who put them together?" Barry asked. His words were clipped as his hands balled into fists.

In the beginning, Patrick had been too wrapped up in his own promotion to question the motives of others. Recent events forced Patrick to reexamine the past. The moves were so subtle they seemed inconsequential.

"Silas was passed over for the promotion that I received. The case of Elijah Stoddard was my first. At the time, I was glad to have Silas on my team. I had worked with Olivia before. I would have been happy to work with her again, but I didn't know that was an option."

After leaving the Bureau, Olivia changed gears and started working for people like Brennon Kane, assessing an accused's competency to stand trial with one important stipulation. She only assessed those claiming the drive to commit their crimes came from some external force.

"Why do you say that?" Barry asked, curious to hear Patrick's take on things.

"Providing expert testimony is far more lucrative than any government job. But I guess you know it's not about money for her. More than that, after the Bureau pushed her out I didn't think they would take her back. Let's face it, that's not their MO."

"And you didn't think anything about that?" Barry asked.

Patrick shook his head. "No. I had just been promoted. I was getting married. My life was good," Patrick reflected on the memory he had just relived.

"And Silas?" Barry prompted.

"Putting him with Olivia would not have been my first choice. The nudge to tag him as her chaperone was not mine. My bosses played it up as being a high-profile case due to the kid's stepfather. Silas looks like an FBI agent, but he is more than that. He's action-oriented, adrenaline driven. Having worked together before I knew that about him."

Patrick's description matched Barry's first impression of Silas Branch. "Why didn't he get the promotion? Was playing babysitter to Olivia retribution for something?"

"Silas had some problems. The story your friend Poe alluded to was true about the FBI turning their back on Olivia and ending her career as an agent. The reason Silas wasn't there the night things went sideways is because he was back in rehab."

Barry felt his gut seize. "Back in rehab? That implies he had been there before."

"It started in college, due to sports related injuries. It flared up again with something that happened on the job."

"Were drugs the only thing he was addicted to?" Barry asked. Now that Poe wasn't here, Barry was turning over rocks, looking for darkness.

"There were some women. Allegations were made, none of them ever proven," Patrick revealed. "Knowing Silas as I do, it was mostly about them not getting the version of Silas they thought they were."

"Meaning?"

"Silas knows how to get what he wants," Patrick admitted quietly. His words tasted like betrayal, no matter what Barry said.

Barry wished he could unhear the words. "If faced

with a choice between the FBI and Olivia, what will *your friend* Silas do?"

Barry's words stung, but Patrick figured he had earned them. "Olivia is not the same as the others," Patrick said, knowing the words were already too late for Barry to hear. "I don't know if it was personal or professional. That's the truth."

"Just answer the question," Barry snapped.

"The move to San Antonio shocked me. That Silas asked for it and that it was granted. Station chief is a good position, but given the high-profile cases of the BAU, the ones Olivia worked on, the move was a step back, not a step up. But no matter the how or the why of it, Silas will believe he can have both the FBI and Olivia," Patrick admitted.

"But he can't," Barry proclaimed. "Not anymore. This is bigger than Olivia and Silas."

Patrick wished the words came with more emotion. All Barry gave him was cold resolve. Lines were being drawn, all while meandering down paths no one could retrace. "What are you going to do? If choices are required?" Patrick wanted to know.

"I will be the least of Silas' concerns," Barry told him. "I've seen what Oliva will do when her back is against the wall."

The conversation was cut short by Will Ibarra opening the front door. "You better come look at this."

Chapter Nine

Poe's skin tingled with the presence of a demon. If he wasn't who and what he was, Poe might not have caught the distorted movement in the back of the garden. As he approached, a shimmer in the mid-morning sun morphed into something monstrous. No introduction was needed. Poe had sensed the demon the first time he visited. Olivia said *Alleracsap's* presence had increased as her pregnancy advanced. Poe wondered if the demon planned on taking up permanent residence now that the twins were born. Either way, getting rid of him wouldn't be easy.

Alleracsap was relieved to appear in his true form. For mere humans, it was more frightening to appear in demon form in the daylight. His kind belonged in the dark, but given who he was meeting—a demon hunter—*Alleracsap* was pleased to be himself. Olivia Osborne's garden was a place he could make his home.

Poe didn't flinch at the demon's appearance. This wasn't the first demon he had met and most likely would not be the last. The only thing that interested Poe was what wasn't here. The waves of cinnamon he experienced in the kitchen were gone. Poe had never associated the scent with a demon before. Maybe that was because he only ever dealt with the low-level ones prowling Alzheimer's units, preying on the elderly, and infirmed. Poe knew the cinnamon meant something.

This demon was not the source.

Alleracsap stretched his hulking figure as if waking from a nap. The demon's arms appeared covered in vines, but on closer inspection, Poe saw shades of color. The twisted forms on his arm weren't vines at all, but a knot of snakes, twisting and turning, basking in the sun as the light danced off their scales.

"Cinnamon invokes lust. Maybe the scent is yours," *Alleracsap* greeted him.

"Get out of my head," Poe snapped.

"It was just a peek, I assure you." For once *Alleracsap* spoke the truth, not that Poe would believe him. The demon hunter had a shroud of shielding that could only have come from Olivia.

"Doubt it," Poe told him. "The scent's not coming from either of us. It's something else," Poe ventured.

"Hang around long enough and you will see." *Alleracsap* smiled, showing a row of teeth. If it had been darker, Poe would have seen the glow of his eyes.

One of the snakes broke free from the rest and leered toward Poe. The forked tongue darted out to test the air. Poe watched it without comment.

Alleracsap snatched the wayward serpent and tossed it into the bushes. "Snakes are her familiar. Must be why she has so many of them in her life."

Poe recognized the play on words but refused to take the bait. He wasn't in the mood for demon sparring today.

Alleracsap tried again. "Why are you not at the hospital?"

"I could ask the same of you," Poe replied. *Alleracsap's* presence here was significant. If her demon was here, then who was with Olivia?

"You know the old saying, *we are many, we are legion, blah, blah, blah*. I take it you disapprove of my presence?" *Alleracsap* queried.

"It's her garden," Poe said dismissively.

"Glad you see things my way."

"That's not what I said," Poe snapped.

"Oh, but it is," *Alleracsap* assured him.

"Don't pretend to know me," Poe said.

"But I do. I am hers," *Alleracsap* gloated.

"But you're not the only," Poe wagered.

"Neither are you," *Alleracsap* snapped back. "You might have been invited here, but for the men inside, you disrupt their world. Just as Olivia does. My kind are not the only ones who wish to possess. There are those who want to harness what Olivia has been gifted," *Alleracsap* warned.

Mémé taught magic was both a gift and a trap. Magic must be respected. Incantations could sound like prayers, but it must never be forgotten that magic was given by demons. Because demons were once angels, the one who possesses the gifts, decides how to use them.

Practitioners walked narrow paths between deception and redemption. Good and evil. Darkness and light. Inside the grey was the most dangerous place to be. Amongst the shadows, it was easy to get lost. That's where Olivia was now.

"The answers you seek are in history," *Alleracsap* assured him. "Ask yourself who showed mortals the way? Who gave them the gift of witchcraft? The men inside aren't the only ones who see change coming. Olivia sought you out. Now that she has found you, is it not your wish to pull her from the shadows and teach her what she truly is?"

Poe didn't like this demon in his head. Luckily, he was still skirting the edges.

"Familiarity will win," *Alleracsap* promised. "But which one?"

****

The shadow man was waiting for Dillon when he left Silas's room. "You think you might have pushed him too hard?"

"Not really," Dillon quipped.

"You didn't want to save something for later?" Douglas pressed.

"Like what?"

"The feed from the prison. That was dramatic. She scared me." It wasn't so much what he saw but how she made him feel. It was like stumbling upon a predator in the dark.

"Watching it had the same effect on him," Dillon confirmed. "And he was there for the live show."

Douglas realized what Dillon was getting at.

"Imagine, if it can have that effect on him, what will it do to the general population? That's what I want him thinking about, what his life will be like if she succumbs to her true nature. If she's not controlled."

"And you think you can what, tame her?"

"I'll need his help, that's what this is about. Tame or break, it doesn't matter to me. Just like everything else, she's a tool to be used."

What worried Douglas, and what should worry Dillon is they weren't the ones who made Olivia Osborne.

****

"It seems Olivia was asking the same questions

you were," Will surmised, according to the emails from Kevin Branch.

"I don't want to know how he got this information, do I?" Patrick asked, as he paced in front of Olivia's desk. What kind of data access did Silas' little brother have that he could track Elijah Stoddard into an abyss that had all the markings of some dark covert agency?

"When did she request the info?" Barry asked.

"The night before Silas left for Vegas," Will replied. It wasn't the only request Olivia had sent. The one asking for information on a certain nurse went out days before this one. Will avoided that piece of information for now. It was a personal matter for Barry.

"I knew something happened that morning," Barry said. He and Patrick circled each other as they paced, passing like sentries on patrol. Barry recalled Olivia's mood change after her walk with Silas. He chalked it up to Silas finally telling her about his impending trip. Barry held back because he was hesitant about intruding into her personal affairs. Barry decided he wouldn't make that mistake again.

"Something Silas said must have spooked her," Will said, mirroring what Barry was thinking.

"She hasn't trusted the Bureau for a long time," Patrick revealed. "Add Deveroux to the equation and it wouldn't be a giant leap for her to know Deveroux's useful days were coming to an end. Olivia knew Deveroux was just a tool. She would want to know his purpose."

"Researching her past cases was a good place to start. She hinted that she thought Pittman could have been a Guinee pig," Barry shared. Incarceration was a perfect environment for study.

"Of course, he was," Poe said, entering the room.

Barry realized how much smaller it felt with his presence.

"Look, I know I'm new to the party and maybe you guys need to hash this out, but we don't have time for this. It's the past. We need to prepare for what's coming."

"And what's that, exactly?" Patrick wanted to know.

"Acknowledgement. Everything Pittman told her is true. It's how she found me. There is a collective—if that's what you want to call it and they are obviously way ahead of us. There are varying degrees of 'gifted' ones. Olivia's special, but she's not the only one." Poe turned to Will. "You're dating Kim's aunt, am I right?"

"Kim spoke frequently of you since starting her new job at the same Alzheimer's facility. She said you understood her, just like Olivia did," Will acknowledged.

Poe was glad Kim held him in such high regard. Kim had forged the path between him and Olivia. "Kim's different. You don't know exactly how or why or what it even means, just that she knows things most people don't," Poe surmised, turning to Patrick next.

"The girls Sarah Larsin employs are another kind of gifted. The FBI knew long before Deveroux. There is a peaceful coexistence between them. Sarah Larsin wouldn't want to risk the arrangement, otherwise she would sink from entrepreneur to handler. The bottom line is, we all have a place and a goal. It's always been to keep to the shadows. There are those like Larry Pittman, who always end up getting caught; but it's mutually beneficial. They take out the trash. Enter Rose

Corey, the one who killed the sheriff. She's an outlier, the likes of which no one has ever encountered. She exposes all of us who don't want to be exposed. In the worst kind of way. Rose is tilting the status quo and forcing us into the light. Rose is pushing the limits not only of secrecy but of patience."

"You failed to mention Olivia. The FBI has no choice but to turn to her. She's the only one who understands what Rose is. Olivia is the only one who can stop her," Patrick interrupted.

"But at what cost?" Poe snapped back. "It will depend on what is asked of her."

Barry assessed the threat level and didn't like it. "Olivia has already severed ties with the FBI. What if she isn't agreeable to their terms?" he asked.

"There's always a contingency plan. They've known about gifteds for a very long time, even before Olivia. They will take matters into their own hands," Patrick prophesized.

"And do what?" Barry wanted to know.

"Do what they always do, oust the ones who don't belong. The ones who don't fit the mold," Poe answered first. He grew up hearing Mémé warn of the day the gifts were outed. It's why Mémé liked living off the grid. The swamp was a good place for that. "The only unknown is how? It won't be with full disclosure that would endanger their position. I suspect it will be some kind of fear mongering. It's worked for centuries. There's no better way to sow unrest amongst the populous. Dehumanizing a group makes it easier to take away their rights. They will have neighbor turning on neighbor. Hell, it could be another civil war."

"What if they give Olivia no choice?" Patrick

dared to ask.

"They will wish they hadn't treated her so badly," Poe said. "Olivia has always been in the middle of two worlds, but now, if asked to choose sides, they need to know it's no longer just about her and I don't mean Silas Branch."

Poe glanced down at his phone and then back to Barry. "You and I need to go. We don't have time for this." Poe looked at Patrick one last time. "Go find Silas Branch. Or don't. I don't care. He's a wild card and everyone in this room needs to understand what side he's on."

Poe didn't speak again until he was behind the wheel and Barry was in the passenger seat, silently contemplating whatever he was reading on his phone.

"What are you thinking?" Poe prodded him.

Poe couldn't see it but it was a text from Will.

—We need to talk —

Barry could only assume it was something more Will found in Kevin Branch's emails. It was why he was on Olivia's computer.

"I'm thinking about the bonds we make," Barry admitted, sounding philosophical. "I heard what you said about the archbishop not helping Ginny Larsin. Maybe he felt responsible."

Poe doubted Mendoza felt anything.

"He lied for me." The words spilled out of Barry's mouth. "I wasn't with the archbishop the morning Amanda died." Barry felt relieved to finally say it out loud.

Poe knew Olivia was the only one who could have persuaded the holy man to do such a thing. "He did it to keep you in play. We all have a part to play," Poe repeated.

"At the time, the archbishop had you if things went bad," Barry reminded him. Poe was supposed to be the stopgap preventing Olivia from descending into darkness. As her watcher, that was Barry's role until the birth of Olivia's children.

"If you're wondering about the archbishop, his obligation will always be the Church. I'll handle the demons, like the one in her garden, while you handle guys like Monahan. You're from their world, I'm not. And I'm not talking about the underworld. Your knowledge of law enforcement could come in handy."

"You predicted a pretty somber view of things to come," Barry reminded him.

"I'm just thinking about history," Poe replied.

"History repeats itself," Barry cautioned.

"Yea, it does," Poe confirmed. "The desire to cast out those who don't fit."

"I was thinking of Salem," Barry said. One of Olivia's ancestors died in jail there.

Poe actually smiled. "Guys like Monahan and whoever may have Silas Branch are in for a rude awakening. They've never faced real witches before."

"Is that why you said you didn't care if they found Silas or not?" Barry felt the need to know.

Poe's knuckles blanched white as he gripped the steering wheel. "I think it would be in all of our best interest if he was dead. That way, they can't use him against her."

Barry nodded. "That would only hurt Olivia."

Maybe. Maybe not. Either way, Poe elected to keep the secret Renaye shared a little while longer.

Chapter Ten

Gran was crying — again. Gran had been doing that a lot since Amber's birthday party. It seemed people wouldn't stop talking about what happened. Olivia didn't understand. All she did was tell the truth about the magic man. He was a really bad man who would have done really bad things given the chance. Amber's parents should be glad she told. Instead, they were angry with Gran.

Somehow, things had gotten all twisted, and now people were asking questions about her living with Gran instead of with a mommy and daddy. Olivia didn't understand why people who didn't live here were trying to tell Gran what to do. The school was supporting Gran because she had something called "custody". Olivia had heard the word before–it meant she could live with Gran instead of her mom. The only way Olivia knew these things was because she heard Gran on the phone even when the door was shut, and she wasn't supposed to be listening.

It was all very confusing. Thinking about all of it made Olivia's stomach hurt. She didn't understand why all these adults, whom she didn't even know, were talking about where she lived and how. Olivia thought Gran should be a lot madder than she was. Instead, Gran just cried. Olivia vowed that when she was older, she would make the people hurting Gran sorry for what they did.

Now they were trying to make Gran take her somewhere called 'counseling'. Olivia looked it up. Counseling meant she was supposed to talk to a stranger about her feelings. Gran said she didn't have the time or money for that. None of this was new. There was never enough money, but Gran had to make everyone think she was listening. Gran would do what they said because if she didn't, someone could come and take Olivia away.

Olivia decided she wouldn't go–no matter what they said. They couldn't make her. Olivia wasn't sure why she felt that way. She just knew the same way she knew the magic man was bad.

When Olivia didn't want to listen to Gran on the phone anymore, she escaped to the backyard and into the little wooden building her grandfather had built. That's where she went when she was in trouble. Today, her head felt full. When that happened, she would put her head down and drift. She was sleeping when the whispers began.

"Do not fret, my child. Ginny will find a way and when you are older, so will you. You are the one who has the power. No one can take that from you."

Olivia opened her eyes to see yellow ones. "You're not supposed to be here," she whispered.

"Neither are you, my child. Time to wake up. Your stay here has come to an end. They are coming for you. The time has come for you to make them pay. I bid you farewell—for now."

****

Olivia felt a push and a gust of hot wind against her face. Her eyes flew open, and she found herself bathed in blinding light. She gagged against the resistance in her throat. Panic gripped her. She heard a rattling sound as she pulled her hands free from the soft restraints. Only then did she see the massive shape lurking in the corner.

Olivia grew still, her struggle forgotten as he glided toward her. His head would have touched the ceiling if it wasn't bowed. Snow-white wings perched above his shoulders. Untucked, they would fill the room. He was the most beautiful creature Olivia had ever seen. Bathed in his light, her panic evaporated. The figure slowly brought a finger to his lips as he placed a hand on the head of the man in the chair next to her bed. Olivia watched a lone white feather float free. Watching its lazy descent, she became still. Olivia knew no fear as she closed her eyes and yanked the tube free from her mouth.

****

Poe's predictions joined the thoughts inside his head and took Barry to places he had previously buried. For his own well-being, Barry needed to focus on the here and now.

"Is there a name for what she is?" Barry asked. Olivia's mother's side was full of witches, and her father was a demon. "There must be some kind of designation. All she is going to hear is the word demon," Barry cautioned.

"Cambion is the more traditional term, or changeling," Poe explained.

"I'm assuming she gets to decide which path she will take?" Barry asked.

"Like any halfling, she has three choices—demon, human or something in between. The choice is entirely hers," Poe emphasized.

Barry grew quiet as he took an inventory of what he had seen Olivia face so far.

"What was it like to see her angry? I mean, really angry?" Poe invaded his thoughts again. An image of Olivia's wrath directed at the ones who had wronged her was lodged in his brain. Whether she wanted retribution or not, Poe wanted it for her. She deserved it after how they had treated her.

Barry stared out the window, but he didn't see the traffic stacked before them. The last few days had been surreal, as if he had transcended behind the veil and into another plane of existence. It was strange to see the world still marched on with or without them. The hair on his arms rose with the memory of the barn roaring with fire only to see Olivia emerge unscathed.

"Gloriously frightening," Barry finally answered Poe.

Poe knew then the demon *Alleracsap* was correct. Familiarity would win. Olivia's familiar was the snake for a reason. She was the epitome of transformation. No matter what history or legend said she would forge her own path.

****

The room was so dark. It felt like the longest night of his life. Maybe it was the concussion they told him he had that was messing with his mind. Or it could be the drugs. He had experienced time lapses before. Either way, he had no idea how long he had been here.

Silas raised the head of his bed, giving himself a moment to orient to his surroundings. Straight ahead, he could make out the TV mounted on the wall. Not wanting to think about the images that came with it, he looked to his more immediate vicinity and saw the outline of a bedside table. He was fumbling around it when a streak of light pierced the room.

"Looking for something, Agent Branch?"

It was Dillon again.

"My cell phone," Silas answered.

"Missing. I sent agents to scour the area of the explosion," Dillon explained.

"I need to speak with my wife."

"Don't worry about her. Your old friend Patrick Monahan has already spoken with her. So has Agent Sharpe."

The door swung open again, ushering in the nurse. "It's time for your pain medication, Agent Branch."

Silas didn't recall asking for any, but he wouldn't refuse. His knee hurt, and so did his back. He had been in bed too long. Before he could protest, he felt the familiar peace of backing out of the room.

Dillon waited until the nurse was gone and Agent Branch was sufficiently under the influence. "You were right to be worried about your wife. In your absence, she has been in contact with a man named Rogan Poe. Based on what little we know about him, he is a bigger threat to your way of life than Rose Corey will ever be."

****

Olivia unclipped the pulse oximeter clamped to her finger and peeled away the blood pressure cuff wrapped around her arm. By the time she was finished, all the machines in the room were chirping.

Free of her restraints, Olivia tried to reach Brennon, but the burning pain in her lower abdomen made her rethink the crawl she had planned across the bed.

Down the hall, Renaye stepped out of the supply closet to find a lab tech leaning over the desk in the middle of the unit. He was reporting a ray of light. After last night's electrical disturbance, the charge nurse wasted no time picking up the phone to call maintenance and request they send the electricians back.

Renaye heard the tech say room number seven. At the same time, a cacophony of beeps rang from down the hall. The charge nurse looked at the screen and across the desk at Renaye.

"Your patient just went offline."

Renaye didn't have to ask which one.

Fighting against her sluggish muscles, Olivia reached behind the head of her bed to push the code blue button, adding more alarms to the chorus.

Hearing the new alarm, Renaye shouted, "Call respiratory," as she sprinted down the hall.

****

Poe and Barry were waiting to take the elevator to the sixth floor when they heard the overhead page of *Code Blue—ICU.*

Barry watched Poe's crystal blue eyes go black. Poe frantically scanned the immediate area for an alternative. "It doesn't mean it's her," Barry said, hammering the elevator buttons. The lights above told him the elevator was coming. Barry turned to tell Poe, but he was gone, the door to the stairwell slamming in his wake.

Renaye slid into the room, grabbing the privacy curtain to save herself from falling. She couldn't believe what she was seeing. Her patient was out of bed and standing over the man in the chair. It was the attorney—Brennon Kaine. Rogan Poe hadn't returned to relieve him.

"Don't just stand there," Olivia snapped, "help him."

Renaye joined her on the other side of Kaine. He was slumped in the chair, his eyes closed.

He looked clammy, and there was saliva on his chin. His muscles were slack. Olivia was holding his head to the side to prevent aspiration.

"What happened?" Renaye asked.

"He was seizing," Olivia explained.

Renaye listened but felt frozen as she tried to process. Less than five minutes ago, her patient was intubated, in a sedated sleep, and now she was upright and issuing orders.

The tube that had been breathing for her was cast aside in the bed along with her cardiac leads. Her IV was still intact, but it was in a losing battle as blood oozed from Olivia's arm and dripped onto the floor. The only thing that remained intact was her catheter. The tube was still in place, with the bag attached to the bed. Luckily, it was on this side of the bed or Renaye feared she would have pulled that out too.

"No, I meant, what happened to you?"

****

The ping of the elevator stopped Barry from following Poe. Luckily, only two people were waiting to depart. Others had gathered to take the ride with him and were waiting for their chance to enter. Securing the elevator for himself, Barry blocked the doorway, hands on his hips. It was a reflex. For decades, a gun and a badge rested there, a silent signal for others to keep away. Even without them, Barry got his point across. In silent unity, they all elected to wait for the next one.

Barry burst through the door to the visitor's waiting room outside the ICU, finding it eerily empty. Visitors usually had to be buzzed inside. Luckily, the door to the patient area wasn't locked. It must be because of the code blue. Whatever the reason, Barry was glad because he was short on patience.

Rounding the corner, Barry saw what Poe had feared. A cluster of people gathered outside Olivia's room. Barry prayed Poe was one of them. Before Barry could get closer, a gurney emerged. Someone in scrubs was leading the way. Two more were stationed at the head of the bed, one on each side. They turned and headed in the opposite direction. From his brief time here, Barry knew at the other end of the hall was an elevator reserved for patients. It was how he and Poe arrived the night Olivia was admitted. Barry could only think of one place worse than the ICU.

Watching the gurney depart, Barry realized the hall was unnervingly quiet as if the air had evaporated, taking the sounds of alarms with it. Whatever had happened was over now. Pushing himself off the wall, Barry felt a wave of vertigo. He righted himself, forcing one foot in front of the other.

The privacy curtain was pulled. Barry waited a moment before stepping up and doing what he had wanted to do all along—*rip it aside*.

Chapter Eleven

Barry saw Renaye first. Her hands were full of a half-empty bag of IV fluid in one and a tangle of tubing in her other. She was the only medical person left behind. Even as she cleaned the room, she kept watch over her patient. Renaye looked uncomfortable with the scene unfolding before her, obviously conflicted about whether to stay or go.

Barry quickly found what held Renaye's attention, finding himself caught in the same snare. Olivia was awake, unbound by the shackles of this world and the other. Olivia was free. Poe's arms were wrapped tightly around her as he stroked her hair and whispered words too soft for Barry to hear. It could be French for all he knew. Either way, Barry couldn't decipher it for the tidal wave of emotion filling his head. His earlier feelings of vertigo threatened to return.

Olivia untangled herself from Poe and found Barry. Her green eyes shone like never before. Another wave of emotion rose within him and crested, leaving behind only one—*peace*. His world had once again righted itself. Poe and Olivia parted like dance partners as she reached for him. Barry went to her. She clutched him with strength she shouldn't have. Olivia buried her head in his chest and sobbed.

Barry held her tight and did what he always did— *surrender*.

****

Will paced the floor of Olivia's living room. He hated waiting even though he was the one who insisted he wouldn't leave until Kim arrived. She had agreed to stay at the house and keep things running, but she needed a quick tutorial on home security. She was already familiar with the dogs. Barry gave Will cash so she could do whatever grocery shopping she deemed necessary. While Will waited, he kept sneaking glances at his phone. Neither Barry nor Brennon had texted him back. Maybe the texts they received from him got them to talking, and Brennon was busy explaining what they learned from hospital security. It was probably better that Barry hear the story in bits and pieces. Will felt sorry for his former lieutenant. For such a nice guy, Barry was really lousy at picking women. First Amanda Greene, and now Lily.

The knock at the door was a relief. Now Will could get to the hospital. Even if Barry and Brennon had yet to connect, something else could have come up, given Poe's eagerness to leave with Barry in tow. With Olivia in the ICU and the babies in the NICU, it could be any number of possibilities.

Will pulled the door open, expecting Kim. Instead, it was a man he didn't know. Will peeked past him and saw no car. Where did this guy come from?

The visitor looked as surprised as Will. "Uh, hi. I was looking for Silas or Olivia," the man said, clearly uncomfortable.

Will waited for more information before handing out any of his own.

Will's silence raised the man's nervousness by a few notches. The stranger's stare had wandered to the badge and gun at Will's waist.

"Uh, I hope I'm not interrupting, but I live next door," the man said, pointing to the house where Lily lived.

Will scanned across the lawn to see a car in the driveway of the same house. It hadn't been there when Will arrived.

"I'm Ross Forrester," the man said. He almost offered his hand and then thought better of it the longer he stared at the gun. "I'm just looking for my wife, uh, soon to be ex-wife. She and Olivia are friends."

Suddenly, Will was glad he hadn't talked to Barry. He was going to gain some new information. Will relaxed his shoulders and attempted to appear as non-threatening as possible. "Sergeant Will Ibarra. Why don't you step inside, Mr. Forrester, and let me see what I can do."

Ross crossed the threshold while Will closed the door behind him. Neither man sat. Ross glanced nervously around the room. "So is Silas or Olivia around?"

"Not at this time, but maybe I can help you with something. What did you need?"

Ross shifted from one foot to the other, considering his options. Since he was here, he might as well get what he came for. "Lily's not home. I was wondering if Olivia knew where she was. Or if she had seen her."

"I see," Will said with genuine interest. "Maybe I can help. Part of my job is finding people. Why don't you tell me why you're worried she's not home," Will suggested, trying to sound reassuring. "Is she missing?"

"I would hate to say 'missing'," Ross responded with a pained smile. "I'm surprised, that's all."

"Is she supposed to be home?" Will asked. He knew Barry thought so.

"Well no. We were supposed to meet with our attorneys this morning and a real estate agent for some arbitration thing."

"So, let me see if I got this straight. Your soon-to-be ex-wife missed an important meeting." Will was repeating the question, not because he didn't understand, but because the more someone talked, the more they revealed. He needed more information on Lily Forrester and this man could give it to him.

"The meeting was kind of important. It's about the house."

Ross hesitated, but Will waited him out.

"I'm selling the house and Lily can't afford to buy it. It was kind of an important meeting," Ross explained.

The email Olivia sent Kevin Branch began with an inquiry into Ross Forrester's finances. Will had skipped over that part in favor of Lily's past work history.

"Look, I'm not an asshole, really. Her name isn't even on the deed because she hasn't contributed financially to the marriage in twenty years. We weren't in a good place when we bought it, but, you know."

Ross finally stopped talking. Will wondered if it was because he sounded like an angry husband and not a worried one. "Did you call her? Maybe she got mixed up on the time," Will suggested.

"I did. So did her attorney. We both were shuffled straight to voicemail and then I got a message the voicemail was full," Ross explained.

Will nodded. Ross' story matched Barry's.

"I started to worry so I came to the house."

"Have you called friends or relatives? Or her work?" Will asked.

"None of our family lives close. Lily works nights and should have been available for the meeting. I called her work just to make sure, but I got bounced around all over the place. Either they don't trust me because I'm the soon to be the ex or she got fired. It's happened before," Ross said with a shrug. "I came over here because she and Olivia are friends."

Will nodded, taking it all in. "Did you check inside the house, just to make sure?"

"I tried, but she must have changed the locks," Ross said. "We have a side door to the garage, through the backyard. I peeked inside and her car's not there."

"You said she had been fired before?" Will asked. "Is that recent?"

Ross waved him off, wishing he could take back the comment. "It was a long time ago. She hasn't worked in years. I was kind of surprised she got back in nursing after being out of it for so long. I guess there's a shortage of nurses or something. I got a weird vibe from the hospital. Probably just me." Ross tried to smile.

"Do you have a card, Mr. Forrester?" Will asked.

Ross patted his shirt pocket and came up with one.

Will handed him one of his own. "I'll let you know if I hear anything. You should do the same. I don't want Olivia to worry," Will said.

"Sure thing," Ross said. "Tell Olivia I said hello. I also wanted her to know the house is for sale. The sign will go up as soon as I can get the locks changed. The place used to belong to her great grandparents. I'd be happy to sell without going through a realtor. I just want to be done with the whole thing."

Will flashed him a reassuring smile. "I'll be sure and pass along the message."

"You've been very helpful, Sergeant Ibarra," Ross said, referring back to the card. "Thanks again for your time." Ross offered his hand, and Will shook it.

"No problem at all," Will assured him.

Will felt as if he should be thanking him. Ross Forrester had answered questions Will hadn't even gotten around to asking.

****

"So, what the hell happened?" Barry whispered.

Renaye kicked him and Poe out to the hall while she did as Olivia asked. The nurse had been reluctant at first, but Olivia stood her ground. Olivia was insistent on seeing her babies and she wanted the catheter and IV removed before she did. Her wishes soon turned to demands. Olivia refused to wait for anyone's permission. Renaye compromised and agreed to let Olivia go as long as she could tag along.

Poe shook his head, trying to connect the jumble of events to something explainable. "Olivia said she woke from a dream to find Brennon seizing in the chair next to the bed. She extubated herself and then hit the code blue button on the wall."

Barry massaged his forehead. There were gaping holes in her story. Barry could see from the look on Poe's face he was as worried about those gaps as he was, but neither of them was prepared to tackle them. Olivia needed to see her daughters first. Then they could worry about the rest of it.

"I think it's best if we let her open up on her own," Poe said, what Barry was thinking. "If we start asking too many questions, she might bury those memories in a corner of her mind somewhere. Whatever she went through, she's going to need to talk about it."

Barry couldn't agree more. It's how he would handle a victim. "And Brennon?" Barry asked, moving to something more immediate.

"They whisked him down the hall. That's all I know. You don't happen to know his medical history, do you?" It would have sounded like a bad joke, except for how gray Kaine looked when they left with him. Poe hoped for Olivia's sake, he would pull through, but the nurse in him kept him from it.

"Olivia would know," Barry found himself saying. "She and Brennon were close...once. What would make him seize like that?"

"My honest opinion is something happened in that room," Poe said, his eyes not meeting Barry's.

"She's different, isn't she?" Barry asked what they were both thinking.

"You mean in addition to waking up from a full coma and not acting like someone who just had their abdomen cut open? Yea, you could say that."

****

"What the hell just happened?" Renaye snapped as soon as Barry and Olivia passed into the locked unit, leaving her and Poe alone in the visitor room. Poe declined to remain behind while Renaye joined Olivia and Barry on their trek to the NICU. Besides, Renaye needed him for backup when Olivia refused to ride in a wheelchair. Poe argued using the wheelchair was hospital policy at the same time the whispers inside her head reminded her she had just had abdominal surgery. She shouldn't be strolling the halls like nothing happened. Olivia listened to both while erecting a wall that Poe couldn't breach. After kicking him out of her head, Poe could only guess what she planned to do on the return trip.

"She wants to see her babies. Do you blame her?" Poe knew that wasn't the answer Renaye was searching for but it was all he had.

Renaye glared at him. It was probably best to shelve that conversation until later. Renaye shifted to more immediate problems, like how she was supposed to chart what just happened? It was a good thing Olivia was her only patient. The episode had imploded her entire shift. Renaye decided she needed to sit with what happened for a while before she could document the unexplainable. Olivia certainly wasn't the only patient who managed to extubate themselves. Still, she was the only one who demanded to walk off the floor afterward.

"If it's not too personal, can I ask what you said to calm her down?" Renaye asked. Once the attention was on Mr. Kane, Olivia collapsed into Poe, her shoulders heaving with sobs. Whatever Poe said had calmed her down. Renaye wondered what other complicated piece of Olivia Osborne's life she was missing.

"I told her she was back now and there was nothing to worry about," Poe said.

"Back from where?" Renaye dared to ask.

"A place she's been trying not to go her whole life."

Chapter Twelve

The unit secretary caught up with him after he finished his rounds and before his follow-up meeting with the hospital administration. Dr. Hader could only assume the message was a mistake. The girl was probably overwhelmed by the constant ringing of the phone. The topic of his meeting was the same as the message—*the Osborne twins*. The message from the ICU took precedence.

Before Dr. Hader could call and verify the information, he saw who he could only assume was her. The last report he received was that she was still intubated. Now, without warning, she was here, accompanied by the former policeman who had been the twin's only visitor. Olivia Osborne's appearance caused ripples through the NICU. Hader knew he would need to squash the chatter when she left. He had read up on her. She was a doctor in her own right, albeit the initials at the end of her name weren't the same as his. Still as a woman of science, Hader hoped Dr. Osborne was prepared for the task ahead of her. They would all get to know each other well over the next few months.

Barry ditched the wheelchair outside the door at Olivia's request. His hand was ready for her when she stood. After taking a moment to catch her breath, Olivia moved on her own accord. They donned gowns and scrubbed their hands in silence. The hospital boasted the largest NICU in the city with ninety beds. Barry planned to lead Olivia to the private room that housed her daughters. Instead, she led him. The unit grew quiet with her passing, punctuated only by the hum of machines.

Genevieve and Gwendolyn's room was tranquil, the color of twilight. Each baby was secure in their own isolette, sealed tight against the elements, and programmed for the needs of infants who weren't mature enough to regulate their own body temperature. There were openings on either side of the clear box for clinicians to slip their hands through to care and comfort them. The lid was detachable for when they were mature enough to withstand the elements of an open room. The tiny babies were dressed only in a diaper. Their heads were covered with crocheted caps handmade by volunteers. The different colored caps undoubtedly helped the staff keep track of who was who, but Olivia knew her daughters instantly. She didn't need the name cards at the end of the isolettes to know Baby A was wearing pink and Baby B purple. Olivia teared up when she saw that someone had added their names, Genevieve and Gwendolyn Osborne. The information could only have come from Barry.

The twins were on their backs, their eyes closed as if sleeping. Olivia watched as each tiny chest moved up and down. She was as comforted by watching them breathe as she was hearing the sound of their heartbeats inside her womb. The small tubes in their noses carried a low dose of humidified oxygen. Breathing was tiring, and the extra support kept them from working too hard. Energy was a precious commodity for the two-pound infants. There was another tube secured to their cheek used for feeding. They wouldn't master the sucking reflex for at least another four to six weeks. They each had an IV in the scalp, and stickers attached to their chest for continuous monitoring, not unlike the ones Olivia ripped from her own chest less than an hour ago. Even though they were separated, each baby's free arm was stretched outward as if in search of the other.

"They came out holding hands," Barry told her, trying not to choke on his words.

Silently, Olivia reached behind her and squeezed his hand, afraid if she looked at him the tears would fall harder. Barry squeezed back, soothing her. As their fingers drifted apart, Olivia moved closer, placing one hand on each of the isolettes, signaling her daughters she was there.

Dr. Hader watched from the doorway, allowing her to take in the sight of her babies before joining them. The doctor introduced himself and began filling her in on the last forty-eight hours. Olivia absorbed it all, with few questions. Trying to get to know her better, Dr. Hader asked some of his own. "Their names are beautiful, regal even. Do they have special meaning for you?"

Olivia nodded. "Genevieve is after my grandmother. She was named after the patron saint of Paris. Gwendolyn is also named after a saint. Both of them, in their own way, dedicated their life to God, by fighting paganism."

Dr. Hader noted the infants had opened their eyes at the sound of her voice. "I'm glad you're getting to see them when they're not crying. Genevieve is typically the one to start. Gwendolyn, I think, joins in as a sign of solidarity," Dr. Hader told her. "Each assessment is an opportunity for them to remind us what a great set of lungs they have. They've been very lucky. They have yet to need ventilator support, even at twenty-eight weeks."

"Is that uncommon?" Olivia asked.

"It's not uncommon for a single birth, but for twins," the neonatologist shook his head. "Let's just say I am amazed by their progress every day."

Olivia nodded, a smile of pride on her face.

"They know I'm here," Olivia whispered. She closed her eyes, blanketing her progeny with gentle thoughts, just as she had when they were inside her womb. Managing the onslaught of their emotions jumbled with hers had been challenging in the first weeks of pregnancy, leaving her to hope the connection would severe with birth. Now, Olivia was grateful the connection remained despite the distance between them. She didn't know how long it would last, but she knew she would never wish it away again.

Dr. Hader stood silent as mother and offspring shared a private moment. He couldn't shake the eerie feeling something was happening. The lights overhead dimmed, hovering somewhere between twilight and night's first blush. The hair on his arms rose, but there was no chill. He became aware of the hush that had swallowed the whole unit. It was eerily quiet for a place where every patient was attached to some device.

Dr. Hader couldn't shake the sense he was an intruder watching these tiny babies who were as mesmerized by the presence of their mother as she was theirs. Both babies locked eyes with her, staring at her no matter how impossible. At their age, the muscles in their eyes didn't work that way. The thought evaporated as the little ones who fought so hard against their frequent assessments grew silent. He watched their eyes grow heavy as they slipped back into slumber. Maybe she was right and they did know she was there. Her presence was the signal they were waiting for to slip off into unencumbered sleep.

The connection severed, and Dr. Hader braced himself for the questioning to begin. He had heard enough theorizing from the staff. He chalked the stories up to a busy night with a harrowing delivery. What the staff didn't know was he had called no less than a dozen colleagues seeking answers. They could give him none. They had never seen what he was describing. He had promised himself he wouldn't bring up the color of their eyes until she asked, yet she didn't. She just looked at him seemingly unbothered. He felt the urge to speak but no words would come out. The silence grew awkward until thankfully, she shattered it.

"Anything else, doctor?" Olivia asked.

Under her scrutiny, Dr. Hader grew strangely uncomfortable. It wasn't a familiar feeling. He graduated top of his class. He had fifteen years of clinical experience, yet he couldn't help but wonder if she was baiting him or trying to root out something he was keeping from her. The flash of green in her eyes didn't match the monotone of her voice. Perhaps it was a trick of the light, a counter effect to the dimness earlier. He heard there were electrical issues in the ICU overnight. Maybe those same problems had found their way to the NICU. He made a note to have the overworked secretary put in a call to maintenance, just in case.

Eventually, the doctor's discomfort migrated to Barry. He rested his hand on Olivia's shoulder, dissolving whatever spell Olivia had cast over the physician. Dr. Hader took a deep breath as Barry let out one of his own.

"With that behind us, I would very much like to hold my daughters now," Olivia told him.

Her words were soft, but it was clear they weren't a request.

****

While the nurses made arrangements, Barry left the NICU to find Poe. Will was with him in the waiting room, minus Renaye. Poe and Will went mute as he arrived, telling Barry something was up. "What?" Barry asked.

Poe's eyes shifted toward Will, indicating he wanted him to go first.

Will decided to lead with good news. "I got Poe's text in time to grab the bag Olivia requested. I passed it off to Renaye and she took it upstairs with her."

"Olivia's neurologist called. I think there's some pressure from the charge nurse to boot Olivia out of the ICU already. I think they need the bed. But it's up to the neuro after he sees her," Poe explained.

Barry knew Olivia didn't want to go back to the ICU even if they hadn't talked about it. If it was the doctor's decision, perhaps she wouldn't put up a fight like the one over the wheelchair. "As long as it's safe," Barry said.

"How's she holding up?" Poe asked.

Barry smiled for the first time in days. "If it wasn't for the babies, you would never know she just came out of the ICU. She's getting ready to hold them, but it's going to be a few minutes. I came out here to tell you the nurses have some paperwork for you to fill out," Barry told Poe. "They said you could get it from Labor and Delivery. They're kind of swamped in the NICU right now."

Poe was curious. "What kind of paperwork?"

"Olivia wants you to be able to visit the girls. Fill it out and bring it back to the NICU and they'll let you back there with us," Barry explained.

Poe was unnaturally quiet, humbled by the news. He glanced at Will before heading off.

Barry's smile faded as soon as Poe departed. "So, what do you have to tell me?" Barry didn't want to ask but whatever the news, it was inevitable.

"I need to brief you on the meeting with hospital administration." Will didn't say it, but he wondered if the ICU needed Olivia's room for Brennon Kane. Renaye told him what happened when he dropped off Olivia's bag. Brennon was awake but not coherent. The way the nurse talked, Will got the distinct impression something other than a medical emergency took place, but that was a discussion for another time.

"Brennon's presence got their attention. I think the hospital is preparing themselves for the worst once Olivia gets wind of what happened."

After witnessing her demeanour in the NICU, Barry would concur. "I'm guessing that means it wasn't a drill." Barry folded his arms and listened as he would to an admission of guilt.

"The alarm was real," Will confirmed. "It was activated by a door located in the back of the NICU, near a stairwell used exclusively by hospital personnel. The rooms in the immediate vicinity were empty.

Security reluctantly acknowledged the monitor that set off the alarms was assigned to Genevieve. Camera footage from the hallway showed someone wearing a surgical hat step out of the NICU. They passed something to a person in the hallway wearing scrubs. It was hand to hand contact, so whatever it was, it was small."

Barry grew more alarmed by the moment. "Like that narrows it down." The person could still be around.

"I think they already have a suspect," Will told him. "Things got interesting when Brennon pressed them. They said the internal investigation was ongoing, but they felt confident the threat had been removed," Will explained. "I don't think they would dare lie to him."

"Then that means they know who, but aren't prepared to say," Barry surmised.

"Because it implicates them in some way," Will finished for him.

Barry stared into space, searching for answers. There were no good choices. "There's more," Will cautioned him. "I know what Kevin Branch was so eager to share with Olivia. I'm betting it's connected."

Barry's stance told Will he didn't want to have to ask.

"Apparently Olivia asked Kevin to look into Ross Forrester's financials," Will planned to roll the information out slowly, allowing Barry the leverage to jump in at any time.

"Lily was upset that she couldn't keep living there, but she was relieved that she would get something out of it once the house sold. Knowing Olivia, she probably wanted to make sure Ross wasn't holding out on Lily,"

Barry explained.

Will decided to save the answer to that question for last. "During the search, Kevin stumbled across information on Lily. When she and Ross first got married, she went to work in another NICU but that didn't last long. The reason for termination was ambiguous. According to Kevin, he didn't find disciplinary action with the state board, so he doesn't think it was medical in nature, not in a direct patient way. Makes me wonder if it's not something like now. Some kind of breach. Something a hospital wouldn't want to fess up to," Will suggested.

"Get rid of the nurse, get rid of the problem," Barry translated.

Kevin's hypothesis wasn't wrong. A similar scenario had played out before. Jamie Smythe wasn't the only serial killer that had haunted San Antonio. This city had its own serial killer nurse. In that case, instead of the hospital fully investigating their suspicions, they implemented sanctions, forcing the nurse in question to leave of her own accord. The hospital was fortunate. They stopped the nurse before lives were lost at their facility, but like any other predator, she just found a different place to hunt. The next place wasn't so lucky.

"So, what happened to Lily this time?" Barry wanted to know.

"No one named names, but it looks like those with direct access to the twins were placed on administrative leave. That would include Lily."

Will watched Barry, wondering how much the lieutenant was beating himself up.

"If it's any consolation, Olivia was right. Ross was holding out on his wife," Will told him.

"How do you know that?" Barry asked.

"Not long after you and Poe left, Ross showed up. He was looking for Lily, just like you. They had some important meeting this morning about the house. Instead of finding out how much money she was going to get from it, Lily was going to learn her name wasn't even on the deed. Ross doesn't have a clue where she disappeared, but he asked if I would put in a plug with Olivia that the house was for sale. He sounded desperate."

Realizing how it must have sounded, Will wished he could take back the comment. Barry was dealing with a lot right now. Olivia and the babies were the obvious things. Will hadn't stopped to consider what effect Brennon Kaine's condition might have on Barry. Like Lily, the attorney had recently become an integral part of Barry's new life.

"Why don't you tell me how you're holding up?" Will floated the idea trying to get a handle on Barry's feelings.

"Olivia is awake now. That's all I can think about. That's all that matters," Barry said, the relief streaking his face.

Will couldn't say he was surprised at the answer, but it wasn't what he had expected. The next question was something else Will had been saving, but since Barry opened the door, he might as well ask. "What did you tell Olivia when she asked about Silas?"

The question seemed to catch Barry off guard.

Before he could answer, a nurse poked her head outside the NICU and called to Barry. "She's asking for you."

Barry's gaze wavered between staying with Will

and leaving to go to Olivia. The look on Will's face reminded him he was supposed to say something. "She never asked."

Will stood alone watching his former partner hurry back to the NICU, remembering the man Barry was when they first met. Before Amanda Greene and Lily Forrester, there was only Olivia Osborne.

Chapter Thirteen

Olivia's recovery was rapid, surprising everyone except maybe Poe. He was relieved she was awake, but her revival brought about its own set of problems. One in particular.

"So, you're going to let her go?" Poe asked. He and Barry had waited outside Olivia's room while Dr. Murdoch made her rounds. When she was done, Barry slipped back inside to be with Olivia while Poe followed the doctor.

Tammy Murdoch ignored him while she stopped briefly at the nurse's station. "Dr. Osborne will be discharging later today." Aware Rogan Poe was following her, the doctor made sure they were far enough away from the nurse's station before she stopped ensuring no one would hear their discussion.

"Medically there's no reason she should stay," Tammy Murdoch explained. Since she had Olivia's permission to speak to both Poe and Barry, she seized the opportunity. "Even if I could find a reason to keep her, do you honestly think she would stay?"

Poe gave a shake of his head.

"After nine years of doing this, I thought I had seen it all, then there's her," Tammy confessed. "Her recuperative powers are amazing, to say the least. From what I hear from the NICU, her daughters have the same genes."

The doctor stared him down, looking for an answer Poe wouldn't give.

Poe sensed her need for reassurance, so that's what he gave her. "Olivia won't be alone, we'll make sure of it," Poe told her. What he didn't say was Olivia had already resumed control.

Free from the ICU, Olivia's first move was to shift Barry to night duty. The postpartum unit was more accommodating to overnight visitors. Barry even had a bed. Olivia wanted Barry with her when she visited the babies at night. He would wheel her away, but Olivia would ditch the wheelchair as soon as they entered the elevator. Poe was not so accommodating, but that wasn't why Olivia ousted him. Olivia said it was because he was the only one employed, and he had other obligations. It wasn't that simple but Poe went along with the charade.

Beyond the hospital, Olivia took charge of fortifying her base. Part of that included resuming control of her emails. She weighed the pros and cons of keeping Kevin Branch in the dark. Ultimately, it was too difficult to explain her absence. Kevin was an asset and she needed him. He could get into places she couldn't. The ease with which Kevin agreed to keep the rest of his family out of the loop regarding Silas' absence did not go unnoticed. Olivia shoved aside the implications of such a move just as she did her own thoughts of Silas. She employed previous coping habits by pushing him into the dark and dusty corner of her mind where he used to live when they were in between assignments.

With Kim already on board at Barry's request, Olivia tasked Kim with managing the house. That meant the dogs, groceries, and the delivery of the furniture Olivia bought with the click of a button. She was furnishing her upstairs with more than baby beds, making room for those she wanted to hold close. Kim was as eager to stay as Olivia was to have her there. Kim called the gathering a collective, which also included Barry. With his condo pending sale to Isaac Kaine, Barry would soon be homeless. It only made sense for him to stay with Olivia. While Poe had his reservations, he couldn't argue with her logic. Besides, Olivia didn't seem in the mood for resistance.

Needing to put his own questions to rest, Poe had no choice but to turn to the doctor for answers. As luck would have it, Dr. Murdoch was looking for the same.

"When you say *we* will make sure she's not alone, does that mean you and the policeman or her husband?" Tammy asked. "I know it's none of my business, but Olivia didn't mention Silas in her discharge plans. In fact, she hasn't mentioned him at all," Tammy probed. "The last update I got it sounded like he was missing, or worse. Is that still the case?"

"None of us know where he is, but he's not dead." Poe realized his response was blunt. Maybe because the visit from Agent Jon Sharpe still weighed on his mind. The information should have come from Patrick Monahan. Poe amended his statement. "Silas should be home in a few days." It was what Agent Sharpe told Olivia.

The doctor hesitated, but Poe stifled any more questions with one of his own. "Does Olivia know everything that happened during delivery?"

Tammy stepped close, keeping the conversation private even though they were the only ones at the end of the hallway. "You're talking about us losing her on the table, aren't you?" The scene played vividly in her mind. There was so much blood, so many alarms going off, Tammy Murdoch could still hear them in her head. She had never lost a mother before. She went into the operating room with three lives in her hands and she wasn't willing to leave any other way.

Poe's face said what his words didn't.

"She made me tell her. I think she already knew, but she needed to hear me say it," Tammy confessed.

Armed with what he needed to know, Poe and the doctor parted ways, but not before Tammy encouraged him to reach out to Renaye. Poe wasn't sure if it was a personal recommendation or if it had to do with Olivia. Either way, he went on about his assignment. Olivia wasn't the only one who was making plans.

After eighty years in the bayou, Mémé had decided to take a trip. Poe spent hours on the phone coordinating airport transport and arranging her discharge from the assisted living facility, giving them no return date. Dire warnings were issued about availability should Cloteel Bouvier decide she needed to return. Poe knew that would not be an issue. Once Mémé left that place, she would never go back. She had never wanted to go in the first place.

Barry was loitering in the hallway when Poe returned. "I didn't expect to find you out here," Poe said exactly what he felt.

"The lactation nurse is in there," Barry explained. The babies might not be mature enough to nurse yet, but Olivia's milk had come in and the nurse was helping her through the process of pumping and storing her breast milk. When Olivia returned for visits, she would bring what she had collected to add to the supplements the babies were receiving through their feeding tubes.

"She's going home later this evening, with strict instructions not to come back later in the night. Dr. Murdoch was firm about Olivia getting some rest," Barry informed him.

"Good luck with that," Poe told him.

"I'm keeping her keys until she's released to drive," Barry said, employing the same restriction Silas had used before he left town. "When is your grandmother coming?" Barry asked hopefully.

"Please don't call her that or Cloteel. She prefers Mémé. She'll be here as soon as I can arrange a direct flight," Poe reminded him.

"Olivia will be happy to hear it. She's preparing a compound." Barry said, as glad as Olivia to be free of the hospital and its rules. They needed time to deal with what had happened, and this was not the place. Hospitals were supposed to be for healing and recuperation. In reality, Barry wondered how anyone could find peace with the constant stream of people in and out of the room. Olivia spent half her morning completing the girls' birth certificates. It was a task Silas Branch would regret missing.

"What you call a compound, Mémé would call a coven. It's Olivia's way of nesting," Poe explained, wondering if Barry was even listening. "Olivia will never be the same again," Poe prophesized.

"I think I like this version better," Barry mused.

Poe saw Barry's motivation was different than his. With Dr. Murdoch's confirmation of Olivia's death, no matter how brief, Poe understood the implications.

Olivia's union with Silas was severed. They either have to find their way to each other, or go their separate ways. It was a reset with Barry in the middle.

"What are you willing to tell her about Silas?" Poe wanted to know.

"Everything," Barry admitted, his eyes focused on the door with Olivia on the other side.

Poe expected as much. "I don't think you're the best person to discuss Silas Branch. Olivia needs to develop a conclusion on her own. She's a smart woman," Poe reminded him. "I don't doubt that she will be just as suspicious as we are."

"The visit from Sharpe did that," Barry recalled. The agent's story confirmed that whoever had Silas wasn't done with him. Olivia called Jon a puppet to his face. "Either Silas is injured worse than they're saying or they want him isolated for a reason." Nothing good could come of either of those scenarios.

Poe couldn't argue either theory but he didn't need Barry going down rabbit holes. "Still, we need her to connect those dots for herself."

Barry looked like he wanted to argue, but Poe stopped him. "I'm just looking out for you going forward," Poe cautioned him.

Poe could see the predictable end. The groundwork was laid long before he came along. The only variable now was how much carnage would ensue in the meantime. Even though he had never met him, Poe doubted Silas Branch would go quietly. "If Olivia feels like we're making up her mind for her, she will resist."

Barry felt like there was more Poe wanted to say but didn't. If that was the case, that meant it was personal. Barry knew what was eating Poe. Barry was worried about the same thing but he was powerless to stop his feelings.

"You're right," Barry conceded. "We should let someone else tell her things she doesn't want to hear. She called Patrick Monahan. Let him do it for us." The issues with Silas began long before him or Rogan Poe.

Poe couldn't argue with the suggestion. "Then let's cross that bridge when we get there," Poe suggested. He glanced down at his watch. "You have somewhere to be. And I have travel arrangements to make." Now that Olivia had a firm discharge date, Poe wanted Mémé here sooner rather than later.

Chapter Fourteen

A wave of déjà vu smacked Barry in the face as he walked the parking lot. Familiar smells rose to greet him, sparking a rumble in his stomach. It was no wonder. Barry hadn't eaten anything except hospital food for a week. Still, he could turn around and leave with no regrets. The course of his life had changed, the bend in the road clearly marked by the twin's arrival. He was perfectly content to stay on that path, but Rogan Poe insisted he accept the invitation.

Barry spotted his party right away. Zavalla wasn't alone. Texas Ranger Hershel Gaines flanked him. Barry wondered what other surprises were in store.

"There he is." Zavalla smiled as if he and Barry were old friends.

They might have been in a life Barry no longer lived.

"I figured if I bribed you with food, you would come," Zavalla wagered.

Zavalla's forced cheerfulness, along with the ranger's presence, told Barry Poe was right.

He might be done with his old life, but apparently, it wasn't done with him. This wasn't just lunch between friends to shoot the shit. Something was up.

Barry was mute as he took his seat across the table. Lolly arrived right behind him with a large drink in her hand. She and her sons owned the restaurant that began as a mobile food truck near police headquarters. Barry was a frequent customer at both locals and one of Lolly's favorites.

"Where is your beautiful lady friend?" Lolly inquired.

Barry's last visit here had been with Olivia and Brennon. Two weeks might as well have been a lifetime. "She had plans today," Barry said politely.

"Tell her to take good care of herself and those babies."

Zavalla took the lead as soon as Lolly was gone. "You're a hard man to pin down. I was starting to take it personally when you didn't answer."

Barry took his time with a long sip of tea. "I've been busy," he finally said.

"I was sorry to hear about Brennon Kaine. I hope he's going to be all right," Zavalla probed.

"He's hanging in there." Barry wondered if Zavalla's intel included Olivia.

Barry saw Herschel Gaines flash a rare smile. It was aimed at the young girl who had stepped up to take Lolly's place.

"We're gonna be a minute," Herschel said before the waitress even had a chance to pull out pen and paper.

"What do you want?" Barry preempted Zavalla. If the captain happened to ask about Olivia, Barry wasn't sure his face wouldn't give him away.

"I asked him to set up this little soirée," Gaines intervened, slicing the lingering friction between Barry and his former captain. Gaines didn't blame Barry but now was not the time. They had bigger fish to fry.

Barry turned from Zavalla to concentrate on

Gaines.

"Do you know why the Feds are bigfooting the case in Atascosa County?" Gaines asked. Like all recent cases associated with the small county, it was a jurisdictional clusterfuck. "Agent Branch requested the rangers assist given the sheriff was pending questioning in a federal case. Now, unbeknownst to us, it appears that the offer has been rescinded. The local field office has gone radio silent, just like Agent Branch and that other fella, Deveroux. At the same time, the Feds have seized Sheriff Tennent's house. It's closed to all other jurisdictions by order of the UAD under the governance of the FBI, Dallas Harrington, Director," Gaines read from the photo he had taken of the notice tacked to the front door of Tennent's house.

Gaines slid the phone to Barry for a look. The names weren't familiar, but that didn't mean anything. The perimeter alerts clanged too loud for Barry to absorb the acronym. At first glance, it was a sign of the future, but he shut down those thoughts too. Barry slid the phone back to the ranger and concentrated on what he did know. He had seen pictures of the deceased sheriff's demise while sitting in this restaurant, at this very table. Olivia hadn't discussed details with him, but Will had. According to Will, the sheriff became a dead man walking.

"Why not ask Will Ibarra?" Barry offered.

"Ibarra doesn't belong to me anymore. The feds have pulled him. He's theirs now," Zavalla explained.

Will had mentioned being fast-tracked. Barry hadn't heard from him since Patrick Monahan's visit. The days were slipping past faster than Barry could keep track.

"They also confiscated whatever forensics Frank's team collected, along with Meeks' autopsy results. They even took the sheriff's body," Zavalla explained. Lucky for them, no one in Tennent's family was interested in his remains. "There's talk of exhuming Dr. Greene's body. I don't have to tell you there will be no opposition from the family," Zavalla warned. Amanda had four brothers, all in law enforcement. They would seize any opportunity to blame someone other than Amanda for what happened the day at Barry's condo.

For Barry, the last piece of information was like a blow to the head. "What? Why?" All he knew about the circumstances of Amanda's death was the cleaned-up version Brennon provided. Olivia walked the crime scene at Zavalla's request yet she had never discussed the details with him. What did she see that motivated her need to secure him an alibi?Barry scrambled to find his way. This conversation felt eerily similar to the one he had with Patrick Monahan, where nothing was as it seemed.

"Meeks must have something to say," Barry insisted. Meeks performed the autopsy on both Amanda and the sheriff. Barry also knew the crusty coroner had no love of the Feds.

"It's what he won't say," Gaines told Barry.

"He quit. On the spot," Zavalla said.

"How's Dr. Osborne?" Gaines cut in.

"You need to leave her out of this," Barry snapped.

Gaines held up his hands in retreat. "The last time I saw the doc, she didn't look so good," Gaines explained. "That's why I'm asking."

Zavalla didn't heed the warning. He leaned in for a final blow. "I don't think she can sit this one out. The

Feds pulled my notes on your case as well. They know I asked Dr. Osborne to take a look."

Zavalla gave voice to Barry's already racing thoughts. "Do they know what she found?"

"It was off the books. She wrote nothing down," Zavalla assured him, "but they know she's the one who called Kaine and the archbishop."

His holiness was the one who provided the alibi that allowed Barry to go free. The district attorney had mentioned authenticating the alibi the day the archbishop arrived in Zavalla's office. At the time, Zavalla had ignored him. Now it was all Zavalla could think about.

Barry's gut tightened. A lie told to win his freedom had the power to threaten not only his future but Olivia's. It was time to restore trust and end secrets. "Olivia had the babies. Silas is missing, and Deveroux is most likely dead."

The two men across from him took a beat to digest the information. Gaines recovered first. "That may have slowed the Feds, but it won't stop them from coming," the ranger cautioned. "Tell me how I can help."

Barry said the first thing that came to mind. "Tell me what Meeks wouldn't say."

****

His secretary tried to warn him, but she was as powerless as he was to stop the woman who had just invaded his office. Mike Murphy's business was financial oversight of the hospital. He wasn't accustomed to dealing with patients. Numbers were his thing. Yet she was here, and she wasn't alone. At least it wasn't another cop. Instead, it was a younger version of the attorney who also happened to reside within the hospital. Murphey didn't get involved in the daily minutia. But he had been monitoring the discharges for both her and the attorney. Hers was set for today. The attorney was pending transfer to an out-of-state sanitorium, a fancy name for a psych ward.

Murphy stood to greet his unexpected visitors. "Dr. Osborne, I could have come to you," he boasted.

"You could have, but you didn't," Olivia said, savoring the element of surprise. It's why she came herself. "This is Isaac Kane," Olivia said, letting the last name speak for itself. "I wanted to follow up on the code pink involving my daughters."

"I'm not at liberty to discuss ongoing matters," Murphy stammered.

"I think you should reconsider that position," Olivia cautioned. "I know who it was. You granted Lily Forrester access to my daughters, not to mention countless other infants."

Murphy felt his back break out into a sweat. "I can assure you her access has been suspended," he quickly replied.

"If you had done a proper background check, she wouldn't have been here in the first place," Olivia suggested.

Murphy wasn't used to interference. "I'm not sure what you want me to say. She's already been suspended."

"You can fire her, and report her to the nursing board. That way, she will be prohibited from endangering any more babies. Otherwise, I'll have no choice but to tell my story."

Murphy stiffened. "Are you threatening me?"

Olivia smiled, throwing him another curveball. In

Murphy's experience, most crumbled when he challenged them. He was a powerful man with a pen, but she wasn't impressed or intimidated.

"I believe my suggestions are more than reasonable," Olivia said, giving him time to rethink her offer. "I'm told my daughters are going to be here for at least eight more weeks, so unless you want me in your office every day of those eight weeks…" Olivia let the silence speak for itself. She had just handed him a thread. All she needed was for him to pull it. It didn't take long.

Murphy felt the queasy sensation of the floor falling out from under him. "You are threatening me," Murphy stammered as he felt his stomach right itself.

"Your words, not mine," Olivia emphasized.

Murphy's eyes narrowed as realization washed over him. Everyone wanted something.

"If you are not agreeable to my terms, which I believe are very reasonable considering the circumstances, you could challenge me," Olivia suggested.

Her voice was non-threatening, but there was lightning in her eyes.

Olivia could almost see the swirl of options inside his head. He was looking for a way out, with his usual avenues unavailable. He was a man used to getting what he wanted. He liked pushing people around. In this new era of health care, the money men had more power than the medicine men, but today, he was hopelessly lost.

"I'm not one of the physicians that you employ," Olivia reminded him. "I'm the mother of two helpless infants. My protection of them is boundless. My terms are non-negotiable."

"What do you want?" Murphy heard the words coming out of his mouth, but they didn't sound like his.

"For starters, untethered access to my daughters for myself and those I designate. As the chief financial officer," Olivia said, giving him a nudge back from the hole he'd fallen into. "I'm sure you can think of something."

Olivia let herself out with Isaac Kaine in tow.

"You didn't need me for that," Isaac said once they were in the elevator.

"Did you find it distasteful?"

"Quite the contrary. It was an impressive performance," Isaac admitted. As a young child, he would eavesdrop outside his father's home office. Isaac had heard men with names he couldn't pronounce speak the same way.

"Your presence told him I meant business," Olivia added. "He can't pretend he doesn't know who you are."

"I think it was the eyes," Isaac confessed. "My father said your eyes were electric. I didn't know what that meant—until now."

"Eyes are the silent communicator. At our root, we're all animals responding to unspoken cues. The flight-or-fight response is an embedded psychological response to a perceived threat. It was that instinct that kept our ancestors alive," Olivia explained. "I believe Mr. Murphy responded accordingly."

****

Poe was waiting for her when she returned to her room.

"I went to the NICU. You weren't there," Poe

greeted her. Seeing her out of bed reminded him she didn't look like someone who had just given birth. Her hair and makeup were done and she had shed the standard hospital gown in favor of something personal.

"I had another errand," Olivia explained.

She sounded distant. "Don't think I don't know you're avoiding me." Poe watched as Olivia fidgeted. "It's because I've been in your head, isn't it?"

Olivia stiffened, avoiding his eyes, telling Poe he was on the right track.

"I can read you, but not any better than a profiler. You've fortified your walls and shut me out. It's the equivalent of slamming the door in my face. I no longer have access to your thoughts," Poe assured her. Her memories had become his. "For us to share, you will have to open the door." Poe saw her shoulders relax with the news.

"Tell me, did you shut me out on purpose, or did it just happen?" Poe asked.

At last, Olivia looked at him. Her eyes were sad and tired.

"It just happened. A defense mechanism or instinct, I don't know. I'm doing so many things without thought, just an ever-increasing drive to do them," Olivia explained, wondering if she was experiencing her own fight or flight.

"You took a walk on the other side. What you're experiencing is a residual side-effect." Poe couldn't stop her feelings, but he could try and explain them. That had to count for something. "I'm not promising I can help you, but I am willing to try. Where do you want to start?"

Olivia looked uncharacteristically unsure. Poe

started with something close to home, proving he was serious. "I saw your past. Jason was important. While he might not have understood what you were, he saw it. I'm sorry that he was taken from you." Poe couldn't help but wonder if that wasn't part of some demon's diabolical plan. They were crafty like that, always playing the long game because they could. From her fragmented memory, Poe deduced her demon was involved, but that was *after* Jason. As far as Poe knew, *Alleracsap* had never lied to her. *Something* else had been in play.

Olivia pursed her lips, holding back a wave of emotion Poe couldn't fathom.

"Go on," Olivia encouraged him.

"Jason's loss, while tragic, pushed you to explore what was always waiting for you," Poe emphasized, feeling his way through the wave of her emotions. He might not be able to read them, but that didn't make him immune.

"When is Mémé coming?" Olivia asked, seeking confirmation from a woman she had yet to meet.

"A couple of days," Poe promised. "Until then, you're stuck with me, Barry and Kim."

Poe watched her gather herself, removing the mask of the past and replacing it with a new one. Olivia was regal in her new role. She was not someone to be challenged. No wonder Barry preferred the new one.

Chapter Fifteen

It wasn't the homecoming she expected, but it was the beginning she needed.

Dr. Murdoch said it was normal to feel sad. Depression ranked high among women who left the hospital without a baby cradled in their arms. Back inside the walls of her home, Olivia felt anything but empty. Mentally, she was connected to her daughters. The feeling was like the soft brush of a feather against her cheek. Physically, she had those gathered around her dinner table.

Olivia marveled at Kim, a young girl who should be broken but wasn't. On either side of her were two men who started out as enemies, only to grow into trusted confidants. They were the unified foundation Olivia needed to build a future for her daughters. One where their gifts were nurtured—not shunned. Sadness wasn't what Olivia felt. Under the gratefulness of survival, she felt the slow burn of vengeance.

With Daisy and Alvin following her every step, Olivia retreated to her backyard oasis. After learning of her pregnancy, she completely took over the space that she had created for another. She was on her way resurrecting the garden Gran once grew. The seedlings were remnants from her great-grandmother, Abitha, the Apothecary. Olivia already had plans for a pool.

Poe's voice pulled her from her wanderings. He

was apologizing for his tardiness. Olivia hadn't noticed. Then she remembered he stayed behind on kitchen duty so Kim could get Adelyn to bed. Kim seemed fretful when Olivia returned home. She didn't realize why until Kim requested a moment alone with her. The young girl stumbled over tears as she asked Olivia if she and Adelyn could remain with her. Olivia's reaction was immediate. She opened her arms and held Kim close, reassuring her that sending her home had never crossed her mind. It was not until later that Olivia considered the possible meaning behind Kim's tearful request.

Kim was gifted with an internal receiver, her frequency tuned to places and objects. Poe had called her a *listener*. Olivia mistakenly thought Kim only heard echoes of the past, but maybe her gifts also included the present. Kim's feelings were now resonating with her. Olivia had felt a constant, low hum of background noise since coming out of her coma. She had attributed it to the hive mind of the hospital, with so many people and emotions pressing against her. While the white noise had considerably lessened once she was discharged, something else took its place.

Olivia felt poised for fight or flight. It could only mean something was out there, slowly circling, stalking like a predator in the dark. Whatever it was had the potential to shatter the delicate world they were creating here. Whether it be the tranquility of the dinner table or the burning embers of the night.

Poe passed Olivia a cup of warm tea. "One of Mémé's recipes. It's supposed to increase milk production and tighten the uterus." If not for Olivia, Rogan Poe would never have uttered those words in the same sentence. He was still acclimating to his new role. Where he had once been a hunter of demons, answering to no one, he found himself acquiescing to whatever Olivia needed from him.

Olivia accepted his offering. The contents smelled sweet, like syrup with a touch of sugar browned by fire. Olivia savored the first sip, giving herself over to the magic of the tea. When she opened her eyes, she found Poe surveying the perimeter for what was lurking in the shadows.

"*Alleracsap's* not here," Olivia told him. "He's watching over the girls."

Barry waited for Poe to object. When he didn't, Barry did. "Is that a good idea?"

"I trust *Alleracsap* more than whoever sent Lily," Olivia explained.

"But he's a demon," Barry stressed the obvious.

"It's about loyalty. *Alleracsap* is a low-level demon, taking orders from something much more powerful than himself. For Lily, or someone like her, unemployment is the result of her failure. *Alleracsap,* on the other hand, risks an eternity of punishment should he do the same," Olivia explained, before addressing Poe. "You are the one who told me *Alleracsap* could not take my offspring without my permission," Olivia reminded him. "You just failed to tell me why. Now I know." She should have known it from the beginning. "*Alleracsap* never did what demons do – *possess*. He didn't even try with me because he knew he couldn't."

No matter how chilling her answer, Poe knew it made perfect sense. One demon could not possess another. Olivia was only part demon, but one drop of it was enough to keep others away.

Olivia waited for Poe to speak his mind. When he didn't, she employed another method. He may no longer have full access to her thoughts, but that didn't stop her from sending him a message.

"Too close to the dark side for you?"

"It doesn't feel right."

Olivia studied him, making sure they were past his disapproval. While she didn't need his permission, she was seeking his understanding.

Poe gave her a slight nod of submission.

With the matter settled, Olivia moved on. "So, who does the car down the street belong to?"

"Your former employer?" Poe speculated.

"I pegged it for FBI too, at first, but I think the make is outside of their budgetary bounds," Barry surmised. The car looked too expensive for government use.

"The agent who came to see you at the hospital didn't mention it?" Poe asked the obvious. Something about the FBI being concerned enough to tuck Silas Branch away, yet they left his wife and the mother of his children defenseless didn't feel right. Unless they knew she wasn't.

"There are a lot of places to hide in this neighborhood," Barry said. It was the same concern he had since Jamie Smythe invaded their lives. It wasn't two weeks ago that someone left flowers for Olivia on the porch. To him they were a token but of what Barry had no clue. "The car down the street could be a diversion that keeps us from looking elsewhere."

That kind of thinking reminded Poe that Barry was a cop.

The assessment assured Olivia they were all on the same page. "We trust no one outside this coven," she proclaimed. Her voice was quiet, but her words were firm.

The use of the word wasn't lost on Poe. "Does that include your husband?" he dared ask.

Olivia didn't hesitate. "I can't think about Silas right now or I'll go down a rabbit hole that will blind me to everything else."

"Maybe that's the point," Barry theorized, still in cop mode.

"That's the predictable response," Olivia mused. "Those watching from afar sent Agent Sharpe because he was a familiar who could placate me but I know Sharpe asked for a transfer the day of Sheriff Tennent's murder. That means he's no longer in play. Meeting with me was the last useful thing Jon Sharpe could do for his handlers," Olivia theorized. "If the FBI was intent on informing me they would have sent Patrick Monahan. Since Patrick's not answering my calls, I'm relying on the two of you to tell me what he told you. And don't lie or I will know," Olivia cautioned. She could feel the change within herself. Any other time, Olivia would have gathered information. But since she was demanding loyalty, by creating a coven, she must become something more.

Given Olivia's demand for the truth of what transpired during her absence, Poe did the talking. Under Olivia's scrutiny, he told her exactly what he cautioned Barry not to do. Poe could deliver the information without emotion, something Barry could not. Poe repeated what Patrick Monahan shared, from his surprise escalation to BAU director, to Silas' pursuit of her. The only thing Poe kept to himself was Silas' drug habit. According to Patrick, it predated Olivia, so Poe saw no reason to add it to the burden he had just given her to carry.

Olivia didn't flinch. She didn't interrupt. She sat passively and listened to the words she knew Poe did not want to speak. They left her feeling hollow, unsurprised, and absolutely convinced there was more betrayal to come. Those feelings had been with her since she woke from her coma and Silas wasn't there.

"It tracks," Olivia affirmed. "I even considered it myself, but if the FBI knows there are others—*a collective*," Olivia said, using Larry Pittman's words, "then what changed?"

"Atascosa County," Barry said. He wasn't just talking about the barn.

"During your time with the Bureau, did you meet one, other than Pittman?" Poe asked. The obvious answer was staring them in the face, but Poe was now the one gathering information. He hadn't shared the news of a young killer who wasn't behind bars because he wanted to hear if Olivia's answer mirrored Monahan's.

"Elijah Stoddard. He was the stepson of some up-and-coming Virginia politician. What he said to me then, I did not understand," Olivia answered without hesitation.

"What do you mean?" Poe pressed.

"Elijah told me there was a demon who wanted to know if I would come when called."

"Was he like Pittman?" Barry asked. Larry Wayne Pittman admitted to gunning down two twelve-year-old girls because he could see the evil inside them. Pittman referred to his role as a *cleaner*.

Olivia focused on the flames, retracing her steps before stumbling onto an answer. "He was part Pittman, part something else." Elijah's attempted exorcism got Father Dominic in trouble with the church. "I was woefully ignorant," Olivia mused. She had cautioned Dom against exorcism. Whichever demon chose Elijah was transient. He wasn't interested in staying. In the end, it was Elijah's mother who insisted Father Dominic help her. She believed something had always followed her son. Olivia wondered where the woman was now.

"No matter the decisions you made then, you knew the kid was different," Poe assured her. Olivia had been used in more ways than one by the Bureau. Eventually, the reality of that would sink in. Poe could only wonder what the realization would do to her. "If it makes you feel better, your data guy, Kevin, traced the kid to a black hole that could only be government-related."

Olivia wondered if uncovering that detail prompted Kevin's recommendation for increased protection. She would get the details on Elijah another time. They had more immediate problems.

"Kevin is searching for what Lily could have taken from Geneviève. I think it has to be blood. It's the one thing she could acquire without drawing attention to herself."

"Will saw the video feed taken outside the NICU. Whatever it was, it was small enough to pass from hand to hand," Barry added.

Olivia looked at Poe given their shared medical background. "A tube of blood is small."

"It makes sense," Poe agreed. "Who hasn't had to

give a blood sample? It would make one hell of a tracking system."

"That's why I gave Kevin names of the other gifteds I know. That includes you," Olivia told Poe. The list was longer than she had anticipated. Most were accumulated in the last two years, but she didn't stop there. Olivia included Gran, Marceline Roche, and even her own mother. With the age variables of the individuals, Olivia hoped Kevin might also be able to determine when the tracking began.

"We need to add Franklin Pope to the list," Poe reminded her. Frank was Mémé's brother. Frank spent time in prison for killing his neighbor. It wasn't until after the neighbor's death that stories began to leak that the neighbor was the local peeping Tom who may have crossed the line to rape. Frank did his time and stayed in Texas. Well into his eighties, Frank resided at the same skilled nursing facility where Poe worked. Pope, like Pittman, was also a *cleaner*.

Barry was strangely quiet. He caught Olivia looking at him, hoping she could not see his thoughts. "Blood, DNA. Poe is right. It's widely available, not to mention it's how we,"

"Track the bad guys," Olivia finished for him.

"What did Zavalla want?" Olivia asked. When Barry returned to the hospital, they were too focused on her discharge to discuss what happened at lunch.

"It wasn't just Zavalla. Herschel Gaines was there too," Barry told her. "They wanted to know why the FBI sealed off Sheriff Tennent's house and seized all information associated with the investigation. That includes the forensics. Even the body."

Barry didn't realize he was being selective about

the information he shared. It wasn't intent, but instinct.

"They found something they had never seen before," Poe cautioned. "No doubt this has been a long time coming."

"The gifted have suited their needs. I'm guessing the lower-level ones are plentiful. The cleaners like Pittman take out the trash, leaving less bad guys to hunt. The seductresses are employed by people like my mother. Sex sells, so do the potions my great grandmother used to concoct. Then there are the fortune tellers." Olivia stopped talking. She could already see a tangled road ahead.

"They hide in plain sight, while the listeners, like Kim and the hunters like me, fly right under the radar," Poe finished for her. He hoped the interruption stopped Olivia from spinning wherever she was going. He had never seen her angry yet he sensed that was where she was heading. Barry said it was comforting. Somehow, Poe didn't think this was the same.

"Then there's me."

Olivia's tone dripped with bitterness. The clench of her jaw paired well with the sparks in her eyes. She was not concerned, but defiant. Poe wondered if he was watching the unraveling of the bond she shared with Silas or something more.

"I played a part. I tracked the monsters they couldn't catch. I also found the most frightening gift of all. *Necromancy*. Rose Corey gave them a reason to fear us. Raising the dead violates the natural order of things. The FBI and all those other three-letter agencies want order more than they want anything else."

Olivia looked like there was more she could say, but something in the flames caught her attention.

At the same time, Poe felt a strange quiver on the back of his neck. He looked beyond the flames, searching for the demon that raised his alarm. He almost wished it was *Alleracsap*. Instead, it appeared a new player had entered the game. Poe felt the pull of Olivia forcing him to focus on her. She knew the demon was there too and she was not concerned.

"I need to ensure that my daughters know their heritage. I cannot do that until you tell me mine," she told Poe.

Olivia returned from the other place, knowing her father was a demon, relieving Poe of the unenviable task of telling her. Now she wanted specifics. Not all demons were created equal. *Alleracsap* taught her that. There was a hierarchy even in Hell.

"Does the smell of cinnamon mean anything to you?" Poe asked.

"Gran called it my *secret* ingredient. I was especially fond of adding it to my favorite cookies," Olivia explained. "Why?"

"Mémé's been researching. It's a little-known fact that cinnamon is associated with certain types of demons. I have never encountered one myself, but I did smell it here and in your hospital room the day you woke up," Poe explained. He resisted sniffing the air now.

"So, it's not *Alleracsap*?" Olivia clarified what she had already decided for herself.

Poe could not refuse her and he knew it. Especially since this appeared to be a test. She knew there was another demon present and it wasn't *Alleracsap*. Her trip to the *other side* gave her insight Mémé would never find. No one in Mémé's coven had traversed the shadow plains, at least no one that came back. "Most demons smell like sulfur. According to Mémé, there's a myth that instead of smelling like sulfur, these particular demons emit a cinnamon scent."

"What sets these demons apart from the others?" Olivia asked.

"Rank, in other words, royalty." Poe couldn't decide if knowing or not knowing was the worst. At least the list was short. "It means he would have been one of Lucifer's closest allies originally sent to earth while still an angel. There is only one demon who is referenced in the Dead Sea Scrolls and the Bible. He's also thought to be part of the storey of Yom Kippur, the Jewish day of atonement. According to the Torah, there were two goats. One was sacrificed as an offering to God. The other absorbed the sins of the Jewish people and is pushed off a cliff, demonstrating the casting aside of wrongdoing, thus the *scapegoat*."

"A lofty position as a demon, no doubt," Olivia surmised. "Because of his status, he can command another." She trusted *Alleracsap* with her daughters because he answered to a higher power. The sneaking suspicion *Alleracsap* had been on duty her whole life had been with her for weeks.

"Finally, according to the book of Enoch, a collective of angels were sent from heaven to earth to watch over God's creations. While doing that, they fell in love with the daughters of man. Love led to fornication and they fell, finding themselves cast out along with Lucifer. In turn, they bestowed the humans with gifts. If all of these things are true, Mémé's best guess is *Azazel* is your father."

The mention of the name sent Olivia's heart into

overdrive. Her ears roared with the sound of a wave coming for her. Digging her toes into imaginary sand, Olivia waited for the truth to sweep her away. "Why him?"

"Because of the gifts he gave," Poe told her. "*Azazel* gifted men war and women witchcraft. Your family was full of witches, but their gifts were waning. Your mother possesses the *allure*–it's why she trades in flesh and harbors girls who carry the same gift. *Azazel* may have chosen her specifically or maybe it was a chance encounter. Your mother, the seductress, seduced a man possessed. You are the product of that union. It's the demon blood that sealed your fate and bestowed your power."

Chapter Sixteen

Poe left them with an excuse Olivia didn't believe but didn't care enough to ponder.

Barry felt reluctant to leave Olivia alone so he busied himself tending the fire. Poking the smoldering coals and watching the sparks fly gave him something to do while Olivia contemplated her lineage.

Concealed by shadows, Olivia wasn't contemplating as much as she was observing. For someone who had lived without a yard for a long time, Barry seemed to have regained his footing. He seemed more relaxed since leaving the hospital. The magic of her sanctuary had overtaken him and his peace flowed back into her. Olivia drank in the shared tranquility, but she could only bask for so long. Barry's presence was a stark reminder that for all her thoughts of the future, there was a *before time*. Reality was heading her way, threatening to steal her harmony. Remnants of the not-so-distant past would get their turn with or without her consent.

Olivia might have renovated her childhood home, but her plans had not included the sanctuary she found herself in now. Ensuring the dogs had enough space to roam and preserving Gran's small garden had been her only plans. Then everything changed. She added the patio, and the fire pit was a wedding gift to Silas. *Did she dare consider what she thought was shattered was merely rearranged?*

Barry put the poker away and sat down next to her. "How do you feel, really?" Earlier, she needed Poe's counsel, but not now that they were alone.

Olivia's first thoughts were of her daughters, but she didn't have to tell Barry that. He missed them too. There were no words that could fill their void so she didn't even try.

"Like I'm seeing everything for the first time. I was forced to bury so much, now all of it is resurrected. The first step toward the future is letting go of the past. Gran painted a portrait of a life that was never real. What's happening now is the way it should have always been."

Inside the flames, a veil lifted and Olivia saw everything. "There was never a ghost in my house. I never had a guardian angel. There was no Alice, only *Alleracsap.* And when I decided to stop listening to the whispers of the dead, Jamie came for me but he did not come alone. He dragged me into a world that should have always been mine."

If anyone else had been telling this story, Barry would have felt pity. But the words slipping past her lips sounded nothing like pity. They sounded like liberation.

The clap of the back door shattered the moment. Olivia and Barry were on their feet when they saw it was Poe. He should have been gone already.

Barry said what Olivia was thinking. "I thought you were leaving."

"I'm glad I didn't," Poe answered, bypassing Barry to speak directly to Olivia. "I have good news and bad news. The good news is I know who was in the car down the street."

"And the bad news?" Olivia asked while a musty smell pricked her nose.

"I know who was in the car down the street," Poe told her. "It's your mother, and she didn't come alone."

****

Inside her house, her past had shown up unannounced.

"I love what you've done with the place," Sarah Larsin said, gazing around the room like a prospective buyer.

Olivia was mesmerized by the woman who was her mother, yet looked young enough to be her sister. The only difference was the red hair and the same blue eyes as Gran.

Poe snapped at her mother. His words were muffled, drowned out by the thoughts flowing from the man in the corner.

"Only one of the things waiting for you."

"I'm not that vain," Olivia clapped back.

"I doubt you're here for a tour." Poe was still snapping when Olivia tuned back in.

Olivia raised her voice over the others. "Leave her." It came out sounding like an order. "She's hardly the most interesting thing in the room." Olivia was aware she had spoken, but her voice didn't sound like her own. There was a strength behind it she had yet to use.

"You are the most interesting thing in the room."

It was another thought inside Olivia's head courtesy of the mesmerizing man in the corner. He had cinnamon-colored skin accented by coal-black hair with delicate threads of silver running through it. His close-clipped beard was a combination of more silver than ebony. Blue was too simple a word for the color of the double-breasted suit he wore. It looked like it cost more than most people spent on a car. At his throat was a paisley ascot. On his nose were round- framed glasses that made Olivia think of a dead rockstar who died too soon. The lenses were dark. She wondered why he bothered to wear them. No one got close enough to look him in the eyes.

"Not willingly."

"Until now."

The words were a hiss inside her head, but Olivia knew the man could hear her.

Olivia slipped past Poe's grip, but he did manage to stop Barry. "She has to do this," Poe cautioned him.

"You don't look like you belong here," Olivia said, gliding past her mother.

"It has been more than a century this time. Still perfecting the process."

So, this was the elusive Samael Knight. No wonder Interpol had a hard time identifying him. The body he inhabited shouldn't be living. Olivia invaded his personal space, gazing at him unflinching, with only one goal in mind. She very much wanted to see what was behind the glass. Before she could finish her thought, his glasses were perched just far enough down his nose for her to stare into ebony eyes surrounded by flames of orange. They reminded her of the fire burning outside.

Olivia leaned in, her face not far from his. She watched his pupils constrict and knew her emerald eyes were giving him their own show. She closed them and inhaled loudly. "You smell like death." Her words were a hiss. "You have no power over me, do you?"

Samael attempted what Olivia could only guess was a smile. The skin was too tight on his face, making him look like some comic book villain. "What makes you say that?"

"My father sent you," Olivia quipped.

From her periphery, Olivia watched Sarah flinch. "What, you think he wouldn't tell me?" Olivia asked, referring to Poe. She left Samael for the moment to turn on her mother. "Don't tell me you didn't know."

"I didn't, I swear, not that night. I was just glad I got out of there alive. He didn't come to me in his true form until the day I found out I was pregnant. Even then, I didn't know his name. He said it was his greatest wish to have another child."

"Another one?" Olivia wheeled back to Samael.

"It is an age-old story, same rules, same ending. Do not taste the forbidden fruit or the world will end. I hope you were not hoping for a family reunion. It has been a few millennia since he made one stick. He just cannot seem to stop trying."

"Why?" Olivia asked.

Samael shrugged. At least this attempt to appear human was better than his smile. "Why does anyone keep trying? They are hoping for a different outcome. He feels like he has a pretty good shot this time. For one thing, you have managed to stay alive longer than any of the others, even if it took you longer to find your powers. The show in the barn was impressive. It is still talked about. It seems Ana was not so useless after all. Your mother mistakenly thought you could learn something from her but it looks like you were the teacher."

"It was the last lesson Ana ever learned," Olivia agreed, her words cold.

"Tell me, what was it?" Samael asked, not because he did not know, but because he wanted to hear her say it.

"Not to cross me."

"And what of Mr. Roche?" Samael probed.

"He wanted a demon so I gave him one."

The flesh on Poe's arms reacted to the sound of her voice. He snuck a glance at Barry. The former cop was unaffected by the change.

"Clever girl. You are a natural."

"I had good intentions," Sarah murmured.

Olivia turned back to her mother, looking annoyed. At the same time, the lights in the living room blinked.

Poe turned to Barry.

"Let her be. She can handle this," Barry repeated Poe's own warning.

"Really? Is that supposed to be an apology?" Olivia stared down the woman who abandoned her decades before.

"Livie."

Olivia locked eyes on her mother. "Don't call me that. That's what Gran called me."

Sarah flashed a thin smile. It looked like one Olivia would use one day when her daughters were testing her patience. "*I* called you that," Sarah corrected her, sounding like a disapproving mother. "I thought Olivia was too big a name for you at such a young age. It was too much responsibility. I never wished you to feel the same weight of what I carried." Sarah waited for another interruption, but Olivia appeared to be listening to her, maybe for the first time. Sarah pressed on because she may never get another chance.

"Even at seventeen I knew you were extraordinary and I had no idea what to do for you or what you needed. Neither did your Gran, for that matter. I did the only thing I was capable of doing–leave. I hoped my mother would find you help or guidance. Instead, she froze in place. Just like she did when my father died.

"You have great gifts and I'm sorry for you–but you absolutely cannot freeze in place. I'm afraid you have no other choice but to act. If you don't–others will do it for you. Believe me, you don't want that for you and especially not for your daughters. You have the power to free the gifted–*do it*. Use what's yours," Sarah told her.

"Like you?" Olivia asked. It wasn't a cheap shot. It was a real question.

"No, not like me. I have no extraordinary gifts. The ironic thing is I can sense it in others–that's why I try to help the girls who show up at my door. And I surround myself with the likes of Samael. He's never been here for one before. He's here for you."

Olivia was ready to end the conversation, but Sarah couldn't let that happen.

"One of Gran's faults was she saw everything in black and white. You're not that, Olivia. There is more than one path. Embrace the gray, Livie, and make your own way. It is what your father wants."

Olivia's patience was waning. Barry wasn't sure if he was seeing it or feeling it. Either way, he knew what would happen if he didn't intervene.

"What can you tell us about the UAD?" Barry asked, breaking the connection between mother and daughter. It's what he would do in an interview room to catch a witness off guard. He had listened to Sarah's speech to Olivia. It was as much an apology as it was a warning.

"What's the UAD?" Poe wanted to know.

"Something Zavalla asked about," Barry told him quickly. When he looked back up Barry noticed he had Sarah Larsin's undivided attention. He felt a momentary sense of lightheadedness. It could have been the abrupt absence of the energy radiating from Olivia or the sudden attention from the demon in the corner.

"The UAD stands for the Urban Affairs Division. It's operated in secret for decades," Sarah conceded.

"What is it?" Poe joined the conversation.

"They're the ones who track *us*," Sarah said.

"Through our blood?" Poe suggested.

"How do you know that?" Samael was quick to ask.

"A tube of Genevieve's blood was taken without permission," Olivia explained.

Samael and Sarah exchanged information but kept it to themselves.

"You need to tell us what you know about the UAD," Barry insisted.

"It's a reasonable request," Poe echoed.

"I have a lot of high-profile clients. The girls in my establishments hear things they shouldn't. In turn, we exchange information with certain compromised government agents so there are no surprises. It has been mutually beneficial, but no more. We have been shut out," Sarah explained.

"Why? How long ago?" Barry pressed.

"The same time Agent Deveroux and Silas Branch

went missing."

"Any idea why?" Barry wanted to know.

"My guess is Rose Corey gave them the push they needed to go public. Alliances are being drawn and wagons are circling. It's one thing to kill a washed-up sheriff. It's another thing to kill a federal agent, even one set up by his own agency. Mason Deveroux is dead," Sarah revealed. "I saw the video, before it was taken down. He's walking around an empty parking lot at three a.m."

"What's he doing?" Barry asked.

"Nothing. He's dead," Sarah said with a shrug.

"We were told the last phone call Silas Branch made was to you." Barry left the rest for Sarah to answer.

"Unfortunately for him, he made a pit-stop at Deveroux's, just in time for the explosion. As far as we know, Agent Branch survived the blast. We figure the agency had eyes on Deveroux's place, hoping to catch Rose. Since Silas is not here, my guess is he's being handled, redeployed, incentivized, whatever you want to call it," Sarah hypothesized.

"How can you be sure your information isn't compromised?" Poe asked.

"You don't think I have access to an empath or two?"

The disclosure piqued Olivia's interest despite the fact there was a demon in her living room, not to mention her mother. "An empath? A true one who does nothing but scan the thoughts of others?"

"Granted they're hard to find and they don't last long, but they are valuable." Sarah didn't seem to understand the curiosity.

"What do you mean, they don't last long?" Olivia wanted to know.

"They're an open receiver without an off-switch. They kill themselves rather than being institutionalized." Samael was nonchalant, like discussing the weather.

Olivia looked to Poe, telegraphing her thoughts.

"What else are you not telling me?"

"Anyway, I know this doesn't make up for me being a shitty mother, but I am thinking ahead." Sarah pulled an envelope off the mantle. Olivia hadn't noticed it before. Sarah must have stashed it when Poe went outside to get her and Barry.

Olivia tore it open. She didn't look past the first page. It was a bill of sale for the Forrester's house. Poe mentioned something about Ross stopping by and asking for Lily. After hearing Lily's name, Olivia stopped listening. "I can't accept this." Olivia shook her head and slid the papers back inside the envelope.

"It's not for you," Sarah corrected her. "It's for my granddaughters. They're going to need a place to come home to. That house and its secrets belong to our family. My mother only sold it because she needed the money. I don't blame her, but now I have the money to take it back."

Olivia continued to shake her head.

"Don't make your daughters pay for your feelings for me. You think you may know what's coming, but you don't." Sarah waited for a response from Olivia but got nothing.

Barry watched Sarah square her shoulders and drop the mask of confidence she wore.

"I'm asking for grace." Sarah waited, but when she

could wait no longer, she slipped out the front door, never looking back.

"*Grace*. Who uses that word?" Olivia asked.

Samael moved from his place in the corner to go to Olivia, invading her personal space as she had his. "Sarah is asking for grace first because she does not want to be put in a position to beg for mercy. After what she did to you, you would be well within your right not to grant it. I feel the need to caution you that what you will have to do to protect your daughters and secure their future, you must become ruthless because our enemies will not go quietly. Your mother may be the first to ask for grace but I guarantee you, she will not be the last to beg you for something."

Samael paused, giving Olivia a chance to speak, but she didn't. He reached out to touch her shoulder. "Do not doubt yourself. As you ascend to your rightful place as the one to lead the gifted out of the shadows, many will ask for favor, grace and most certainly mercy. Before long, you will grant none of those. I rather look forward to seeing you that way."

"What way?" Olivia snapped.

"A mere fledgling on her way to becoming what she always should have been—a ruler, a queen. It has been far too long since I have witnessed fire and brimstone."

"I'm no queen – I'm just a woman standing in the way."

Samael smiled. He liked that she didn't flinch when he did it. "Keep the attitude. It will serve you well in the days to come. I would be amiss if I did not point out that a changeling is so much more than a mere woman. I am curious, if you are not afraid of me, what are you afraid of?"

Olivia stepped closer and locked eyes with what she knew lay behind the dark glass. "God. You should be too."

Chapter Seventeen

The buzzing in her head calmed considerably with Samael's departure. Still, Olivia needed more quiet, if that was even possible. She couldn't listen to Poe's ranting. She threw her hands up in desperation. "Please stop talking," Olivia snapped. "Even I don't trust me right now."

"What does that mean?" Poe looked ready for an attack. If he didn't do what she asked, he might get one.

Olivia struggled for words while telling herself to focus on the reason behind Poe's. Fear drove him, not anger. "Unpredictability, chaos. Last time I felt like this there was fire, snakes and a demon."

The realization was chilling. "I think that's what *It* was hoping for," Poe refused to use Samael's name.

Olivia trusted Poe and she desperately needed his guidance. He was more than a confidant, more than a friend, but if she stayed here any longer, she would give him the show Samael wanted. She headed for the backdoor, removing herself before the confrontation spiraled out of control.

Barry stepped in to stop Poe from following. "I know you mean well, but I don't think following her is a good idea. She needs a break," Barry cautioned.

"That's the second time you've done that," Poe snapped, not liking the hostility in his own voice. The demon might have left, but his essence still permeated the room."

"Done what?" Barry asked.

"You stopped her. Just now, and when you confronted Samael. That's why you started asking questions. I doubt he has many naturals speak to him without being compelled," Poe surmised. Poe and Barry had learned to trust each other quickly, but Poe had yet to appreciate Barry's role as watcher until now. Poe had yet to develop the patience his own vow to Olivia required. It would come with time, but Sarah's visit told him time was in short supply.

"What is he?" Barry asked.

"An abomination," Poe said, his distaste palpable.

Before he could say more, Kim appeared at the bottom of the stairs, her arms stretched tightly across her middle. In that moment she looked her age, a teenage single mom. It was easy to forget that she should be in high school thinking about proms and football games, not how to raise her daughter while she still struggled to find herself.

"What's happening?" She sounded on the verge of tears. "I heard voices and it feels weird in here," Kim said, as her eyes frantically skimmed the room.

"That's an understatement," Poe conceded.

With a nod from Poe that he would handle Kim, Barry slipped outside

Olivia was pacing in front of what was left of the fire, clutching herself much as Kim had done. Barry approached carefully waiting for her to make the first move.

"A person could go crazy thinking about this stuff. I don't want to do the things everyone tells me are coming." Olivia felt the omnipresent oppression rising like a wave threatening to sweep away the life she had just started to build.

"You once told me that demons are great deceivers. They trick and they lie to get what they want," Barry reminded her.

Olivia looked at him through a vale of tears. "I'm one of them."

Barry shook his head slowly. "No, you are not. You chose to call yourself a changeling for a reason. There's a meaning behind your choice. Poe believes you are free to choose your own path. That's what I see now and in the barn."

"In the barn I chose to end two people," Olivia reminded him.

"They gave you no choice," Barry reminded her.

"I used magic as a weapon. That is all anyone will remember."

"Not me. What I remember is that I owe you my life. You're too focused on the how rather than the why. What you did was fight for not just your life, but mine and Kim's and Rose's and countless other girls Roche would find if you didn't stop him. He would have killed us both and I dare say your end would have been so much worse than mine. We both made choices about our lives long ago to protect and serve. That's what you did. Samael was right when he said you could be a queen, but I know the most important thing you want to be is a mother. Your daughters are not the only ones who will come to you seeking safety. What I see is a woman who will grant it to those in need."

Olivia bit her lip, the tears falling with every word he spoke. "That's now, but what about after? What if I lose myself in the process?"

Barry shook his head. "I won't let you," he promised. "You have me. I will always remember who you are."

Barry went to her. Olivia slipped easily into his arms. She clung to him as the tears fell in an avalanche. Behind him, Olivia heard the pop of the fire. Through her tears, Olivia saw a cascade of ash reach for the sky. As it floated back to the ground, she realized it wasn't ash, but the whitest of feathers.

****

Dallas was the one sent to break the bad news. Dillon was his charge, but it didn't feel that way. The obsessive agent was slipping through his fingers.

"You can't keep him," Dallas said. "It's been too long. The other side has already made contact. The longer he's away, the less hospitable she's going to be."

Dillon didn't seem to be listening. He was sitting behind his desk in yesterday's shirt and tie, staring at the monitor to his left.

"The plan is to gain her cooperation," Dallas reminded him.

"Have you seen the video? The one of her at the prison?" Dillon asked.

Dallas felt the knot he carried in his stomach tighten. He had seen it—once. That was enough. In his opinion, Dillon had watched it too many times.

Dillon didn't wait for an answer. "I've been thinking. Who's going to believe a teenage girl killed a sheriff and an FBI agent? We need a scapegoat."

****

They didn't notice her until Barry had turned into the driveway. He turned off the ignition and looked at Olivia. "What do you want me to do?"

"Make me the breakfast you promised. I'll handle her."

"Should we invite her?" Barry asked with a wry smile. Olivia's mood had improved drastically after seeing the girls. So had his. He wanted to hold on to the feeling.

"Don't be ridiculous," Olivia told him.

"I waited until the girl and the baby left before coming," Sarah explained. She knew the demon hunter had departed the night before. She was still awake when her daughter and her watcher left. It wasn't hard to guess where they went. "How are your little darlings?"

"I don't feel like discussing them with you," Olivia told her.

"Can you at least tell me their names?" Sarah prodded.

"Genevieve and Gwendolyn."

"Strong names. I have no doubt under your rule they will live up to them. Your Gran would have been pleased by the choice."

Barry slipped out the front door to hand Olivia a cup of tea. "Would you like some tea, or coffee?"

"Isn't he a gem?" Sarah flashed her daughter a smile that Olivia quickly vanquished.

"She's not staying that long," Olivia answered for her mother.

"I'm already up past my bedtime," Sarah added.

One last long look at Olivia and Barry was gone.

"He's par for the course, isn't he?" Sarah asked, looking amused.

"I'm more interested in why you're on my porch when you should be sleeping," Olivia countered.

"You were conceived in New Orleans. I bet you

didn't know that," Sarah mused.

Sarah Larsin was correct. Olivia did not know this. "I bet there are a lot of things I don't know, but that's not what this is about." No matter how much Olivia disliked sharing the same space with the woman who had birthed her, she had interviewed enough suspects to know when to sit back and let them talk. Often, when revealing something important, they took the long way. It helped soften the blow and deflect the horror they had inflicted.

"I was free to roam the city while my mother went to see someone who could help her contact my father. She loved that man so much. The version I got of him was of a damaged man forever encased in memories of war and the depravity men in control inflict on the weak. It was a haunting that killed him. He carried the atrocities of war with him for the rest of his life just as raw as when he experienced them for the first time. Maybe it was a form of dementia. Only he didn't get to trade memories every day. He was stuck reliving the same ones over and over. He considered himself broken, but in my mother's eyes she forever saw him as the man he was when she met him, the one before the war—the same one she fell in love with."

Olivia felt the prick of tears in her eyes and a tightening of her abdomen. She wanted to tell herself it was postpartum hormones or even Mémé's tea she was drinking, but Olivia knew it wasn't. It was her own flashback to the words Barry uttered last night. *I will remember.*

"I digress, but I think it's interesting that New Orleans is the same place your demon hunter wants to take you." This was definitely not something Olivia knew. "The swamp will provide the cover you're going to need and it will be a hospitable place. There are a lot of gifted there. I'm here to extend the same offer for you and your daughters, your watcher and whomever else you've included in your coven to come to Vegas."

Olivia slipped out of last night's memories, feeling unsure of what her mother meant.

"Of course, there is the concern that Vegas will be the first place they will look for you. Southern choices would be Savannah, Charleston, Saint Augustine, and of course, the closest would be where Poe wants to go—New Orleans. It's easy to get lost in the swamp. Lots of things are hidden there not just collectives. Those contacts could be very valuable in the long run. Besides, New Orleans is what, a seven-or-eight-hour drive?"

"These are all places with a lot of gifteds?" Olivia asked.

"Yes, sorry." For one so powerful, there was so much her daughter didn't know. "I would avoid air travel if possible because it leaves a paper trail. To the north you have Chicago, west is San Francisco and east there is Salem, but I would avoid that place like the plague. If you feel the need to go farther, I can arrange travel abroad, it will just take longer to plan. Regardless of where you go, I will cover all expenses. My funds are unlimited, thanks to Samael."

"You already gifted the girls the house next door," Olivia said, not wanting to be anymore indebted to her mother than she already was.

Sarah leaned forward in her chair and reached for her daughter, but Olivia recoiled.

At that moment, she felt childlike in her mother's

presence.

"You don't understand. The agency will come to you with an offer. I don't know the offer, but after last night, I know you. You won't take it. The price will be in compliance with their agenda. Rose is the example they want and they need you to find her. I've seen the video of the FBI agent in the parking garage. I've heard there's one of the sheriff, maybe even one of you."

Olivia shook her head, unable to recall. There were no cameras in the barn.

"Your visit to Pittman. Prisons have no privacy. You must learn to govern your emotions."

Despite her absence, it was frightening how much her mother knew about her. Her actions at the barn and the prison were born from the same place. *Protecting someone she loved.*

"What do you think seeing those images will do to the masses? There is no middle ground. You and those who choose to follow you to the swamp or wherever will have to be off the grid, as they say, for an undetermined amount of time. What's coming will not blow over in a day, a week, or even a month. There will be civil unrest. Gifteds will be hunted and lives will be lost. On both sides."

"Don't you think you're getting ahead of yourself?" Despite the slow dread slipping over her like a cloak, Olivia did not want to believe her mother.

Sarah's smile was cynical this time. "What are you waiting for, Olivia? I just said the quiet part aloud for you. I know you feel change coming. Even I feel it. You were part of that agency world. I catered to it. I was scared at first at how much Mason Deveroux uncovered. Then, when the agency had what they wanted, I watched them let him twist off into the wind and destroy his career for uncovering exactly what they asked him to find. Now instead of forcing him into retirement, he's dead by one of us. We might could have ridden out another generation or so, but not now, not after what Rose did. The time for *us against them* is looming."

The conversation her mother was having with her brought up too many memories of the one she and Silas had shared just before he left.

"I'm surprised Samael isn't here to deliver this news. It seems like something he would want to share," Olivia countered.

"I wanted you to hear this from me. Mostly, I wanted to ensure that your anger toward me doesn't blind you to the very serious threat we're facing."

"Samael appeared intrigued by the thought that we could be tracked. Is it true?"

"We think so. Blood makes the most sense. Owning a brothel, my girls are required to undergo testing regularly. The same could be said for the incarcerated. Both would make an excellent baseline."

Larry Wayne Pittman said being behind bars he was nothing more than a rat in a lab.

"Demons may be superior when it comes to manipulation, but technology is still a stumbling block for them," Sarah revealed.

"But you have an empath?"

"I do, but we've also heard the agency has one of their own. Do you know anything about that?"

"I was recently informed they have someone. He was just a child when I interviewed him. Looking back on it he had to be some kind of gifted, but what kind, I had no idea." Her time spent with Elijah Stoddard replayed in Olivia's head. "I barely knew what I was."

"Don't spend time worrying about past transgressions. Fix it by finding him. If he's been turned against us, that's problematic."

"What can you tell me about Rose Corey? She worked for you. Could she do the things the FBI thinks she did?"

"Practicing dark magic, absolutely. She probably learned it from Andre Roche's mother. The boldness of her escapades even concern Samael."

"They concern me," Olivia acknowledged.

"Imagine how the agency feels. I have to warn you, even as the chosen one to lead the gifted out of the shadows, there are those among our own kind who will fear you almost as much as the naturals. Most gifteds lump themselves under the umbrella of witches where certain gifts run in the family and knowledge is passed down. Witches like Rose and the Roches, who lean toward the dark side, are taboo. Then there is the *other* kind of witch - the myth. The kind like you, the one who is demon made."

Rogan Poe had warned of the same. At least everyone was on the same page.

"Where does Samael come in? What is he? He's not *just* a demon."

"A demon sent here to watch over me and now you," Sarah confessed.

"I thought that's what *Alleracsap* was for," Olivia corrected her.

"Ironic, isn't it that you sent him to watch over your girls?" The move surprised Sarah and pleased Samael. "It is a wise choice on your part, to protect them with him. He is once again the babysitter. His time of watching over you is done, although I'm sure he won't wander far. Now you have Samael. He is your handler."

"What if I'm not interested in being handled?"

"*Azazel* will not yield. Do not ask him to send another. He will see it as a sign of weakness. Samael was chosen specifically," Sarah explained with a tone that did not waver.

"Why?"

"He has spent more time in the company of naturals than any other demon in the last few centuries. Samael is what you would call a *surrogate*. The body he inhabits is a *host*. It's a choice, not a possession," Sarah clarified.

Olivia carefully dissected what her mother described. True possession was something a person was afflicted with unbeknownst to them. They experienced missing time, perceptual distortion, and hypersensitivity. The altered behavior was most often believed to be related to drugs or a physical condition. That was why, before performing an exorcism, the Church demanded a medical and psychological examination before proceeding.

"So, it's a symbiotic relationship?" Olivia asked.

"Sort of. The *host* accepts the possession as a willing participant. The host is aware of what is happening and allows it."

"Despite consent, Samael is clearly in control," Olivia added.

"Of course. When the host becomes dissatisfied, which isn't often after so many years, Samael is quick to remind him of the opium den where he found him slowing killing himself."

"What does the host get out of it?" Olivia asked.

Sarah shrugged. "This is the only host I've ever known. He was some Persian prince too far down the line of succession to ever rule anything. The prince had a keen mind but bored easily. After a while, the riches weren't enough and the vices caught up with him. That's when Samael came along and offered him something money couldn't buy – prolonged life."

"And Samael, what does he get out of it?" Olivia asked.

"Assimilation amongst the naturals. And the prince, for all of his vices and vanities, he was a shrewd businessman. Demons need as much help with that as technology. Swapping favors is one thing, accumulating wealth is another. Building an empire isn't what it was a century ago."

"How long does this kind of relationship last?" Olivia wanted to know.

"Samael has inhabited the same host for close to a century, maybe more. He'll need a replacement sooner rather than later, but even I don't know when or how he makes that choice," Sarah conceded.

Olivia filed the information away and moved on to more immediate concerns. "How much time before the agency shows up?" Olivia asked.

"Now that I've made first contact, not more than twenty-four hours," Sarah predicted.

"Do you know who they will send?" Olivia wondered if that was why Patrick Monahan wasn't answering her calls. Maybe he was already on his way.

"The person they believe you are least likely to say no to. Your husband."

Chapter Eighteen

Her mother was right about everything. Even the timing. Olivia and Barry had just left the hospital after their nightly visit with the girls when the first call came.

Olivia saw Patrick Monahan's name on the screen and answered. Barry never heard her part of the conversation, for the buzz of his phone. It was Poe.

Neither Barry nor Olivia had seen or talked to him that day. Olivia chalked it up to Mémé's impending arrival. He also might have needed some time to cool off following the showdown with Sarah Larsin and Samael Knight's arrival. Barry suspected it was more to do with the latter.

Olivia was still glowing from their visit with the girls. She held both babies while they received their first taste of breast milk. Since they were too young to have mastered the sucking reflex, it was delivered through a tiny tube in their nose, but Olivia didn't care as long as they were back to sharing.

Barry hovered nearby. Seeing Olivia cradling her babies was all the magic he needed. He wasn't finished savoring the moment. The last thing he wanted to do was fall down some new rabbit hole Poe had discovered. All Barry longed for was a few hours of normal, but now was not the time for calls to go unanswered.

Poe passed on a greeting. "Where are you?"

"Just left the hospital. We were thinking about dinner." It was true. With Kim working the evening shift at the Alzheimer's unit and Adelyn with Jessica, Barry had managed to talk Olivia into an outing. He thought it would be good for both of them. "Care to join?" Barry asked.

As the words crossed his lips, Barry caught a glimpse of Olivia out of the corner of his eye and he knew. Nothing would ever be normal again. Poe's words were confirmation.

"Dinner's postponed," Poe told him. "I'm at the house. I just met Silas Branch and we've already decided we don't like each other."

****

Silas may have returned home but nothing was as he left it. His arrival marked another homecoming with failed expectations.

Olivia might not recall the events of that first night, but even if she did, it would forever be overshadowed by what happened next when Silas met their daughters. It would serve as a blueprint for the following years of their life.

The twins had their own private room. Glass windows looked out into the NICU, a similar replicate of her room in the ICU. Following her talk with the CFO, Olivia had her pick of caregivers overseeing her daughters. It was no surprise the ones who volunteered were the same ones she would have picked. Olivia was learning that healthcare was full of gifteds. It made her think of her great-grandmother, Abitha the Apothecary, who cultivated and sold her homemade medicinal potions. Finding healing in nature rather than man was a recurring theme through time.

"Where are they?" Olivia snapped when she saw her daughter's room was empty.

A strange hush fell across the NICU. Fortunately for the innocent bystanders, the neonatologist appeared. Her displeasure permeated the room. Dr. Hader instinctively raised his hands in a show of surrender.

His body language begged forgiveness. Olivia wondered if she interpreted it that way because of her conversation with Samael.

"I apologize, Dr. Osborne. We just moved them. As soon as we got them settled we were going to contact you," Dr. Hader explained, his words in a rush to free themselves.

"In the future, you should do that first," Olivia told him. She saw the twin's day nurse waving to her from a room two doors down. Their new accommodations looked identical to the previous ones. "Why did you move them?"

"Flickering lights, temperature fluctuations and random alarm bells," Dr. Hader explained, hoping it would satisfy her. He left out the part about two nurses, not ones assigned to the twins, who were convinced there was a shadow lurking in the corner of the room.

"*Entirely my fault*"–came Alleracsap's familiar whisper. "*I may have been a little too zealous on my first watch.*"

Olivia suppressed a smile. "Thank you," she said and headed for her babies.

Her heart didn't stop pounding until she reached their isolettes. She greeted them as she always did, with a hand pressed against their plexiglass home. Olivia closed her eyes and blanketed them with her presence. If she hadn't been so overwhelmed by her own ricocheting emotions, she would have known where they were.

Olivia felt a change in frequency. It was subtle and familiar all at the same time. She opened her eyes to find Genevieve and Gwendolyn staring back at her. A smile spread across her face. Their eyes were a gorgeous indigo this morning.

In the background, Olivia heard the neonatologist launch into an account of Genevieve and Gwendolyn's birth and their progress so far. Olivia didn't turn from her daughters. She knew Silas was approaching before he reached her. The girls were tracking his every move.

"They know who you are. Your voice is familiar," Olivia whispered. "Do you know they came out holding hands?"

Silas moved beside her, captivated by the sight of them. "They're so small," he remarked. "They don't look like real babies."

"They only weigh two pounds. They're supposed still to be in the womb," Olivia said. She was trying to be patient, reminding herself most people's version of a baby was not one with spindly arms and legs hidden away in an incubator.

Silas stepped closer for a better view.

Olivia studied him closely, hoping for what, she wasn't sure.

"What's wrong with their eyes? Is that normal?" Silas asked.

Olivia couldn't gauge the tone of Silas' voice. Was it a concern or something else?

Knowing the neonatologist had expected her to ask the same thing on her first visit, Olivia fixed her gaze on Dr. Hader. Having been deprived before, he was dying to tell someone who would listen.

With no opposition, Dr. Hader finally got his chance to speak. "We are closely monitoring for retinopathy. After lung development, eye afflictions are a common concern in babies born prematurely. Your daughters will require follow-up eye exams as they grow older, but for now, everything looks good." Dr. Hader tried to sound reassuring, but he was slowly crumbling under Silas' stare.

Silas looked at Olivia, but it appeared she and the doctor were locked in a silent stalemate. "That doesn't answer my question," Silas interjected, not caring who answered.

That tone Olivia was familiar with. She had heard Silas use it during investigations when he knew someone was hiding something. He wasn't wrong then or now.

"No one truly has purple eyes," Dr. Hader hedged.

Silas looked at the neonatologist and back to his daughters. "Their eyes look pretty damn purple to me." His tone morphed from request to accusation.

"There are certain medical conditions," Olivia suggested. "Albinism for one."

"Albino?" Silas repeated, turning back to the doctor, looking for a better answer.

At that moment, Dr. Hader wished he was closer to the door. "We tested for that. There is no evidence your daughters carry the gene." He wanted to look at Dr. Osborne but didn't dare.

"There are various non-medical possibilities," Olivia suggested. "Some cultures believe violet eyes are a sign of spirit people, or witches. There's also something called the Genesis myth," Olivia explained.

"Those born with violet eyes are said to be full of vitality and abnormally long life-spans."

"None of it means anything," Dr. Hader felt the need to add. "It could be a trick of the light," he suggested, pointing to the ceiling. "Fluorescent lighting isn't the best," the doctor suggested while he beelined toward the door.

"Oh, but I think they are significant," Olivia said, halting his exit. "I choose to believe purple eyes represent spiritual awareness. In ancient times, they signified a blessing from the gods. You bear witness to the miracle of life daily, doctor. Surely you have seen things that are without explanation."

****

"What the hell was that?" Silas asked once they were alone in the elevator.

"You're going to have to be more specific," Olivia told him.

"You. In the NICU. They're all afraid of you."

Silas' voice was way too loud for the enclosed space, but since they were alone, she guessed it didn't matter.

"I'm sure if you asked the CFO he would agree," Olivia told him.

Silas was almost afraid to ask, but couldn't stop himself. "What does the CFO have to do with it?"

Olivia reached over and hit the emergency stop button, grinding the elevator to a halt. Silas grabbed hold of the side rails to keep his balance. The knee immobilizer was gone, and he hadn't put on the brace, at least not for the trip to the hospital. It was too bulky to hide under his suit pants. He was back to looking like the FBI agent he was. He had opted for the cane instead. He had initially rejected it, but the physical therapist was stern. Even before the surgery, his knee was already compromised from previous abuse. He didn't need to further impede the healing process. The cane had been beneficial during his trip home so he opted for it again today, just like the driver waiting outside. Olivia had been pissed when she found out he intended to go to work after their visit.

"Is that what you think I was doing? Scaring people?" Olivia watched Silas run through sample responses, wondering which one was safest. "Am I scaring you?" she asked when he couldn't seem to make up his mind. "You didn't seem to mind when I talked to the ones who wouldn't talk to anyone but me."

"This is different," Silas said, struggling to keep his voice civil. His head was beginning to throb in tune with his knee. Luckily, he had the pain pills in his pocket. "You could have also spared the other worldly stuff."

"That *other worldly stuff* was what you needed from me. It's what I do."

"This isn't a case. This is a hospital," Silas redirected.

"The same hospital where a code pink alarm sounded the night our daughters were born."

Silas' face told her what she already knew. He had no idea what she was talking about.

"A code pink is the alarm for an infant abduction," Olivia explained. "They tried to tell me it was a false alarm but video footage showed Lily Forrester handing something off to an unknown person just outside the NICU."

Silas still looked confused. "Lily? What? Why?"

"Our daughters were born in the early morning hours with limited staff and no available parents. Maybe if one of us had been around, Lily wouldn't have thought she could get away with it. Instead, I was in the ICU and you were, wherever you were. Just in case you're interested, Lily doesn't work here anymore. The hospital suspended her and no one knows where she is. Even if she does come back, she won't be living next door. Ross sold the house. If anyone should be afraid of me, it's Lily. As for the CFO, he's scared and rightly so because I threatened to sue him for hiring Lily in the first place. She had a history."

"Do I want to know how you got hold of that information?" If true, the CFO wouldn't have told her willingly.

The look Olivia shot him told Silas he needed to talk to his little brother. Kevin and his sleuthing skills teetered closer to hacking than data mining. Her use of Kevin could not continue. "Not answering is an answer, Livie," Silas said, her silence infuriating. "If Brennon Kaine's still in town, I'm sure he'll be happy to take the case," Silas clapped back before he could stop himself.

"As a matter of fact, Brennon is still in town. He's in this hospital. He had a seizure. He was at my bedside when I extubated myself."

"What?" Silas asked.

"In his defense," Olivia made herself stop. She had told no one what really happened. Not Poe. Not even Barry.

Silas knew enough to take a pause. When she didn't resume talking, he did. "It sounds like you're mad at more than just me."

"If   you'd   finished   reading   *Exceptional*

Expectations you would know that female hormones are a little out of whack during the postpartum period," Olivia told him, referencing the book that still sat on his bedside table. He neglected to take it with him to Vegas. Olivia told him, referencing the pregnancy and beyond book that was still on his bedside table.

Her eyes smoldered as she hit the red button again, releasing the elevator.

"I told you if you left you would miss the birth of your daughters," Olivia said quietly. "I wasn't wrong. I never am."

The doors opened. They both got out. People were waiting. Silas kept walking but Olivia moved to the elevator next to the one they just left. She had already pushed the up button before Silas realized she wasn't following. He retraced his steps so no one could hear their conversation.

"I can have the driver drop you at home before he takes me to the office," Silas offered.

"I'll figure it out," Olivia replied, watching the numbers count down until the elevator arrived.

"Where are you going?" Silas asked.

"Back to the NICU to feed out daughters before I leak through this shirt."

Silas looked confused. "I didn't know you could hold them."

"You didn't ask."

"I'll send the driver back for you. He'll text you when he's here," Silas offered.

"I'm sure I can find a ride," she assured him.

Silas hesitated. For one fleeting moment, Olivia wondered if he was going to stay.

"If you weren't awake for the birth, how do you

know they came out holding hands?"

This time, Olivia did look at him. "Barry. He was there."

Chapter Nineteen

Poe heard the bedroom door open. It was a short walk to the kitchen where Barry found him at the table with his laptop open.

"I made extra coffee," Poe said, pointing Barry to the cup on the counter.

Barry followed the sweet smell. It reminded him of some fancy cigar room Mark took him to when he made lieutenant. "Smells good."

"It's the chicory," Poe told him. "It's a Louisiana thing, a contribution from the French. Mémé taught me to give credit where credit is due."

Barry leaned against the kitchen counter savoring the taste and wondering what prompted the memory of Mark to bubble to the surface. It had been a while since he thought about his former partner. Maybe it had to do with his own recent trips down memory lane. So much loss of what had been and what would never be.

Barry redirected himself to the present. "What time is your grandmother's flight?" He was going to have to clear out of Poe's apartment. With Silas' return he didn't think Mémé would be staying with Olivia. Neither would he. Barry pondered his options, his thoughts crawling back to Mark.

"She'll insist you call her Mémé," Poe reminded him. "It looks like all flights out of New Orleans are delayed."

"Weather?"

"There's something going on with check-in. People are being turned away. The flights that are getting off the ground are all late." Poe closed the laptop in frustration.

"Computer glitch?" Barry asked, pulling out the chair across from Poe.

"One would think, but there's been no confirmation. No announcement that it's one airline in particular. There's also nothing that tells people not to come," Poe said, drumming his hands on the closed computer. He had been about to check other cities when Barry wandered into the kitchen.

Barry sipped his coffee, unsure what to say.

Poe was distracted. He wasn't even sure if it was just about Mémé. He called her as a precaution, unsure if she even knew what was waiting for her. Poe confirmed her ride was coming as scheduled but he prepared her for a possible delay. If her flight was canceled, Poe assured her he would arrange another ride back to the assisted living center. No one was going to give away her room. The staff was quick to inform him of the waiting list of people trying to get into the place.

"She picks today of all days to fly for the first time," Poe muttered, shaking his head.

Barry hated flying any day. He let Poe stew some more.

"Thanks for letting me crash here last night and take over your room," Barry finally said.

"It's okay, I found another one," Poe said.

Barry wondered if it was the girl he and Olivia saw leaving the day they met Poe. He tried not to look interested.

"The nurse from the ICU, Renaye," Poe answered Barry's unspoken question.

Barry tried not to look surprised and quickly changed the subject. "I also owe you another bottle of liquor."

"The bottle was almost empty," Poe joked. "There's always more. You looked like you needed it."

Barry felt uncomfortable.

Poe held up his hands. "You don't have to explain it to me."

Poe's reaction signaled Barry that Poe could read his moods as easily as his thoughts.

Admirably, Poe quickly changed the subject to something they both had in common. "I'm going to be honest. I don't know how you've put up with Special Agent Branch as long as you have."

Barry was glad for the change, even if the topic was Silas. "It's not been easy," Barry admitted.

"Why do you think he bailed you out of jail?" Poe wanted to know.

Barry shook his head. It was a good question. One Barry didn't want to talk about because that would bring him back to what Zavalla said. If the FBI did look into Amanda's death, they wouldn't have to dig very far to find out his alibi was a lie.

"I meant what I said about Silas Branch," Poe stressed. "The dislike was instant. He's an angry, self-serving man ripe to become the agency's next useful idiot. He covets and he lusts and I'm not just talking about women. I'm talking about power and not with the FBI, but down to the smallest details of his own life. I'm curious to know how he will react to his daughters." Poe didn't mean to go that far. Not yet. He quickly reversed course so as not to lose Barry. There was more.

"Special Agent Branch is a dangerous animal who feigns domestication when he needs to. Not because he's smart but because over time, he's learned he can get away it. He honed those skills long before he went to work for the BAU."

Poe's words were like knives, peeling away carefully layered lies. Barry ripped through the veil, forcing himself to see Silas again - from the beginning. Their introduction began even before he arrived. The constant buzzing of Olivia's phone was followed by the call from Zavalla.

"The Feds are here and they are asking for Dr. Osborne."

As Barry wondered why he had been pulled from the biggest case of his career, he watched Special Agent Branch pace the interrogation room like a panther in a suit. *Everything Barry needed to know was inside the thin blue folder. He just didn't know it yet.*

While he, Olivia, and Mark hunted a murderer, Silas Branch was stalking gifteds. Roche, Anna and *Olivia.* Silas Branch showed Barry what he was from the beginning yet Barry refused to see it. Maybe because in some ways he and Silas were hunting the same thing. *Olivia.*

Again, Poe said the words Barry didn't.

"We can never forget he was good enough to charm Olivia."

"You think I can?" The words spilled out before Barry could catch them.

Barry had reconciled himself to his fate, at least

that's what he thought. Now he felt like he was starting all over again. Maybe that's why memories of Mark decided to resurface. Mark Austin was the one who brought Olivia into his life and things had never been the same since. Barry guessed he hadn't buried those feelings as deep as he thought.

"You should know, her bond with Silas is broken."

"You think?" Barry snapped. "Leaving Oliva when she needed him the most would leave a mark on any marriage. I've had been married—twice. I know what absenteeism does to relationships."

"It's more than that." Poe got up from the table. Without asking, he took both their cups over for a refill.

Poe reached inside a nearby cabinet and snagged another bottle of something, adding a generous dollop to each of their cups.

Barry felt another lesson coming.

"Whiskey," Poe promised as he returned to the table. "I have no more hyssop tea, not that it would do you much good now."

Hyssop was used to suppress feelings. It's what Poe used to curb the free flow of emotion between him and Olivia. Originally, Barry thought it was because she and Poe were both gifted. Now he knew it was because Poe was a demon hunter and Olivia had demon magic flowing through her veins.

"It seemed to help you," Barry said. The interaction between Poe and Olivia now was more like rival siblings—a definite improvement from before.

"What helped was Olivia giving birth," Poe admitted. "Mémé suspected it would subside once the twins were born. Thankfully, she was right. Dealing with three of Olivia at the same time was, um,

185

challenging to say the least."

"So, what are we talking about?" Barry asked. "More gifted history?"

"I'll be as brief as I can. This is about nature and natural selection. The bond that Olivia made with Silas is strong. Even though he isn't gifted. Think back to our ancestors—the ones that roamed the plains and lived in caves. Someone like Olivia, small in stature, fair skinned, beautiful would stick out. She would need protection and then there are her gifts. Back then, they wouldn't have been as easily concealed. The word *witch* has ostracized and polarized populations for thousands of years. To procreate, she would need someone like Silas who is more than your typical alpha male. As such, he would have his pick of women. People have been making up and breaking up since the beginning of time, thus the need for a strong mating bond in her situation. Without this kind of protection, someone with Olivia's attributes or afflictions, depending on how you want to look them, wouldn't last long."

"So, if this bond is so strong, what does it take to break it?" Barry asked.

"Death."

"But no one is…"

"Dead?" Poe said what Barry didn't. "Olivia died on the table, remember? She didn't have to stay that way, she just had to cross over. So, no hyssop tea will save you."

In that moment, Barry knew the answer Poe asked earlier. Silas bailed him out because he knew that was what Olivia would want. It was a great building block for trust.

"She's unbound. She may not know it yet, but she will." Poe could see Barry was processing. "I think we all know how this threesome ends."

****

It was obvious Olivia had been crying, but she pushed her own troubles away in favor of Poe. "What's wrong?"

Poe's living room faced the small balcony where he was pacing and talking frantically into the cell phone pressed to his ear. He didn't look happy.

"Something's going on in New Orleans. Mémé's not coming today," Barry explained. He paused, hoping Olivia offered an explanation of her own. Barry needed to know the reason behind her tears but she was fixated on Poe. Finally, Barry realized something he should have noticed earlier. In all fairness, the text announcing her arrival did go to Poe. He was on the phone then too and only pulled it away from his ear long enough to show Barry her text.

"Hey, how did you get here?" Barry asked.

"Silas has a driver. After I got him to pick me up from the hospital, I had him take me home. Once I was sure he was gone, I drove myself over here."

There were so many things wrong with that story that Barry didn't know where to begin.

Olivia sprang from her place on the couch at the same time Barry heard the scrape of the patio door. Poe was off the phone.

"*Unfuckingbelievable*," Poe announced.

Olivia stepped in to intercept him. She couldn't stand more pacing. She needed to see his face. "Tell me," she insisted.

Poe stopped to take a breath. "I don't even know

where to begin."

"Barry told me Mémé wasn't coming today. It seems like you're stuck, so is she and so am I. Does that tell you anything?" Olivia said.

Barry had gotten up when Olivia did, but now, he thought he should sit this one out and let them talk. Olivia was obviously feeling something.

"As I was checking Mémé's flight today, I noticed there were delays. I had the driver pick her up and take her to the airport anyway. She got through security without a problem, but when she got to the gate, there was not only a ticket agent checking boarding passes, but another person was taking everyone's temperature. Mémé watched a few people being pulled aside and not allowed to enter the jetway to the plane. They were redirected to another line away from everyone else. When it came Mémé's turn, she too was pulled out of line and asked to remain. After everyone was checked in, those pulled to the side were told they were running a fever and not allowed to board the plane. They were each issued a card that the agent attached to their ticket. They were then loaded on to a transport and driven to a glassed-in room where there were others were waiting."

"These other people weren't on Mémé's plane?" Barry asked.

"No," Poe said quickly. "Mémé called the place a holding cell. The passengers were instructed to remain there until they either got a ride back from where they came or one was arranged for them. The only other instructions were that they inform their doctor. And keep the card with their ticket so they could get a refund."

Now Olivia knew what all the pacing was about.

"That doesn't make any sense. Does Mémé feel sick?"

"No, that's just it. The few who were talking said the same thing. Mémé never runs a fever. If anything, she's colder than most. She always said if she was feverish, I better call a priest," Poe said.

Olivia didn't want to interrupt Poe to say it was the same for her and Gran.

"While she was waiting for a ride, did she speak to any of the others? Were there any commonalities?" Olivia was looking for a pattern. It's what she did. As a nurse and especially as a profiler.

"Most were older women, not as old as her, but middle age at least. Same for the men. Other than initial anger, there was little talk. But that didn't keep the whispers out of her head. Mémé knew then she wasn't the only one. She thinks they were targeted."

"It's because they are gifted," Barry said.

"I told her we don't know that," Poe said, his voice raised.

"What happened when she got back to the home?" Olivia asked.

"She was told she couldn't go back to her old room. She was shuffled into an empty wing. Others she knew were already there. They too were told they were running a fever. The nurse said she would send the doctor around to check on them later."

"Yet none of them felt sick."

"Not a one," Poe confirmed. The incident at the airport had rattled Mémé. He saw the same effect on Olivia. The sparks started to swirl in her eyes.

"What facility like that has an empty wing?" Barry asked. Tracking Poe's employment records before they met, Barry learned not just nurses were in short supply, but so was housing for elder care. There were still plenty of baby boomers around and they were all living longer than their predecessors.

"Did you ever check other airports?" Barry asked, leaping ahead to Silas and Poe's recent encounter. "Is it just New Orleans?"

Barry didn't wait for an answer. He headed back to the kitchen and the laptop, with Olivia and Poe trailing along behind. They found a section of the kitchen counter to lean against to keep them from hovering over Barry's shoulder as he searched. He was methodical. It was an agonizing long time before he told them anything.

"Okay, first things first. Still no information from any airline on the reason behind the delays. My search of airports reporting the most are as follows: Portland, Oregon, San Francisco International, Chicago O'Hare, Charleston, North Carolina, Jacksonville, Florida, New Orleans, Louisiana, San Antonio, Logan Airport in Boston, Savanah, Georgia, and Harrisburg, Pennsylvania." Barry leaned back and looked at the list again. "Not what I expected," he admitted. "I thought JFK, LaGuardia, LA, Regan National, Dulles and Atlanta would have made the list given the amount of people in and out of there every day."

"It seems kind of random," Poe agreed.

"It's not random," Olivia said quietly.

"Why do you say that?" Barry wanted to know.

"Working for the BAU, you wouldn't believe the travel miles I accumulated. I'm more familiar with airports and their surrounding cities than I want to be, but more to the point, the places with the delays all feed cities my mother mentioned."

Poe perked up immediately. "Sarah was discussing travel? Do I want to know why?"

"She said you would want me to go to the swamp," Olivia told him. "She said lots of things are hidden there."

This was news to Barry, but the shadow that crossed Poe's face told him Poe wasn't surprised.

Poe shook his head, unhappy with his response before he even said it. "Can't believe I'm going to say this, but your mother is not wrong."

"Can one of you please tell me what you're talking about?" Barry interrupted.

"The airports are important because of their surrounding cities. Those particular cities are filled with a high population of gifteds," Olivia said quietly.

"Why would she tell you this?" Barry wanted to know.

"Because she wanted us to have a place to go we when we can't stay here anymore."

Chapter Twenty

Olivia didn't resist Barry's offer to walk her to her car. As they approached, she used the key fob to open the back hatch.

Seeing his things neatly folded and tucked away, Barry felt the rise of a lump in his throat. It took him a moment to speak. "I could have done that," he offered.

Olivia couldn't look at him or his things. "I thought it was best you and Silas don't run into each other anytime soon," Olivia murmured.

Barry nodded, looking anywhere but at her. "Is it okay if I tell you I miss the girls?"

Olivia nodded, her lips quivering. "Is it okay to tell you they miss you too?" Coming from her, Barry knew those weren't empty words.

"I'll be going back again tonight. You can join me if you like," Olivia offered with a small smile.

His heart beat fast at the invitation. "What about, Silas?" Barry asked, forcing himself to say the name.

"He saw them," Olivia said, the pain on her face evident. "He doesn't like their eyes. He wants them to be *normal*. I don't even like the sound of that word."

Barry stepped closer. His hands had been in his pockets, the stance he usually took with her. This time, he freed them and pressed them to either side of her face, ensuring she saw him. "Normal, like beauty is in the eye of the beholder."

Without warning, Olivia slumped into him, burying her face in his shoulder. "I don't know how I'm supposed to do this."

****

Silas found Olivia outside curled in a lounge chair wrapped in a blanket with the dogs at her feet. Alvin, the little schnauzer, followed Olivia like a shadow. Maybe because she rescued him from a murder victim. Daisy, the lanky greyhound, raised her head at Silas, but she didn't trot over as usual. Greyhounds weren't guard dogs, but that wasn't why Olivia rescued her. She was seeking companionship. It looked like Daisy had abandoned him. Silas wondered if her mistress felt the same. The scene at the hospital could have gone better.

If Olivia had looked his way, Silas didn't know it. She was staring into the fire. He had called earlier and asked if she wanted to join him for dinner downtown at their favorite restaurant. Her response was a curt no. Silas had hoped for a warmer reception.

He extended the glass of red wine he knew she liked. "Peace offering." It was only afterward he noticed Olivia's hands were already full. He could see the warmth of the contents of whatever was in the mug as it escaped into the chill night air.

"No, thank you," Olivia said.

"It's your favorite," Silas tried again.

"Our daughters are too young to drink."

Silas blinked, obviously unaware of what she was saying.

"I'm breastfeeding. I drink, the girls drink."

Silas nodded. Awkwardly, he sank into the lounge chair next to her, more to get off his feet than to share her company. This was not how he would have preferred ending his day, but putting off a conversation wouldn't make it any easier by not starting. He began by hiding the glass of wine from sight. He sat it down on the other side of him, away from her and stretched his legs. Next, he took a long sip of the bourbon he brought for himself. When Olivia left Virginia, they sometimes went weeks, even months, without seeing each other. The feeling he had right now reminded him of those times. He felt like they were starting over.

"What are you drinking?" Silas asked, trying to begin again.

"Herbal tea. It fosters milk production and tightens the uterus," Olivia said, not holding back. While Silas had been eager to read *Exceptional Expectations*, she knew he would have skipped the overly descriptive anatomical parts. Silas preferred beauty over reality.

"A recipe of your grandmother's?" Framing the question with familiarity, Silas hoped to make some headway.

"Someone's grandmother, not mine," Olivia said.

Her eyes flicked over him before fleeing again, leaving the uncomfortable yawn of silence in their wake.

"You said you were going to wear the brace." That was more than twelve hours ago.

"I put it on once I got to the office," Silas assured her. Every word from her seemed like a small victory.

Of course, he did. He hadn't worn it to the hospital because it distracted from his FBI man-in-charge look. He used the cane instead. It was not only useful, but it went with the suit. Olivia was surprised at how quickly she had lapsed into old habits. She hadn't been this critical of Silas since...*when*? The first day he came to

San Antonio and she called him a prick.

Before that, they had a push-and-pull relationship. They were work partners, but it was the quiet time after work when Olivia felt the pull of him. It took hold of her in Florida with the Larry Pittman case. If Pittman had revealed his soul to her the first time around maybe none of this would be happening. Or possibly it would have happened already and both she and Silas would be in very different places, not having hard conversations.

Olivia's standard mode of operation was typically full steam ahead. On rare occasions, she ignored, denied, pushed things aside, or mentally packed them away inside a box. Silas had been one of those things. Until he pushed her and she couldn't find a reason to pull away.

Silas took another sip of the bourbon, looking for liquid courage while waiting for the pain pills to do their trick. Maybe he should do what he used to do when he knew she was angry with him. He would give her a dose of honesty at his own expense. As long as they had known each other, she had never shied away from telling him what an ass he was being.

"I'm failing at this, aren't I?"

"You're not off to a good start," Olivia agreed.

"Not being here when you needed me, I can't change that," Silas admitted.

That was too easy. Silas had a quest for answers. She had worked enough cases with him to know. It's how he slowed the room in volatile situations. Everything was done with purpose. Silas wasn't done. They weren't done. The amount of humility coming from his answer was way more than she expected and too much of a confession she didn't ask for. It meant he wanted something but Olivia doubted it was forgiveness. It was the same tactic he used when the FBI was about to send her on some horrific errand no matter how many times she told them the last case was her last case.

Over the years, Olivia often questioned why Silas was chosen as her chaperone, but none more than in the last few days when there was no Silas. The answer was simple. It had been there all the time. She just hadn't wanted to accept it. At this moment, even she was surprised by the swell of anger brewing inside of her as she realized that the FBI knew she and every other woman that crossed Silas Branch's path had a hard time saying no to him. Having embraced not only her gifts but herself, Olivia had already vowed she would never yield to the FBI again. The path forward for Silas Branch was not as clear. Even she didn't know if she would grant him grace or mercy.

"Why don't you try again."

For an instant, the eyes that slid from the fire to him weren't the green of Olivia's but yellow. They reminded him of a predator. Before he knew it Silas let go of a breath he didn't realize he was holding. He hoped the pain pills weren't getting ahead of him like they had before. He told himself he only needed the extra because he had been on the leg more than he should.

Silas reached for the familiar. In the past, talking about work was how they found their way back to each other. "I was on my way home. I swear to you. I didn't tell you because I wanted to surprise you. But I couldn't get a flight until late. With time to kill, I went looking for Deveroux."

Olivia surrendered, for now. She owed it not just to Silas, but to the life they started together. Most of all, she owed it to their daughters. Olivia knew the moment she laid eyes on them that everything she did from that point on would be for them. This night would be an important day in all their lives or a forgotten footnote of family history.

"Did you find him at least?" she asked. She knew the answer already, but not the details.

"No. But I found enough to know I was too late." Silas only spent moments in Deveroux's house, but the one memory he could recall was the amount of blood. "His kitchen looked like Sheriff Tennent's living room. What happened in Vegas was a wake-up call. Mason Deveroux might have been on his way out, but he was still one of us. It was Rose. She was better at it this time. So much so, she felt the need to commemorate it. I saw it. She posted it online until one of our guys took it down."

"By *our guys*, do you mean the Urban Affairs Division?"

Silas' reaction was subtle. If Olivia hadn't known him as long as she had, she would have missed it. Silas tried to cover by taking another sip of bourbon. He was pausing hoping she would keep going, but Olivia was willing to wait. Silas wasn't the only one who could be methodical. She had to glean as much information out of him as she could before he shut down.

"You heard about that?"

Silas waited for Olivia to answer, but she was waiting him out. "I was going to get to that," he confessed.

"Why don't you get to it now," she suggested.

"Remember the conversation we had the day before I left, when we took the dogs for a walk? The part about *us* and *them*. The UAD has been around a long time, but what Rose did, forced them out of the shadows. While I was recuperating, they were mobilizing. They recognized the threat after what happened to the sheriff and then Deveroux. Now they need you to neutralize it."

For such a monumental task, the words were cold and impersonal. Olivia wondered how many times he had rehearsed them.

"Define *threat*. Is it the ones who are different, the ones who know too much or the girls with the purple eyes?" Olivia felt her composure slipping away the closer they got to the end.

"You're still mad about this morning, I get it. I know it could have gone been better," Silas confessed.

At least this time he managed to sound more genuine than the last.

"Livie, you need to understand that things are changing. The agency, no matter what you want to call them, has known that about your kind for a long time."

"My *kind*? Your daughters' *kind*?"

"Gifteds." Silas watched how Olivia bristled at the word. "They're not going to let this go. Rose uncorked a bottle and there's no putting it back. The UAD wants her stopped. You're the only one I know that can do that."

"You mean, *they* know."

"The video of Deveroux isn't the only one they have. There's feed from the prison where Pittman was. They saw what you did with the guards. They need you now more than ever."

"Why would I want to help them?"

"Because you know what she is. She's a witch, that's why they need you."

"Are they scared?"

"What? Of course, they're scared. What kind of question is that?"

"And what if I don't help them?" Olivia proposed.

"Why wouldn't you? She's a witch. *You* have to stop her."

"I heard you the first time," Olivia snapped, the mug shattering in her hand.

Silas jumped as the shards fell in her lap. Instinctively, he reached for her, but Olivia swatted him away. "I need to see if you're hurt," Silas pleaded.

"Trust me when I say I am not." Her words were slow and deliberate. She shook the remaining pieces free from the blanket. Luckily, the mug was empty.

Olivia closed her eyes and began again. "Let me repeat it back to you so there is no misunderstanding. Rose is a witch and this agency needs me, another witch, to stop her. Is that correct?"

"Yea. That's what I just said." Silas' head was spinning.

"She's a murderer. You should have led with that."

"They know about Rogan Poe," Silas sputtered, grasping for anything to change her mind. "He's on a watch list."

"Why? Do you think he's a witch too?"

"Maybe, maybe not. Deaths seem to follow him. He was working at the facility where your gran passed. He left just after, only to show up back here about the same time as Jamie. You have a set of followers. What if Poe came to do what Jamie couldn't?"

"Are you telling me Rogan Poe is a threat?" Olivia asked, her voice unwavering.

Silas could see the defiance in her eyes. It caused them to burn brighter, solidifying the fact the yellow ones Silas saw before didn't belong to his wife. "He's too much like Jamie or even Roche. His grandmother is considered to be a witch," Silas confessed.

A switch flipped inside of Olivia, filling her with the need to protect a woman she had yet to meet. "Is that why she and others were pulled off a plane?" She could tell the question was unexpected.

"The agency needs to know what kind of numbers they're dealing with," Silas explained. "It will all be over soon."

Olivia saw it for what it was—a threat assessment. "Fearful men do awful things. Is that why their request sounds like a demand?"

"I can't keep you and our daughters safe if you don't get on board." Silas knocked back the rest of his bourbon and swung his legs over the side of the chair, spilling the wine he poured for her. In the firelight, it looked like blood.

Silas took a moment to calm himself and focus on the objective. He had gone too far, pushed too hard. He had to stop—for now. "We shouldn't have had this conversation tonight, I can see that now. I asked my mother to come down. She'll be here tomorrow. I don't think you should be alone."

"I have Kim for that," Olivia told him.

"You need family."

"Kim is my family. I made one while you were gone."

Silas was on his feet now. He turned to stare her

down. "I'm your family. You need me if you want to get through this."

"What you need to understand is that I'm not mad. I'm vengeful. There's a difference."

"You can't go around saying shit like that," Silas said, his teeth clenched. He forgot whatever else he planned to say when he heard the crackling behind him, followed by a rain of fire and ash. He told himself a log must have fallen or shattered, but that's not what the hairs on the back of his neck told him. The yellow eyes were back, boring into him even if he couldn't see them. Silas was overcome by the feeling something was moving in the dark behind him. He was on the brink of a fight-or-flight response when his nostrils filled with the smell of cinnamon. It had to be because he mixed the pills with the bourbon.

Olivia studied him, her eyes blazing as much as the fire behind him. "I'm the woman who walked out of a burning barn. I'm also the one you and your UAD just asked to catch your monster for you. You would do well to remember that."

****

Not long after Silas left, Olivia heard the soft creak of the backyard gate. With it came the smell of death.

"That escalated quickly," Samael said as he slipped into the chair where Silas had been. "I lost control," Olivia admitted. "It must be the hormones."

"The fact it was only the mug that shattered tells me you had more control than you know. I guess this means you will be taking that trip your mother suggested. The only question now is, *when* and *where*."

"When my daughters are ready, we'll head for the Louisiana swamps just outside New Orleans."

"Joining Cloteel Bouvier, no doubt," Samael mused.

Olivia gave him a dark look.

"I haven't turned her, not that I haven't tried," he admitted with a smile. "Nevertheless, your instincts are well developed and she will be a valuable teacher. I couldn't have chosen a better place for you myself. There are treasures there you have yet to discover."

Chapter Twenty-One

The first thing Silas noticed as his driver pulled into the driveway was Olivia's SUV was missing. He had gotten home a little earlier tonight. He expected her to be here. After dismissing his driver, Silas headed to the porch to join his mother. He smelled the smoke before he saw it.

"I had no idea," Silas said as he slid into the chair across from her.

Sally took one more puff and blew out the smoke in the other direction. "The last time I smoked was during your father's second deployment to Vietnam," Sally confessed.

"I'm not judging."

Sally rubbed out her cigarette and lined it up next to the other two. She snagged her wine glass and held it up. "Want one?" she asked.

Silas loosened his tie and sank back into the chair as he shook his head. "Nah." He was putting off the bourbon until he saw his wife. Olivia was dodging him, and he knew he needed all his faculties to confront her again. It had been weeks and Dillon was growing impatient.

Silas saw his mother wrapping her shawl tightly around her shoulders. "I thought you were going to light the fire in the back," Silas said. "The tank is full. There should be plenty of wood." He had been restocking. Olivia's favorite spot was in front of the flames.

"I know how to light a fire," Sally said, staring off into the distance.

Silas felt a squeeze deep inside his gut as he recalled recent events. The feeling something was stalking him, whether it be beyond the flames or at the foot of his bed, hung over him like a virus. The feeling was so strong he bought a nightlight for the bathroom. He considered mentioning the yellow eyes, but words failed him.

"It's dark back there. I kept getting the feeling there was something lurking in the shadows, just beyond the fire. I think I saw eyes." Sally looked over at her son, but he avoided her. "I've heard animals out there, in the alley. Olivia said there were a lot of opossums and raccoons in the neighborhood because of the trees."

"Olivia's right about the critters," Silas agreed, deciding he didn't want to talk about eyes in the dark after all.

"I just thought if it was wild animals, the dogs would have reacted. Neither one of them raised their head."

"I'm assuming the dogs are used to them. The trees in the back are pretty thick. They can play tricks on you," Silas suggested instead.

"I bet they can, when the wind is blowing," Sally added with a hint of sarcasm. It was a hook she hoped her son would take.

Silas stared across the front yard. There was no wind. His mother knew it, and so did he.

"I need to tell you something," Sally ventured.

There were many things, but she had to start somewhere.

"Shoot," Silas told her, bracing himself.

"I wasn't snooping, but Olivia gave me access to her office and her computer so I could keep up with things at home. While I was in there, I noticed she got a ping on one of her accounts. She left a window open and it looked like there were dozens of emails from Kevin. Why would she be getting so many emails from your brother? Are you working on something for your new position?" Sally hoped she sounded inquisitive and not worried.

Since her youngest son lost his job to downsizing, Kevin assured her he was making it on his own freelancing. Kevin made what he did for a living sound like going to the library for a research paper. With his skills, Sally doubted that was the case. Her husband was the only one Kevin talked to about his work. Raymond Branch described their youngest son as one step away from a hacker. He was probably downplaying Kevin's skills. Like their oldest son, Silas, Kevin had a bit of a thrill-seeking attitude, only he did it behind a computer screen and not in the wild chasing bad guys.

Silas felt another cinch in his gut. Talking to Olivia he had deduced Kevin knew early on what was happening in San Antonio in his absence. The thought wouldn't go away, festering just below the surface. So much so, that Silas had planned to confront his little brother about it at Thanksgiving, but he never got the chance. Other family issues took his place. Just after Daniel revealed his next military assignment would be in San Antonio, Olivia announced that the Forrester's house was available.

The weekend imploded, with talk of Daniel, and Rachel, and their two boys renting the house for as long as they liked. Before long, the plans included Sally. When Silas confronted Olivia privately about it, she chalked her lapse in memory up to not wanting to admit her mother bought the house as a gift for their daughters. The girls couldn't claim their inheritance until they were twenty-five. Until then, Olivia could manage the property any way she saw fit. She reminded Silas she was doing that when she invited his family to use it. Silas couldn't stop thinking the offer was cleverly timed.

The day before his family arrived, he broke the news to Olivia that they might need to move back to Virginia for his job. Not surprisingly, Olivia balked at the suggestion. Her reaction wasn't surprising since he had moved to San Antonio so they could start their lives together. What plagued Silas was she could have mentioned the house thing then, yet she didn't. He heard it for the first time in front of his whole family. With Sally's four grandchildren together in one place, Olivia ensured she wouldn't be the only one against Silas' proposed move.

As for Kevin, he kept to himself that weekend, but to Silas, he seemed more distant than usual. Silas typically chalked Kevin's stand-offish behavior up to the age difference between siblings and the fact his little brother seemed to have little social life. Maybe that's why Kevin's entanglement with Olivia sent up red flags. If Kevin had been proactive about Olivia's condition, their mother could have arrived sooner to be here for Olivia. Instead, Olivia was left in the care of

Rogan Poe and Barry while their mother was kept in the dark.

At the very least, Kevin had been a passive bystander. At worst, Kevin took direction from someone other than family. It was that scenario that left Silas feeling wary. He couldn't shake the jealousy and doubt towards his little brother. Who had been calling the shots when Olivia was in a coma? Silas couldn't shake the feeling Kevin knew far more about his wife's new life than he did. Olivia might be avoiding him, but she was not standing in place. Even Silas knew they couldn't keep doing what they were doing. They lived in limbo as the days counted down to their daughter's discharge from the hospital, but that didn't mean his wife was idle. Olivia had already constructed a narrative for the next move in their life. Her offer to keep his family close was reassuring, but Silas remained on guard.

Marriage was supposed to be about sharing, not keeping secrets. But he was in no position to challenge her. Olivia was different since his return, but he wasn't unfamiliar with this version of her. It was the persona she adopted in the interrogation room when sitting across from the monsters they hunted. She left no doubt who was in charge. It was what made her so good at her job. Now, though, it had spilled over into her personal space. He first witnessed it during their trip to the NICU and then with his family. Silas had lost his footing and couldn't shake the feeling he would never regain it.

"I hate to admit it, but your brother and I don't talk as much as we should," Sally confessed, her thoughts parallel with Silas'. "Why would Kevin be emailing

Olivia?"

"She's used him before in her consulting business," Silas explained, hoping he didn't sound as paranoid as he felt. He heard his mother sigh. The sound conveyed annoyance.

"Speaking of business, I don't want to sound like an interfering mother, but as someone who was married for decades, I can tell there's a … disconnect in your marriage." It was the best word Sally could come up with without sounding too nosy. Nevertheless, she felt her son could use some advice. "Sleeping arrangements say a lot about the state of a relationship," Sally said, just in case he wasn't listening.

When she first arrived, Olivia and Silas insisted she take the master bedroom. Silas was already staying downstairs because of his knee. At the time, she thought nothing of Olivia sleeping in one of the baby rooms. As Silas improved, Sally insisted he move back upstairs with his wife. Sally initiated the move on behalf of her son and daughter-in-law, but also for herself. Since the death of her husband, Sally had become something of a night owl, and there was no television in the master bedroom. She had also recently developed a penchant for a snack before bed. Downstairs, she was free to roam.

What Sally no doubt knew, but thankfully kept to herself, was that Olivia and Silas did share a room, but only as long as the rest of the family was there. It was a practical decision, nothing more. Olivia made that very clear when she insisted he move back to their room when the holiday weekend was over.

Silas kept his eyes on the lawn, wishing for the bourbon he didn't have. "She just gave birth," he said.

"I'm not talking about *that*, Silas. I'm talking about intimacy. It's emotional as much as physical. Sleeping next to someone, knowing they are there when you wake up is a whole other level of comfort. I get the feeling Olivia is seeking comfort. Are you meeting her at the hospital to see the babies?"

"I thought you were going with her," Silas said, instead of answering.

He was deflecting, a tried-and-true method for him. "Not first thing in the morning," Sally told him. "I thought you were meeting her. I was trying to give you two time with your daughters."

"I've been busy."

Her son didn't look at her as he said it. It was an indication he knew better.

"That's not an excuse, Silas. Those babies need both their parents."

"How do they know if I'm even there or not?" Silas said.

The force behind his words told Sally he had already had this conversation. "I could go into an entire discussion about what babies know or don't know. Even if you don't believe they're aware, I guarantee you, your wife does." Sally felt a pang of guilt, not realizing sooner what was going on right under her nose, quickly followed by a shot of anger directed at her son. He knew better. Raymond Branch had been an excellent role model. "Olivia needs to know she's not doing this alone."

Silas wanted to say he doubted that was the case, but lashing out at his mother would beg more questions than he was prepared to answer. "Olivia didn't say anything to you?"

"Why would she? I'm your mother, not hers." Sally let out another sigh, attempting to gather her emotions. The last thing she wanted was to argue with her son, but she was appalled by his behavior.

Sally stood up with her empty glass. "Sure you don't want something?" she asked.

His mother was angry, an uncommon emotion for her. Silas just shook his head.

Sally took longer than it should take to pour another glass of wine. "I didn't think Olivia had a relationship with her mother," Sally said, changing the subject. "I looked up how much houses cost in this neighborhood. That was a *very* generous gift and thoughtful. Olivia said the house next door used to belong to her great grandmother."

"Sarah Larsin can afford it. She earns her living the old fashion way," Silas said, sarcasm dripping in his voice. "She owns some of the most lucrative strip clubs in Vegas. She also owns a brothel. There are only six counties in the state of Nevada where they're even legal. The license for one of them makes the price of the house next door look like a cottage."

Sally ignored his outburst. "Sarah Larsin. I'm sure I've heard that name," Sally said.

Silas' interest peaked. It would be good to hear his mother's take on current events.

"She's the woman whose places were raided." It had something to do with testing. It would have made sense if the testing had to do with STDs, that wasn't it. Silas' additional information made the article seem even more bizarre than the first time she read it. "She was accused of using hallucinogens to entice her customers," Sally recanted. "I read a whole thread, or whatever it's called, about witches living in the modern world. *Sorceress*, I believe is the word that was used. Like that's supposed to hurt her business. Sounds pretty creative to me."

"What do you mean by that?" Silas asked.

"It seems every time I turn around, I'm reading something about magic or witches. Funny thing is some of those beliefs have been around for a long time. My grandmother had a garden like the one Olivia has out back. She also kept a sage plant on her windowsill just like the one in your kitchen."

"What do you know about the garden out back?"

Something about Silas' tone didn't sit well, maybe because it sounded like he was accusing her of something. "You don't want to hear how your wife and daughters need you but you're suddenly interested in the garden?"

"What happens back there?" Silas asked again.

"Olivia spends a lot of time out there, with the girl Kim. I think Olivia is teaching her. Kim said she was in nursing school. Plants and roots were basic medicine long ago. We might be better off if we paid more attention to the things that sustained us before there was a pill for everything," Sally mused.

"Witchcraft is dangerous," Silas said.

"Anything can be dangerous in the wrong hands," Sally hypothesized. She took a long sip of her wine, taking a moment to study her son. He was serious. "What's gotten into you? Where is this coming from?"

"The UAD is the one who ordered the raid on Sarah Larsin's places," Silas admitted.

It took Sally a minute to understand what he was saying. "The new group you've been assigned to?"

"The Urban Affairs Division," Silas repeated for her.

"I read a thread about that too. There's an online community that believes the UAD is just another version of the OSS. The Office of Strategic Services was supposed to gather information on our enemies. There was a reason it was dismantled after the Second World War." Sally's introduction to the military didn't come from her husband but from her father. He retired as a colonel. "Your grandfather used to say that while he didn't like war, idol hands were worse. He was convinced if there wasn't an enemy in plain sight, there were parts of the government that would go looking for one. Are you telling me people like Sarah Larsin are enemies now? I thought you said she operated in a place where brothels were legal," Sally reminded him. Maybe Silas passed on the bourbon because he had already had some.

"It's not about sex, it's about witchcraft, about people with special gifts, or charms," Silas said, gauging her reaction.

Sally took a minute to digest what he was saying. Whatever it was, he didn't look like he was joking.

"Off the top of my head, I'd say if Sarah Larsin hires people who are naturally skilled at seduction, then isn't that good for her business? She is selling sex. It's like profiling, isn't it? Isn't that what behavioral analysis is all about?" Saying the words out loud, Sally wondered why her son, who had previously worked at the BAU, was now working for a place with such an innocuous name like Urban Affairs. Like her hacker son describing himself as a data collector. Sally reached for her wine, glad for the refill. Their conversation had just taken an unexpected turn.

"Every case I ever worked with Olivia taught me there are things, many things we don't know," Silas said.

Sally wasn't sure where he was going with this, but if she had to hear this to get to his problems with his wife, she would. Silas had no idea what risks he was taking with his personal life. "I know Olivia is a doctor of some kind. Rachel told me that Olivia helped you catch people who claimed they were possessed or they had been compelled to commit crimes," Sally said, waiting for Silas to correct her. When he didn't, she continued.

"Are we talking about *things* or people, Silas?" Her son was typically not the spiritual or philosophical type. He saw things in black and white. There was no room for gray. He was also her child who had strayed the farthest from his Catholic upbringing. For whatever reason, that was important at this moment.

"Both," Silas said, his voice barely above a whisper.

"So, *demons*?" Sally said what Silas wouldn't. Rachel had told her that part too, but Sally hadn't wanted to say. Now she had to.

"I believe they're real. You should know. Pope John Paul warned us all that we had lost our way and had forgotten there are demons among us. They've always been here. We just chose to ignore them. He warned us of our mistake. What does this have to do with Olivia?" Sally asked.

"The UAD needs her help."

"But she won't help them, will she?" Sally again said what her son would not. Rachel had also told her

Olivia's ancestry could be traced back to the Salem Witch Trials. That's what this was about. Silas' work and home life had collided.

"I can keep her safe, and our daughters, if she'll just…"

"You're smarter than this, Silas. I also think you have severely underestimated the power of a mother's love. How long will it be before your bosses come for her or your daughters?"

"These demons know Olivia. They are the ones coming for her," Silas argued.

"Yet she doesn't follow them. The discernment of spirts is a blessing."

"I'm sorry, I don't see a blessing in any of this," Silas countered.

"Judgment of discernment is a divine gift granted to few individuals. It means she sees not only evil but good. That would mean that Olivia has got to be the bravest woman I've ever met. Your precious UAD pushes her too much, she will become a martyr. History will not look kindly upon these events. And if that's not enough, you have a decision to make."

"It's my job," Silas said, cutting her off.

"For Olivia, it's her family. Only you can decide what is more important."

Chapter Twenty-Two

Silas stepped out of the shower and saw the fire outside. He had checked it after he and his mother went their separate ways. Olivia must be home because it was roaring. He avoided looking at how the flames shifted and swirled. He grabbed a bourbon from the kitchen and headed outside. Olivia didn't look up at his arrival. She was focused on her phone. It sounded like she was singing, but he couldn't make out the words. They sounded soft and wistful, too pretty for Latin, at least that's what he hoped.

"Chut! Plus de bruit, c'est la ronde de nuit, en diligence, faisons silence, marchons sans bruit, c'est la ronde de nuit."

Silas listened while Olivia repeated the string of words at least three times by his count. They were repetitive, rhythmical, like a song. Silas watched as she slid her hand down the screen in a long goodbye. She puckered her lips and blew an air kiss as he watched the phone screen grow black. Silas gave her a minute to compose herself before interrupting her.

"What was that?" he finally asked.

Olivia was slow to look his way, like she was still disconnecting. "A lullaby."

"That didn't sound like *Rock-a-bye-Baby*, to me not to mention that wasn't English," Silas said, coaxing her into a conversation.

"It's a French lullaby called the *Night Watch*. *'Quickly, let's be quiet, let's walk noiselessly, it's the night watch,'*" Olivia said, melancholy washing over her.

She missed her babies while at the same time she worried for the woman who taught her the words. Cloteel Bouvier sang the same song to a baby who grew up protecting the weak and dying from demons who came to steal whatever was left of their soul. Olivia heard the wistfulness in Cloteel's voice as she fondly recalled singing it to Rogan as an infant.

There were other words Cloteel couldn't bring herself to say, yet Olivia knew those too. As the days and weeks dragged on, Poe's beloved Mémé wondered if she would ever see her homestead again at the same time she yearned to sing those words to babies she had yet to meet. She remained on lockdown while others departed for places unknown.

The news from the outside changed daily, along with the reasons behind what was happening, leaving Mémé suspended in a lingering purgatory. What didn't change were the ones who rotated through those rooms with her. All of them were gifted. Even the ones that didn't know it. She remained through it all, the only original sequestered one while others came and went. Cloteel couldn't help but think she was a target leading to fears her rescue would come at the expense of her own family.

"I didn't know you knew French," Silas said, pulling Olivia back to the present.

Olivia heard a thread of accusation in Silas' words. Maybe because he realized where she may have learned it. Her eyes flashed as she glimpsed his thoughts.

Rogan Poe.

"The girls are restless tonight," Olivia told him. What she didn't feel like sharing was that today was the first day their daughters had nursed enough they didn't require additional supplements. Sustaining themselves on her breast milk alone, without major weight loss, was the last step toward home. They had missed her birthday by a few days. Christmas was in a few more. Their freedom was all she wanted. Olivia was weary of living in the void and yearned for release, not only for her daughters but for Mémé as well.

"Why are you still up?" Olivia asked.

"I saw the fire."

Olivia made no comment, forcing him to speak or leave.

"My mother is concerned," Silas began.

"About?"

"Us. She says you're never home."

Olivia finally looked his way. "I could say the same about you."

"I was home early tonight," Silas confessed.

"I'm glad you got to spend time with your mother."

"I would rather spend it with you."

The confession earned him nothing.

"My mother also wanted to know why we weren't sleeping in the same room."

"I hadn't really thought about it," Olivia said off-handedly, clearly signaling she was not interested in changing accommodations.

"How do we get past this?" Silas asked, his irritation showing.

This time, she did look at him. As a show of cooperation, Olivia slipped her phone in the pocket of the long sweater she was wearing. "You said you can't change the fact you weren't here for their birth. I get that—I'm dealing with it," Olivia made her own confession. "What I can't get over is you're still absent from our lives."

"I am here, Olivia," Silas insisted. "I'm working hard every day."

"What's that going to get your daughters?"

The tone of her voice told him it wasn't an ask, but a demand. Silas wasn't used to not getting his way, especially with her. "Safety," Silas said. It was all he had.

As the days and weeks had stretched, Silas saw less and less of the Livie he once knew. He had never seen the belligerent side of her, merely glimpses, all doled out for the FBI, never at him. Silas decided he didn't like the new Olivia. Not only was he missing his partner, he missed his wife.

"You can't ensure their safety when it is tied to their mother's cooperation. The demands will never stop."

"You haven't even tried."

Olivia shook her head.

"We know the archbishop lied," Silas quickly revealed before he could lose her attention.

Olivia paused, wondering if the revelation was a threat.

"This is serious, Livie," Silas emphasized.

She set her jaw. Her eyes locked with his. "Then sit down. I'm not going to stare up at you."

Silas did as he was told, taking the edge of the lounge chair, to face her.

"Are your new bosses planning to discredit an

archbishop of one of the largest dioceses in the country?" she asked.

"He discredited himself. When confronted with the security cam footage, he claimed he got the dates wrong. He said he was influenced by a dark entity. Connect the dots."

They only led to one place. SAPD knew she was the one who called the archbishop. "Am I supposed to be that dark entity?" Olivia inquired, outwardly unbothered by the insinuation.

"I'm not writing this narrative," Silas told her.

Now Olivia was as annoyed as Silas. "Then your handlers should know if I wanted to *influence* someone your UAD would never know it. This is not me."

"Then come to the field office tomorrow, first thing in the morning. Director Dillon and I are meeting with SAPD and Ranger Gaines."

It reminded Olivia of the last meeting she attended. Only that one had been at SAPD headquarters. Apparently, the FBI or the UAD, whoever was running the show, wanted the home-field advantage. The feds did like intimidation. Olivia's eyes narrowed, deciding once again to rip the veil aside and show Silas the ugly truth hiding behind it.

"Why do you think Dillon came to you for this new department?"

The question rattled her husband, and she had just begun her dissection.

"What do you mean, why me?" Silas was suddenly on the defensive. This was supposed to be about her, not him.

"I thought the UAD was overseeing this whole medical crisis. You're not a doctor and the last I heard

Dillon worked in the office of professional responsibility, the FBI's own internal affairs department. He took your statement after we both shot Jamie. You told me he was more interested in me. Is that still true?"

Her words hit their mark, leaving Silas scrambling. His inhibitions were dwindling - the result of too much alcohol and his continued dosing of pain pills. His use of oxy increased exponentially as his knee improved. He had slid back into the open arms of addiction.

"The UAD is designed to protect the homeland from threats. Whether they be medical, biological or..." Silas wasn't so far gone that he couldn't catch himself. Still, Olivia knew the word he pulled back before it could slip past his lips. Her skills had grown, the same as his dependence.

"Spoken like a true believer. I believe the word you're searching for is *paranormal*," Olivia said for him. The term was being used privately but had yet to be used publically. It was only a matter of time. She heard the sounds of a ticking clock inside her head before shoving them into a corner.

"*Unexplained*," Silas quickly corrected her.

"Whatever you say," Olivia said. "So, back to my original question—why you?"

Silas' eyes were shining, like a deer caught in the headlights. Olivia was beginning to think it was more than just the illicit substances—it was indoctrination.

"It's because you're good at hunting people," Olivia said for him, "and categorizing them, placing them in groups based on their actions and affiliations. It's why the UAD is holding certain sects of the population. It all has to do with their behavior, doesn't it?"

Silas was mute. A dread was spreading over him. There were no outward signs, but Olivia didn't need them. She could *feel* them, but she no longer soaked them up like a sponge. She had learned to mask the effects and hold fast against them. She had created a formidable defense so the emotions of others no longer controlled her.

"You're profiling them, aren't you? That's why Dillon has you."

"You're being ridiculous," Silas snapped.

Olivia paused again, studying him. Wondering if he could feel the thin trails of her psyche prowling over his. Twisting and turning until she found what she was looking for. "You fear them, don't you?" Olivia realized. She didn't even have to dig deep. "Dillon scared you early on in the way he took you in and made it seem like a rescue. How convenient he and his men were at Deveroux's house at just the right time. Long enough to have missed the murder, but soon enough to capture you. What a calculating bastard this Bradford Dillion must be. How do you know he wasn't also watching when Rose went there? Did he trade Deveroux's life to get closer to his objective, or was he just lucky?"

"Stop profiling me!" Silas was angry now. "You don't know what you're talking about."

"To quote the gospel of Luke, I know that you and Bradford Dillon *know not what you do*. You're asking for trouble, like poking a hornet's nest with no idea what will fly out."

"Our intel says the *gifted* are fragmented. They cling to their traditions but they follow no one. What kind of defense can they mount without a leader?" Silas suggested.

It was more propaganda. "Wrong question," Olivia snapped. "What you and Dillon should be asking yourself is what kind of defense can they mount when they find one. It's obvious that you, in particular, have no idea what people will do when their way of life is threatened." Her words carried an icy edge.

"Get out of my head!" The words came as a roar. Silas stood to tower over her while the lounge chair clattered on its side behind him. He even spilled the drink he forgot on the ground.

Olivia never flinched. "I'm not in there. I don't have to be."

Just then, Olivia felt the buzzing from her pocket. She grabbed her phone, ready for another call from the girl's night nurse. But the screen said it was Poe. At this hour, it couldn't be anything but bad news. "What's wrong?" was her greeting.

"Sorry, this isn't Rogan."

The use of Poe's first name caught her off guard, and the voice on the other end.

"It's Renaye—from the hospital," the voice said, as if Olivia would forget her ICU nurse. Just now, she recalled Barry saying something about Renaye and Poe. She was why Barry spent more time than expected as Poe's roommate. It didn't matter they were sharing a one-bedroom apartment if Poe wasn't there to sleep.

"Rogan wants to know if you can meet us at Oak Hollow. It's his uncle."

Olivia knew Frank Pope as Mr. Sunshine. She had seen him during her visits to her latest client—which was also what led her to the demon hunter. She had just

Lullaby

never gotten around to meeting the man in question.

"Tell him I'm on my way," Olivia assured her.

"I'll be waiting in front for you," Renaye told her.

Of course, it was long past visiting hours.

"You're leaving?" Silas protested. "I need you at this meeting in the morning."

"Be careful what you wish for," Olivia warned him. She started for the house but turned to her husband one last time.

"Just something to think about your Director Dillon. What did he tell you about Patrick?"

The question had the desired effect. Silas was caught off guard again, just as suspected.

"Dillon didn't tell you?" Olivia asked.

"Tell me what?"

"Patrick flew to Vegas as soon as he heard what happened at Deveroux's house and that you were missing. Afterwards, Patrick was so distraught he flew to San Antonio."

"You didn't tell me you saw Patrick," Silas accused her.

"I didn't. I was in a coma trying not to die. Patrick came to the house and met with Barry and Poe instead."

Silas looked shocked.

"Yea, Patrick trusted Rogan Poe," Olivia answered the unspoken question in Silas' eyes. "You should ask yourself why Dillon didn't tell your former boss, not to mention your friend, that you were safe and definitely not dead. Then, perhaps someone could have told your wife."

"Why didn't Patrick tell me?" Silas wondered.

"Maybe because he never made it home." Olivia received the phone call from Melinda at the same time

223

Poe was calling Barry to tell him Silas had just arrived. Olivia had kept the information to herself. Patrick was still missing. "That was eight weeks ago, Silas."

Olivia watched the weight of the question settle over Silas. She was pleased with the uncertainty. "You know, your government is so predictable, they should really try another approach. It's always, ignore and intimidate. It's their playbook. They ignored me for years and now they are trying to intimidate me."

"It's not working, is it?" Silas dared ask.

"I'm the woman who stared down a demon in my living room and then I walked out of a burning barn. Oh, yea, I also came back from the dead. So, you tell me."

Silas watched her go, leaving the scent of cinnamon in her wake.

Chapter Twenty-Three

At well after one in the morning, Barry could have his pick of any parking spot. He spotted Olivia's SUV sitting all alone and decided to pull in next to her. He was used to the late hour. This was their usual time for a hospital visit with the girls. He wasn't sleeping, anyway. His insomnia had returned about the same time as Silas Branch.

Barry missed his and Olivia's time together in a deep way that couldn't be satiated with visits to the girls or the daily pow-wows at Poe's apartment that Olivia dubbed 'damage control'. Barry yearned for alone time, just the two of them in front of the fire, and sharing the same room. He found nights by her side at the hospital calming. The one night they did spend together back in her grandmother's bed, wrecked him. Barry wondered if he would ever sleep through the night again.

Leaving behind the warm cocoon of the car to collide with the cold night air helped clear his head. Overhead, the stars held their vigil through wispy cloud trails. A clear view of the night sky was the only thing he missed from his condo. Out on the balcony, it was easy to forget everything except for the blanket of stars overhead. Barry's one regret from the move was he never got to share the view with Olivia.

The nursing facility up ahead looked as eerily quiet

as it should at this time. Renaye told him to text when he arrived and she would come out and get him. Clearly, visiting hours were long over. Barry had almost escaped the darkness of the parking lot when his peripheral vision caught an unexpected figure emerging from the dark. Barry thought it was odd he didn't hear a car door. He wheeled around, reaching for a gun he no longer wore. It was still in the car because he wasn't a cop anymore.

The figure came into the light—hands up and open. "Retirement has you keeping some late hours, lieutenant," Silas Branch said.

Barry stared him down. A million scenarios scattered across his mind. There were endless possibilities for how this could go.

Before Silas left to go chase down Mason Deveroux, Barry felt they had come to a truce over their feelings for Olivia. After all, Silas was the one who sprung him from an interrogation room before he even got close to seeing the inside of a jail cell. Silas had even taken him into the home he shared with Olivia, shielding him from the shit-storm that ensued following Amanda's death. A lifetime had passed since then, changing alliances and causing Barry to despise Silas Branch more than ever before. His anger was no longer about just Olivia. Barry's rage now included Genevieve and Gwendolyn.

"Fancy meeting you here," Silas said, clearly waiting for an explanation he wasn't owed.

Barry was not up for a stalemate. So, his response was brief. "I could say the same about you."

"Well, it's my wife who's out traipsing around in the wee hours of the morning."

Barry felt the dig, holding back on what he wanted to say. Silas didn't seem to mind she made hospital visits in the middle of the night. Not that Olivia was alone, but Silas didn't know that. Barry wrangled his temper in favor of some insight. "I'm here for a friend in need," Barry said.

Silas' eyes narrowed, deciphering the meaning behind the words. "It's curious this place just happens to be one of Livie's clients."

"That's not why I'm here," Barry told him, glad that's where Silas' head went. He shouldn't even be talking to him. Barry couldn't help but enjoy the satisfaction of Silas wondering what was really happening.

Silas waited Barry out, hoping for some elaboration, but Barry remained mute. "Speaking of friends, Livie told me you saw Patrick Monahan while she was in the hospital."

Barry was immediately suspicious of the reason behind the question. "He came to check on Olivia." The acknowledgement didn't tell Silas anything he didn't already know.

"How did Patrick know to check on her?" Silas wanted to know.

The question was not where Barry thought they were going, but he would use it, nonetheless. "Not long before I took Olivia to the hospital, Patrick sent Jon Sharpe to the house. He was looking for you. Apparently, Patrick was worried about you after giving you Deveroux's address. A lot of people went looking for you that day. No one, including your wife, knew where you were. Concern turned to worry and you know how the rest went. I can't help but think you

Lisa Compton

being missing contributed to her condition." It was the truth. Barry hoped it made Silas feel something. "When Patrick heard what was happening in San Antonio, he was on a plane to see her."

"Livie told me she never saw him."

"She didn't. She was intubated in the ICU fighting for her life," Barry said, twisting the knife further, hoping he would eventually hit some kind of feeling.

"So, Patrick did what?" Silas asked. Apparently, the description Barry just gave him didn't do the trick.

"He met with me and Rogan Poe. At Olivia's house." It was another dig. Even though they were married, it was still Olivia's house. Barry decided to leave Will Ibarra out of it. Will was edging closer to partnering with Silas at the UAD. There was no sense in screwing things up for him.

"If I was missing, what was Patrick supposed to do?"

Barry blew out a long breath, trying to contain his rising anger. "Let's be clear. At that point, we didn't know if you were missing or dead, but Patrick made a promise to Olivia to find you. When he couldn't, when whoever it was that had you, left him hanging, Patrick still came because that's what he said he would do. Apparently, he takes promises seriously." Barry finally saw a flicker of something. He just wasn't sure what.

"That was a dig at me, wasn't it?" Silas asked, pretending bewilderment.

"You think?" Barry shook his head. "I see no reason someone couldn't, at the very least, have reached out to Olivia. It's inexcusable and tells me your new bosses are assholes."

"Maybe they did," Silas hypothesized.

"I carried her phone in my pocket for days. All my waking hours were spent between her and your little girls. When I couldn't be there, Rogan Poe was. Kim held down the fort at the house. I was scared to death thinking about how those tiny little babies could lose both their parents before they ever got to meet them. I worried about how I would have to tell Olivia she lost her husband."

"You did exactly what I asked you to do." Silas' words were gruff, but Barry thought he saw a peek of clarity. Silas was a different person the day he showed up in Barry's office worried about one of Olivia's visions where she saw his death. That version of Silas had cared about his family. Or maybe it was just Olivia and that was the problem.

"But I didn't die, did I?"

Barry didn't answer him. He couldn't because of the truth that lived inside his head. *No, Olivia was the only one who did that.*

"I called the hospital to learn more about what happened to Livie. You know what they told me? They couldn't talk to me because I wasn't her healthcare proxy. I'm assuming that's you." Silas paused, but Barry said nothing. "She didn't even give them my last name." He was talking about the girls now. Silas had noticed Osborne was their name in the NICU. He assumed it was because, at the time of their birth, Olivia couldn't tell them otherwise. An open piece of mail, which he never would have looked at, but for some reason was drawn to, revealed that assumption was wrong. She didn't even give them his last name.

The response was so Silas, thinking only of himself. Still, somehow, Barry felt the need to wake

Silas up to what he had. Barry had accepted the fact he could never have children of his own, yet in some twist of fate, he found himself bound to a pair of babies that would forever be a part of his world. Words failed him there as well or maybe there weren't any adequate enough to describe how Genevieve and Gwendolyn made him feel. They were the beacon of light in this whole dark nightmare. If Silas could only hear him, Barry would tell him that no matter what was or was not on a piece of paper, there were things that could never be taken from him.

"I'm asking things of Livie she can't give me," Silas confessed, halting Barry's search to comfort this man.

"I can't speak for her," Barry told him.

"You could. You just won't. That's the difference between you and me. We protect differently."

"Olivia doesn't need protection, Silas. She needs understanding. She needs support—the kind she doesn't have to ask for. She needs to be seen and accepted for what she is." When it came to Olivia, Barry could go on and on, but he made himself stop. His pleas were going nowhere.

"You're telling me I can't save her?" Silas challenged him.

"I'm telling you she doesn't need saving. It's really that simple."

"And my daughters? I'm just supposed to let them go too?" Silas asked.

It was at that moment Barry realized he had yet to hear Silas call them by name. Struck with that thought, Barry banished his own feeling of sorrow for Silas. This was about Silas and Olivia. Not Silas and his daughters.

If Silas didn't get it now, Barry doubted he ever would.

"One day Genevieve and Gwendolyn will need the same support I just told you to give Olivia. Right now, though, Olivia is the only one that can protect them. Tired of being the peacemaker, Barry focused on something Silas could understand. "You can't serve two masters. Your bosses won't allow it." Patrick was right. Silas was out for Silas and wasn't leaving the life he had before Olivia.

"Biologically, they will always be your children, Silas. No one can take that away from you. Olivia won't let them forget you are their father."

"And you?" Silas made himself ask. "You once told me that if I fucked this up—you would pick up the pieces and there would be no place for me in her life. Do you remember that?"

Barry would never forget it.

"I believe you," Silas said, not waiting for an answer.

This time the words came easy for Barry. "I am at their service. Whatever that looks like."

Silas nodded, head down. For a moment, Barry thought he was going to walk away. Barry already had his phone in hand. He had never let Renaye know he was here.

"Thank you for that," Silas told him. "I don't deserve it – least of all from you. I was the selfish one. I asked you to take care of Livie because I knew you loved her. Because of that, I think you should know, that for all my coaxing to get her to come in for a meeting with my new bosses, she refused week after week. Until tonight, when I threatened you and your freedom. Your love for her is not in vain. She will keep saving you over and over and over because she can't stop herself. She loves you too. I guess I should count myself lucky we lasted this long."

Only then did Silas fade back into the dark from which he came.

Chapter Twenty-Four

The lights were dim—mimicking twilight. Ahead of them was the nurse's station. The resident halls jutted out from the rounded desk area, stretching like the legs of a spider. The scene was familiar, *and* the smell, but most of all the ambiance. This place existed between two realities, merely a waystation along the path unseen until stepping into the great beyond.

Walking these silent halls reminded Olivia of her time working in a place like this one. More often than not, she was the caretaker of the dead or the *near* dead. It was in those times Olivia knew something from the other side had crossed over in some reverse revolving door. It should have been a clue about the rest of her life. She was a conduit between the living and the dead and the monsters that roamed both places.

A cluster of nurses sat cloistered together. Their hushed whispers told Olivia they were discussing the night's events. Even if death was expected here, each time it happened, they were all reminded of their own mortality. Wisps of fear hung above some of them like fog on the water. They were the ones who knew it wasn't always a beacon of light waiting at the end of the tunnel, beckoning the departed. The rest were blissfully unaware. For a brief moment, Olivia wondered what that was like. None of them looked up as she and Renaye passed. Acknowledging them would validate that death had come again.

The hall where Renaye led her was empty. Franklin Pope's room was next to the last one. Olivia reached for the door handle as Renaye melted into the wall, a signal to Olivia she wouldn't be joining her. Maybe Renaye had already seen what was waiting inside. Maybe Poe had spared her. Beyond the door, hung a web of grief and sadness. Poe wasn't all fire and fight. He felt deeply. His emotions rarely leaked to the surface, but when they did, they had the power of a riptide. Olivia was here to push him back to shore before he drowned. Silently, Olivia left Renaye behind as she slipped inside to comfort the man who had become like a brother.

Poe was seated beside the bed, leaned over, as if in prayer. It reminded Olivia of the vow he took at her bedside just before she was whisked away to the room where she too would die. Maybe Poe was petitioning for a safe journey. Frank, like Poe, had changed his last name, an escape from what Olivia had no idea. It no longer mattered.

Silently, she edged closer to the bed. Frank was on his back, his hands on his chest. It was a casket pose, one meant to convey peace. To the casual observer, it would have worked, but Olivia noticed that his hands clutched the blanket beneath him as if in fear. Frank's eyes were closed but Olivia knew that's not how he was found. Poe was the one who closed them. As she stared down at the body of Franklin Pope, Olivia saw the last of his life.

He was tired. His bones ached. The cold winds of December were wreaking havoc on his joints. He shouldn't complain. In all likelihood, this was his last winter. His plans for the night included catching a couple of hours of sleep before making his nightly rounds. He knew his watchful days would soon come to an end. He just hoped it would be after his nephew left for the bayou. Rogan begged him to leave with him and return home. What Rogan didn't know Frank had bid his last goodbye to that primordial place decades ago. He made peace with his departure. No use changing the end this close to the real one. Frank could feel there was a new stalker in town. One that chased all the others away. This one was unlike anything he had ever seen before.

Despite the fear, Frank died a merciful death. His passing was like marks on a scorecard. He would not be the only one.

Olivia untangled herself from the fragmented memories. The night's events faded like dried flowers in the wind. Olivia's eyes strayed to the windowsill. The salt and cumin were undisturbed. The defense was habit. Habits were good. There was comfort in the familiar. At Frank's age, comfort was hard to come by.

Another memory, one of her own, was heading for the surface when Poe interrupted her.

"There was a demon here, wasn't there?" Poe asked the obvious.

Olivia gave him the truth because that was what he needed to hear. He wouldn't have asked her to come otherwise. "Yes."

"Was it one of yours?"

Poe's voice chased away the memory that dangled just beyond her grasp. "Your uncle didn't know *It*." Of that, Olivia was sure.

"I knew it smelled different in here," Poe said. "Similar, but not the same as in your kitchen, or outside by the fire."

That's when the thing hiding in the corner of Olivia's mind claimed center stage. It was guiding her—wanting her to know. Her memory rushed back. The smoky, sweet aroma of tobacco, leather and wood all rolled into one. *With a hint of cinnamon.* Now Olivia knew where she had smelled it before. In a place like this one, where no one smoked.

"It's the same smell from Barry's condo—the day Amanda went over the balcony."

"You never told me if she jumped or she was pushed," Poe reminded her. Their discussion had been shoved aside for other events. Whatever happened before the babies felt like a whole other lifetime.

"She wasn't pushed," Olivia told him. "And she didn't jump." For an instant, Olivia saw something she hadn't seen before—the view from Amanda's eyes before she went airborne. "She didn't know until it was too late."

Amanda's last thought whipped through Olivia's mind like the wind. *She had not gone there for death. She had gone because Rose promised a life—with the father of her baby.*

Olivia clamped down on the thoughts, taking hold of her own. "Amanda was compelled," she said, spitting the words out before she could choke.

The look on her face gave Poe pause. "You, okay?"

Olivia ignored the question. She needed to focus on the present—not the past. *Or her future.* "Whatever was here was powerful enough to get past your uncle's defenses," Olivia said watching Poe's eyes drift to the window as hers had. "He knew something was coming and he was powerless to stop it."

"So, it's powerful enough to be in your *new* league. Was it one of yours?" Poe repeated.

He had lost his sensitivity filter. Olivia forgave him. These were trying times. "Duly noted. This was not my father," she said simply. "But, I bet he knows *It*." The cinnamon was a dead giveaway.

Poe was up and pacing. Olivia hadn't noticed when he got out of the chair. It must have been when he saw her fade away. "Damn it, this is some demon bullshit fight, *again*. Us, mere mortals, are just collateral damage."

"You have to have faith. We are not alone in this fight," Olivia assured him. Whether Poe heard her or not was another matter.

Olivia remained calm, putting pieces together. The events at Barry's condo were the beginning. It meant this new demon was pushing Rose, using her, to gain exposure, revealing what had been hidden here for centuries. Pushing the Gifted into the light was a recipe for chaos. This force, and others like it, would take advantage of the carnage. Just like the new FBI. Some humans were no better than demons.

"This is an enemy of my father," Olivia conceded.

"Since he taught man war, I'd bet that's a long list," Poe taunted her.

"Not if it smells like cinnamon," Olivia corrected him.

Poe glared at her.

"Look," Olivia said. "Maybe, given what's happened, you should go be with Mémé."

Olivia felt guilty. Poe was only still here because of her. "We can join you later."

Poe's head was shaking before she stopped talking.

"No fucking way. You and Barry and two babies cannot be on the road alone. I have to see you to safety."

"I know you think that, but we'll be fine," Olivia assured him with as much bravado as she could muster.

"You still have no idea what that husband of yours or his people will do. Besides, you'll never find your way to your new home. The swamp is unforgiving and welcoming all at the same time. I have to lead the way."

"Suit yourself."

Olivia knew that would be his response, but she had to give Poe his chance. She was worried for Mémé.

"The girls should be home for Christmas," Olivia reassured him as much as herself.

"Not long, then," Poe said, his hand trailing down her arm like smoke. He had no idea how she had handled the past eight weeks, but she had. She was strong and growing more so every day.

Familiarity pinged Olivia's senses at the same time she watched the color drain from Poe's face. She never would have guessed Rogan Poe feared anything. Poe slowly backed away from her. His eyes focused just over her shoulder.

As Olivia wheeled around, the room faded to something darker than twilight, but not as dark as the hulking mass in the corner. She knew the yellow eyes. They were the eyes of her father.

You look improved.

The language wasn't English or Latin, but still, she understood his words.

I have discouraged these types of.....dalliances.

The yellow eyes trailed over the empty vessel of Franklin Pope.

"Why?" Olivia wanted to know.

Azazel trained his gaze on Poe. *His kind, the hunter, always traces the demon back to the witch. The witches are easier to find.*

This was news to Olivia. Demon Hunter was a misnomer. She couldn't help but wonder if that's what protected them from the witches of the past. Poe had hinted at a bloody history.

If the witches are to take their rightful place, they do not need the association.

A hot wind blew against her face with Azazel's departure. The look in Poe's eyes confirmed the demon was gone but still he remained frozen in place, as if any sudden movement would make it reappear.

"He's gone. You can breathe now," Olivia said. With her words, the lights returned.

"I'm not accustomed to dealing with his kind," Poe confessed. "The ones I encounter are low level, like your former babysitter."

It was ironic that he chose the term for *Alleracsap* since she had dispatched him to the hospital to watch over her twins. She was watching Poe for a further reaction and noticed he was eyeing the windowsill as she had done.

"I'm assuming those were here when you arrived?" Olivia asked.

"Yea. He wouldn't have gone to bed without them."

"Then there's your answer. It had to be royalty," Olivia told him.

Poe dragged a hand down his face. "So, *he* knows?"

"I have no doubt. Let him handle it."

Olivia reached out, forging a connection between

herself and Poe. She could not have him fall apart now. "Your uncle is at peace, no matter what was here," Olivia assured him. "Please don't tell Mémé what happened until we get there," Olivia pleaded. Frank and Mémé were siblings. Mémé was looking forward to seeing Frank almost as much as seeing Rogan.

Poe nodded his consensus.

His eyes slid back to the still body of his great uncle while Olivia debated on telling Poe the one thing she had kept from him—from the day she woke up. A knock at the door kept her from it. Renaye peeked inside. Olivia had no idea how long she and Poe had been in this room. Time had ceased to exist.

"Umm, the funeral home is here. And, do either of you have a clue about the lights?"

Renaye watched the silent yet rapid exchange between Olivia and Poe.

Renaye didn't wait for an answer. "So, it looks like we had reason to freak the fuck out," Renaye surmised. "We're done with that, right?" she asked, her voice breathless.

Olivia nodded her head. "Yes. We are done with the dead tonight."

Renaye let out a sigh of relief. "Good, because the FBI is here."

****

After the twilight of, the fluorescent lights of the entrance to Oak Hollow were jarring. There was a circle drive in front like a hotel. Except the only way to check out was to die or go to a place worse than here. The van from the funeral home was a reminder.

Olivia went outside looking for Silas and found Barry.

"He's gone," Barry said, rising from his place on the bench next to the door.

After his confrontation with Silas, Barry's lack of sleep caught up with him with a vengeance. Either that or the conversation he shared with Silas had knocked him off his feet. Barry never believed he would ever hear the words that came out of Silas's mouth.

"I tried," Barry said, hoping Olivia could forgive him.

Olivia's brow creased. "I don't understand. Why was Silas here? What are you even talking about?" Olivia questioned her own coherence. The days and nights were running together—all while she tried to catch snippets of sleep while spending as much time as she could with her babies.

Barry stepped closer, placing his hands on her shoulders, ensuring she was going nowhere. "I need to tell you something."

Olivia's heart thundered in her chest. "No, you don't."

"Yes, I do."

Olivia lowered her guard, yielding to him.

"I need you to know about that day you came to my condo."

Olivia knew the one. It was after they had buried Mark.

"I turned you away. Not because I didn't want you. I want you more than anything I've ever wanted in my life. But I didn't want you to see me like that."

The story conjured memories of what her mother told her about Gran and her husband.

"I wasn't my best self. It was all me. Not you." Barry squeezed her shoulders for reassurance.

Olivia had no words, but it was okay because Barry kept talking.

"I tried to tell Silas what he has. I tried to tell him what you and the girls need."

Olivia reached up and took Barry's hands from her shoulders, using them to propel herself forward. She stopped mere inches away from him. She dropped his hands, and his arms swept behind her. Safe inside the cradle of his arms, Olivia gazed into his face. His eyes were moist and glistening.

"I tried to make him see," Barry said, a catch in his throat.

"Stop," Olivia whispered, pressing her fingers to his lips.

Barry didn't move.

Olivia's lips were trembling and her eyes were wet now too. "You can't make him. Neither can I. It's over," she said softly.

She felt Barry's lips move beneath her fingers. "Stop talking," Olivia pleaded, closing the gap between them. She pressed her lips to his and got her wish.

Chapter Twenty-Five

The room was familiar, even if she had never been inside this particular one. Only now did Olivia realize she had never visited Silas at his office. Her local collaborations had always been at SAPD headquarters, but not today. It was just her and the FBI. Olivia arrived at the same time as the painters. They were there to change the name on the glass door. No matter what they called themselves, the objective was the same—if they couldn't control it, they would kill it.

As she headed for the closed doors at the end of the hall, Olivia thought back on something Poe said. He called *Alleracsap* her babysitter sent from Hell. Earth had sent one too – only that one was her husband. The betrayal felt like ash in her mouth. Needless to say, she wasn't feeling very married anymore. Olivia would rather be standing in the parking lot with Barry or somewhere more private. Her hormones had switched gears from maternal to vixen. Maybe she should warn him.

The door opened before her, and out stepped Captain Anthony Zavalla and Herschel Gaines, her favorite Texas Ranger. She would miss working with them. They were good men with good intentions. Zavalla still thought about the last time they saw each other. He hadn't forgotten the raging green of her eyes as she watched him haul Barry away.

"Doc," Gaines said with a tip of his white hat. "My wife, Glenda, is in town with me. She wants to drop off a gift for the babies later, if that's okay with you."

Olivia smiled, blinking away the pinprick of tears. She had missed out on a baby shower. "Of course, that's very kind of you."

Herschel Gaines stepped into her personal space and clasped her hand in his. "If we miss you, Glenda wants you to know there's a community in New Orleans. You'll find them much more hospitable than here."

Olivia was immediately on alert. The ranger had given her a hard time at first about all the witchy talk. Working with her he became a believer, or someone close had enlightened him. Either way, it was like throwing her a lifeline. There were *Gifteds* everywhere. All she had to do was open her eyes.

"It's an easy drive, especially with what's going on at the airports. If you're looking to get away," Herschel suggested. He smiled and leaned in closer. "She wanted me to let you know, there's more than just witches there."

Olivia opened her mouth and then closed it. There were too many questions for this short amount of time.

"I'd run too if I was you. And I know you're a whole lot smarter than me. Those men in there," Herschel gave a little nod behind him, "they may offer you an olive branch today, but it's full of thorns. They will come for the lieutenant no matter what you do."

Olivia's eyes grew wide at the suggestion.

"I know you can't abide by that. Check the box of diapers that are a wee bit heavier than the others. I got you something too," Herschel said with a wink as he let go of her hand.

Silas was waiting for her, the door open. "You're a little late," he commented as she passed.

"Like you wouldn't wait."

The table was round, leaving it open to interpretation as to who was in charge. All three men had elected to sit side by side. Only two of them had something with them. Silas had a padded folder. Most of the time it was a prop, but there could be something of interest in there. The other one, Bradford Dillon, had what looked like a tablet. Olivia specifically chose the chair across from him. She remembered him from before. He was the one she had to talk to before getting her gun back after shooting Jamie Smythe in her living room. Dillon was lying then as he masqueraded as a representative of the office of professional responsibility. He would most assuredly lie again today. Deceit was his mission. Regardless of anyone's title, he was the one in charge.

The other man in the suite was Dillon's boss from the looks of the age difference and paunch around his middle. He introduced himself as Dallas Harper. The boy in the corner with a military haircut needed no introduction. Even his overseers didn't give him one, but Olivia knew him. He was Elijah Stoddard, grown from a boy to a man who looked like he spent his time behind a computer screen. He reminded her a little of Kevin Branch.

Dallas spoke first. "Thank you, Dr. Osborne, for being here today. I'm sure there are other places you would rather be."

No one at the Bureau called her Dr. Osborne, but Olivia guessed they weren't in the mood to remind themselves she had once been an agent. They certainly weren't going to call her Mrs. Branch, so doctor it would be.

"I'm sure there are places we would all rather be. But thank you," Olivia said, reminding herself to smile. She meant it. So did Dallas. He didn't want to be here either, but these were the cards he was dealt. If he had known this project would ever come to fruition on his watch, he never would have taken it. Surveillance of the *Gifteds* had been ongoing for decades. There were supposed to be more decades before it became a reality, but the timeline had changed — all thanks to the actions of one girl.

Dillon got straight to the point. "Dr. Osborne, we asked you here to discuss Dr. Amanda Greene's unfortunate death. We're aware you were asked to walk the scene by Captain Zavalla, yet there are no notes. We request you share those with us now."

"How convenient, I ran into the captain in the hall," Olivia mused. Three sentences in and Dillon had already told her he was an impatient man who used intimidation. It was his favorite tool.

Olivia leaned across the table, her voice breathy, almost seductive. "It's the same as saying, *you better tell the truth, or we'll know*. Am I right?"

Out of the corner of her eye, Olivia saw Silas' expression. He looked mortified while Dallas shifted in his chair, uncomfortable already.

Dillon, on the other hand, leaned in to meet her stare. "Something like that." The timing had been perfect. "Why don't you start with what Captain Zavalla told you."

"That Dr. Amanda Greene was found dead in the

parking lot of Cardinal Towers. It appeared she had gone over the balcony of Lieutenant Barry Bartholomew's condo."

"That's an interesting way of saying this pregnant woman fell to her death," Dillon commented.

"At the time, no one knew for sure what had happened," Olivia explained.

"But that's not why they called you, is it?" Dillon asked.

"No. They called me because there were 'questionable' items found at the condo."

"Questionable how?" Dallas asked.

"Drawings on the balcony and a snakeskin," Olivia told them.

"What did those things tell you?" Dallas asked.

"That magic was used. The drawings were done with salt telling me something was conjured. The snakeskin is a sign of transformation. Later I was told it was from a rattlesnake. Knowing what I know now, I believe it was a signature," Olivia explained.

"How did you put that together?" Dallas wanted to know.

"Rose Corey was seen on security footage outside the lieutenant's condo. It made sense since we met just as I escaped a cellar full of rattlesnakes."

"Was she sending you a message?" Dallas asked.

"It appeared that way," Olivia surmised.

Dillon interceded. "Interesting, your use of the word magic and conjure. Are you calling Rose Corey a witch?" Dillon asked, waiting for Olivia to interrupt, but to her credit, she didn't. "I read your dissertation on the *Seven Second Theory*. It came from your ancestor at the Salem Witch Trials, did it not?"

"You obviously already have your answer," Olivia placated him. This was where he wanted to go the whole time. No matter what questions came before.

"So, is being a witch hereditary?" Dillon asked.

"I have no idea. Genetics is a funny thing," Olivia told him.

"So, you're saying you're not a witch?" Dillon asked, with a half-smile, even though this was no joke.

"No, I am not."

Olivia saw the mask of surprise cross her husband's face.

"Then what was your ancestor?" Dallas asked. He was genuinely curious. He wasn't trying to make a point.

"She was a poor woman who made a deal with a demon."

Dallas faded back into his chair.

"So, she wasn't a witch?" Dillon asked.

"I doubt any of those collected in Salem were witches," Olivia explained.

Dillon appeared amused again. "Why not?"

"Real witches would never have been caught."

Dallas visibly shook as if something had just scurried down his spine. Silas didn't look much better, even though he had already heard those words. She said them to him before he ever left for Vegas.

"Look, let's just cut to the chase. Rose Corey had an agenda. Dr. Greene was the first step. She was a sacrifice. Sheriff Tennent was the real target. Rose killed him in order to raise him from the dead. A human sacrifice is required for necromancy. I'm sure you have those notes from SAPD," Olivia suggested.

"We do. What we don't know is why."

It was now just her and Dillon. Dallas looked like he wanted to be anywhere but here. So did Silas.

"To see if she could, who knows? She's a young girl who I think has been taken advantage of."

"By who?" Dillon was truly curious about this one.

"Men. From findings at the sheriff's house, it would appear there was a sexual component to their relationship. And then there was Andre Roche."

"And your mother," Dillon suggested.

"I don't know anything about that," Olivia said.

"Not to worry. Your husband filled us in on his visit to Vegas."

Olivia didn't even glance at Silas.

"All those things are plausible, Dr. Osborne. However, there is an alternative theory," Dillon suggested. "Remind me, how did you meet Ms. Corey?"

Olivia wasn't sure where this was going. Before she could speak, her thoughts were interrupted by a tick inside her head. Like a knock. Someone was trying to come inside. She looked at Elijah. It was him. He was an empath, but he couldn't cross her barrier. She had no idea why, and neither did he. But he was trying to warn her. Of what, Olivia had no idea. What she was about to tell Dillon was already part of an official record. There should be no surprises.

"I met her in the cellar where Andre Roche was keeping her and Kimberly Burleson."

"What was your impression of Ms. Corey?" Dillon wanted to know.

"She didn't seem concerned about her captivity."

"Why do you say that?" Dillon asked.

"She was too busy playing with a snake to care if

she had been rescued."

"Is that what you were there to do, rescue her?" Dillon wanted to know.

"I didn't even know she was missing."

"What did you make of that?" Dillon asked.

"No one had listed her as missing or she wasn't a captive." The first was true and so was the second, but Olivia didn't know that at the time. Since then, she had learned from Rose's grandmother that Rose was a professional runaway. Olivia and Barry didn't spend all their time with Poe in pow-wows. Some of it was spent doing good old-fashioned police work.

"Do you think Ms. Corey knew who you were?" Dillon asked skipping ahead.

"We didn't exchange names," Olivia told him.

"If Ms. Corey was seeking your attention, what part did Dr. Greene play?"

Olivia got the sense they were at another place Dillon wanted to go.

"You and Dr. Greene were friends. She dog sat for you. You attended her housewarming party," Dillon said, not even giving her a chance to lie.

"Dr. Greene didn't have friends," Olivia told him.

"Really? Then what were you?"

"A tool," Olivia answered.

"For what?"

"Lieutenant Bartholomew." Dillon didn't need her for this. "Why don't we just skip to the chase?" Olivia encouraged him.

Dillon leaned forward again. "How do I know that you and the lieutenant didn't conspire to kill Dr. Greene and you used Rose to do it?"

Olivia was stunned into silence. It was also a way

to keep him talking. Dillon was a man who was impressed with himself.

"I have all the elements of a crime," Dillon said. He had spotted the exchange between Olivia and his protégé. "*Opportunity.* Your alibi and the lieutenant's, or should I say, former lieutenant, are shaky. The only person who can corroborate you were at home when you said you were, and that Mr. Bartholomew arrived when he said he did, is your neighbor. Unfortunately for you, I have to be the bearer of bad news and tell you Lily Forrester is deceased. She killed herself in some motel near the Mexican border after losing her job at the hospital and finding out she would get nothing from the sale of her house. Which, by the way, you now own. I heard her husband sold it for a song. He was either grief stricken or afraid."

Olivia didn't like that she was glad that Lily was dead, but she was.

"We know you talked to the archbishop before he went to Captain Zavalla's office and gave Mr. Bartholomew an alibi," Dillon added.

If Dillon was going to play court, so was she. The drama now was just for Silas. Olivia hoped he would see this man's crazy and sever his ties before Dillon took him down too.

"The archbishop is a close, personal friend," Olivia answered. "He blessed my house as a wedding gift. He sat with me by my hospital bed, or so I'm told. I've requested he bless my daughters as soon as they're home. I also feel the need to remind you that he is an archbishop who oversees one of the largest dioceses in the country. If you still feel the need to question him, proceed at your own risk."

"Is that a threat?" Dillon asked.

"It's a statement of fact," Olivia corrected him.

"Well, that would be very bad form of me, considering the archbishop is residing in the same hospital where you once were."

This was news to Olivia. Was that what Elijah was trying to warn her about?

"*Means,*" Dillon continued. "According to Captain Zavalla, the archbishop went to see him at your request."

"I called the archbishop and told him the lieutenant could probably use some spiritual counseling, considering what occurred at his condo," Olivia explained. "What the archbishop did with that information was entirely up to him."

Dillon's eyes narrowed at her answer while Dallas looked at Dillon.

"Then there's motive," Dillon said, coming to the end of the three elements. "Dr. Greene was pregnant and Mr. Bartholomew wanted nothing to do with her or the child."

According to Zavalla, the UAD intended to exhume Amanda's body. They would desecrate her final resting place for no reason. Barry was not the father.

Dillon leaned forward again. "Agent Branch managed to get in touch with the urologist Mr. Bartholomew told him about."

On cue, Silas slid a paper from the folder in front of him. Dallas passed it on to Dillon, who pushed it in front of her. "Turns out, Mr. Bartholomew isn't sterile after all. His sperm count is low, but it only takes one, right?"

Chapter Twenty-Six

"Ignore and intimidate, a page right out of the government handbook. I've been ignored, for years, working for the likes of you. What makes you think you can intimidate me now?" Olivia asked.

Dillon smiled, but it was more forced than before. It's because she wasn't as breakable as he thought. He expected more hormones.

"Then let's begin again, shall we?" Dillon suggested.

"You're the one that has an agenda," Olivia clapped back.

Dillon nodded. "I feel the need to tell you that we confirmed that Barry Bartholomew was nowhere near the archdiocese the morning of Dr. Greene's death."

"Not my problem," Olivia told him.

"It could be a problem—for you. I'm supposed to take your word for it that you spent the morning on your porch drinking tea, eating cookies and discussing your ancestors."

Dillon had just slipped. The only person who could have given him those details was Lily. Dillon had to be the one who ordered the unauthorized blood draw from Genevieve. With that knowledge, Olivia slipped on her own mask. She had to control her rage until she didn't.

"Sounds almost like you were there," Olivia observed. "If you don't believe me, then I'm sure the police officers who showed up on my lawn can verify that. Or Captain Zavalla. You should have asked him that when he was here. Next question."

"You said you're not a witch. Do you go by the other term, gifted?" Dillon asked.

"It has been established that the FBI hired me for my claircognizance skills," Olivia reminded him.

"The gift of knowing," Dillon said. "You consider it a gift, correct?"

Not always. Olivia glanced over at Elijah. The look in his eyes confirmed he had received her thoughts, but only because she initiated the contact. "Yes, I've come to terms." Olivia admitted.

"So, no one taught you this?" Dillon clarified.

"No. That's why it's called a gift. It's instinct. Primal, even. Think of a prodigy—they just know how to do something. They're born that way."

Dillon reached for the black case in front of him. Olivia hadn't given it much thought when she arrived. It didn't stick out like the folder in front of Silas.

Dillon's fingers moved nimbly across the tablet, bringing it to life. As it came to life, he slid it her way. "Tell me what this is. A gift?"

The scene was almost too dark to see. If Olivia hadn't been to the sheriff's house, she might not have recognized what she was watching. The picture found its focus when Jim Tennent, the former sheriff of Atascosa County, took his turn in the kitchen and began his slow walk toward the one filming. His jaw was slack, his eyes grayed and filmy. He wobbled like a sloth or a zombie until he fell, never to rise again.

Olivia was about to pass the device back when another scene replaced the first one. This time the lights were better even if they were fluorescent. The buzz was a dead giveaway. This one was taken in what appeared to be a parking garage. Olivia saw movement to the right. Given the lot was virtually empty, it made it easy to spot the meandering figure of a dead Mason Deveroux. He walked, never looking at the one filming. He only stopped when he ran into a concrete barrier. He shuffled and bumped until he ran out of juice like a wind-up toy. Then he leaned too far over the edge and disappeared head-first into the blackness below.

"It's a good thing we arrived at Agent Deveroux's house when we did. We didn't get there in time to save Deveroux, but it could have ended very differently had the UAD not been there for Agent Branch."

Olivia noted the use of the term agent and not station chief. Somewhere, there had been a transference of power that Silas neglected to share.

"Your husband could have been Ms. Corey's next victim. I'm guessing this isn't the kind of magic you want people to see."

Dallas leaned forward in his chair, obvious concern on his face. "How did Ms. Corey do those things? She's just a teenage girl." Dallas might have been seeking answers, but his voice sounded like he really didn't want to know.

"I'm guessing this isn't something every witch can do, can they?" Dillon asked.

"Rose is a murderer," Olivia confirmed. "What she did after – she didn't do alone. This," Olivia said pointing to the black screen, "was not just Rose. She made a request. To make the dead walk requires not only a bodily sacrifice but a demon. In simple terms, it's black magic, meaning it violates God's divine plan.

Why do you think the Catholic Church forbid necromancy a thousand years ago? The Church believes resurrection is reserved for God. To proceed without him is considered blasphemy. Without the assistance of God, the only choice is summoning and this could only have come from a demon."

Dillon seemed to consider her words. "She summoned a demon? So, it's not just witches we need to worry about? It's demons too?" Dillon asked, leaning forward. "I wonder if Rose had something to do with what happened at the barn in Atascosa County. According to the dear departed, Dr. Greene, she told Agent Deveroux there was a demon there. How did it get there? Did Rose bring that one too?"

Dallas paled at the suggestion. Olivia leaned back in her chair for the first time. There was a clamoring in her head now. She clutched her hands to keep from screaming at Elijah to back off.

Dillon snapped his fingers. "My bad. Every statement I read from that night says Rose was never in the barn. Refresh my memory, why didn't Roche and that woman, Ana Lutz, not leave when they could? Was there something stopping them?"

Olivia deflected the question. "Roche told me he was looking for a demon. You can't do the things he did without catching the attention of a lot of bad things. Maybe he found one. It's been my experience that demons show up whether asked or not."

"Do you have a demon?" Dillon asked.

Silas looked away. At least Dillon couldn't see him, but Olivia could.

"With my gift, they have been known to make an appearance. Before I came back to the FBI, those were the types of cases I consulted on."

"You mean killers, claiming to be innocent," Dillon corrected her. "So, let's summarize. Rose Corey is a witch, who colors outside the lines. She practices black magic, meaning she's going to give the rest of your gifteds or collective a bad name? That about right?"

Olivia's eyes narrowed. There was another brush inside her head—like a buzzing mosquito that wouldn't go away. She didn't bother to look Elijah's way this time. She needed to be free from here. "What do you want?"

"In the interest of cooperation, I want you to catch the bad witch."

"I catch killers, Olivia reminded him, not for the first time. "That's what Rose is." Dillon's use of the word witch set off alarm bells off in her head. The clamoring was getting louder the more they talked.

"That she is," Dillion agreed. "The UAD is all about keeping our homeland safe. We are fully prepared to acknowledge witches and gifteds, or whatever they want to call themselves. That's why we will be charging Ms. Corey with maleficium. It's a Latin term for evildoing or practicing dangerous magic with the intent to harm others. Ms. Corey will be an example. While we want to be inclusive, we also need to demonstrate that no one is above the law."

Olivia concentrated on her breathing. She could hear another keeping pace with her. It was Elijah attempting to suppress or cushion whatever she was about to do.

Olivia pushed her chair back from the table. Fleeing this room would help Elijah perform his duty.

He wasn't strong enough to contain the rage building inside of her. "Then I can't help you."

Dillon looked up at her. "You can't or you won't? Big difference."

Olivia reached over to grab her purse. "My departure should give you your answer." Down the table, she saw the fright on Silas's face. The slight shake of his head was a warning signal. He knew the signs of her building displeasure.

"I think you will want to stay for one more question," Dillon encouraged her.

Olivia caught the tablet as it slid back her way. The screen lit up with the scene at the prison. Without missing a beat, Olivia flicked it back towards Dillon. "I've seen this."

"What do you call this?" Dillon asked. "Primal? Your use of the word, not mine."

"It's a transference of energy."

Dillon leaned back in his chair, waiting.

"What do you think gives people the impression some places are haunted? Theaters, hospitals, churches and in this particular case, prisons. It's because of the amount of energy exchanged there. By energy, I mean human emotion."

The explanation seemed to calm Dallas. His shoulders sagged as he let go of the tension he had built up since being here. Olivia had determined he did better with logic. Most people did. She spent her career striving to explain the unnatural in logical terms. It helped the non-believers and kept fear at a minimum.

"Doesn't a haunting imply something bad or nefarious?" Dillon asked. He clearly didn't want a natural explanation.

"Not necessarily. It's collected energy. Think about it, people are very emotional at all those places I just described. It doesn't matter if the emotion is sadness or joy. It stores just the same."

"So good and bad?" Dillon asked. "Kind of like magic. It was obvious from your explanation of Rose's actions that the magic was the bad kind. Please forgive me, I'm just a natural kind of guy, but what you just described and demonstrated very effectively on this video looks like something called psychokinesis. I'm just wondering if you know how many witches can do this? To a novice like me, it looks like an advanced skill. If you're not a witch, what are you?"

The tablet came back her way. He had frozen the screen on her face, her arm stretched out, her lips curled in a scream, her eyes shining like emeralds. "Pretty scary stuff," Dillon commented.

"You should listen to what I'm saying. *Prohibere.* It means stop," Olivia said, each word measured. It was her own control mechanism.

Dillon smirked, seemingly pleased with himself. "Guess I didn't need to translate the Latin for you after all."

"I'm asking you to stop."

"Telling or warning? Your words say one thing, your eyes another."

Olivia kept her mouth clamped shut.

"Have I crossed a line? Am I being a bully?" Dillon prodded. "I heard that's what you called Roche. I also heard you're not fond of bullies. Those words came from Marc Singer, another departed one. I'm sure you remember him from the DOJ. I heard he bullied you and he ended up dead in his hotel room that same night."

"According to the Justice Department, Mr. Singer suffered an unforeseen medical event," Olivia repeated the party line.

"Is this transference of energy a gift also?"

Olivia made no move to answer. Not that she didn't want to, but she knew her silence enraged Dillon. His rage that would tell her exactly what she needed to know. It might not happen today or tomorrow, but she would have to answer for her actions today. So would he.

"I'll tell you what I think," Dillon said. The table was too large to infringe on her personal space but that's what he wanted to do. "If evidence of this gets out, it could become difficult to distinguish between the definition of gifts and weapons. Do you really want to begin this whole new journey into a changed world without clear boundaries? I have to say this display draws a very thin line between a woman such as yourself and Rose Corey the necromancer," Dillon warned. "What will it be — murder or maleficium? Even the word is scary, don't you think?"

"I think you scare easy," Olivia observed.

Next to Dillon, Dallas's face broke out in a sweat. His hand clutched at his tie, tugging it loose. Maybe it was the rising temperature in the room. It felt like someone had turned the heater to blast. Sweat dotted everyone's upper lip but Olivia's. At the same time, the lights in the room dimmed. The cold December clouds allowed little light through the big picture windows. The room fell into twilight—that magical time when the dark and the light swam together as equals.

"You're doing that, aren't you?" Dallas asked. His

cheeks blazed red, obvious signs his blood pressure was rising.

"Is this what you did in the barn?" Dallas asked as the lightning bolt shot his right arm. He flexed his hand. It felt full of pinpricks—like he had slept on it wrong and it was trying to wake up.

"No, it is not," Olivia said.

"How are you doing this? You said it had to be a place full of energy. This isn't one of those places," Dallas pointed out, frantically searching for an explanation. True to form, he was seeking logic, searching for an answer that made sense. It was an easy one. The choices that caused the paunch around his waist had clogged important arteries with plaque. His heart couldn't keep up with the strain, but it would keep thundering until it couldn't.

"The pounding in your chest is your flight or fight mechanism. It's a gift from our ancestors. It warns you when a predator is near. As a man who chases other bad men, you just have heightened senses. Self-soothe. Take some shallow breaths, it should help."

Dallas did as he was told. He nudged Dillon rather than waste his energy on talking.

Dillon shrugged. "In the spirit of Christmas, I'm going to *gift* you a few days to think about what we discussed. I know you have a lot on your mind. I hear your daughters are due home soon. I also heard the hospital is as eager for them to leave as you are. Something about electrical issues in the NICU. I wonder how long it will be before you know what their gifts are? Do you even know?"

"You slipped up today. The only way you could have known what was talked about on my front porch the day Dr. Greene died is if Lily Forrester told you. I'm telling you to stop, and to stay away from my daughters."

Olivia gave Bradford Dillon one last steely glare before she turned around and walked out the door.

She didn't hear Silas coming after her. He caught up to her at the end of the hall. He had to grab her arm to make her stop.

"I tried to tell you." Silas was pleading.

"I tried to tell *you*," Olivia accused him, snatching her arm back from his grip. "Get out of my sight," she said slowly, lingering on each word. "Right now," she added when he didn't budge.

"Livie,"

"Don't call me that."

Olivia reached for the door. The painters were still there, standing on the other side, admiring their handiwork. The door shattered before she even touched it, their morning's work crunched beneath her feet as she walked across the scattered glass.

Chapter Twenty-Seven

Even though she had returned to Vegas, Sarah Larsin still knew the daily goings on of her daughter. Olivia suspected Samael still lingered. She just didn't know if he was a scout or a babysitter. For some reason tonight, Olivia wanted to know. Sarah's response was surprising.

"I told you. I have an empath."

Reexamining the morning's events, Olivia could only come to one conclusion. "Elijah?" It was surprising and not, all at the same time. She knew there was something about him, but what? "Do you trust him?"

"Poor, unfortunate Elijah was put in a precarious situation a long time ago. After serving his time in the mental institution, he had nowhere to go. His mother, unable to cope with losing both him and his brother, never recovered. She found her solace in the bottom of a pill bottle. With his natural father in the wind, hopefully dead, and a step-father who was the newly elected senator from Virginia, complete with a new family, Elijah had nowhere to go. That's when the shady Mr. Bradford Dillon scooped him up," Sarah explained.

"Does Dillon know what Elijah is?" Olivia asked, skipping ahead, looking for leverage. Poor Elijah had been taken advantage of his whole life.

Lisa Compton

"In as much as any natural born knows about the gifted. Dillon never bothers to find out the real origin. But Dillon and those like him are good at studying. I'm sure you've figured out by now that prisons and mental institutions are full of the gifted. The more prominent the gifts, the longer they stay and the more attention the naturals give them."

"Lab rats," Olivia said. It was a theory she realized when visiting Larry Wayne Pittman in prison.

"How much of what you're doing now is learned or instinct?" Sarah asked.

Olivia paused.

"Sooner or later, you should examine what you know and how you know it."

Sarah was as confusing as a demon.

"Anyway, Elijah is my empath. He reached out to me when he heard my name."

Warning bells should have gone off in Olivia's head, but they didn't. "Have you worked with Dillon before?"

"Dillon, Deveroux, they're all the same. Much like you, I provide a valuable service. Unlike you, however, I don't rock the boat—until now, of course. You deviated from the path. More than that, you scare them. Fear is a very valuable tool. You're a natural. It is your fate now."

"Back to Elijah. Do you trust him?"

"Implicitly. He knows what would happen to him if he lied to me," Sarah explained.

Olivia knew her mother meant Samael.

****

Olivia ended the conversation and tucked the phone inside the pocket of her sweater. Silas thought it was Barry on the other end.

"You didn't help yourself today," Silas said. He was looming over her, an empty glass in his hand.

"You're biased. You only see things on Dillon's terms. There will be no inclusion. Only examples. All things considered, you should be amazed at how well I'm holding myself together," Olivia warned.

"You lied," Silas accused her.

"I asked and answered all of his questions," Olivia replied.

"Deveroux told me you were a witch. Barry all but confirmed it. You alluded as much. Yet today, when Dillon asked, you said you weren't."

"In all fairness, Deveroux had no idea what he was talking about. Barry didn't know because I didn't know until I learned who my father is."

No amount of alcohol Silas had consumed that night could mask the surprise on his face. Barry had warned Olivia's father was a wildcard. Silas had never counted on having to deal with him. He was wrong. About so many things.

"You found your father? He's still alive?"

Silas' voice had changed. Olivia didn't know if it was excitement or dread. "He found me. As far as being alive, let's just say his existence is endless."

Silas' face folded. It was dread, not excitement.

"Don't try and figure it out," Olivia encouraged him. "You don't want to know."

Olivia grew tired of looking up at him. She was exhausted, both mentally and physically. She needed to catch a few hours of sleep before seeing the girls. The night visits gave her time to be with Barry. With Sally's arrival, his visits had been curtailed. There was no way

Olivia could begin to explain the situation.

She stood up to go, but Silas blocked her path. Olivia knew the look in his eye. He had always wanted her, but it was nothing more than allure, the same thing the women her mother employed. Olivia saw it as an opportunity.

"A man like Dillon doesn't see your gifts," Silas mused.

"He sees weapons," Olivia echoed. "What do you see?" she asked, invading the circle of his arms.

Silas softened while other parts of him grew strong. His hands went to her hips. His breath quickened. "I'm right here," Silas whispered. "I never left you." He bent his head, angling for her lips.

"No. You left our daughters."

With that, Olivia slipped from his grasp, stepping just beyond his reach. "Gifts can become weapons, depending on who is wielding them. Bottom line is they can be anything I want them to be. That's what your new boss can't handle. Neither can you. I'm not a pawn in his game or anyone else's. I can be the queen of my own kingdom. Dillon is too blind to see that. My protection of the gifted won't end with Rose."

When she left, Silas was still shaking.

****

Olivia and Sally were having breakfast. It was one of the better mornings. Thanks to Sally, the house looked and smelled like Christmas. Olivia had made no effort. Growing up with just Gran, Christmas was a low-key event. After Herschel Gaines and his wife's visit the day before, Sally took the initiative. As the wife of a career military officer, mother of four, and an active member of her church, hosting events was what

Sally did. With the departure of the Branch family at Thanksgiving, the loneliness of the house had only grown louder. Purposeful planning for the future chased away the emptiness.

Sally's enthusiasm was infectious. For the first time since delivery, Olivia was looking forward to something other than her next visit to the hospital. Will and Jessica were coming by later with homemade tamales, a staple of Christmas Eve in San Antonio. Their presence also meant Kim and Adelyn. Olivia realized how much she missed them all. On this morning, the small talk with her mother-in-law was easy.

"Good days are ahead," Sally insisted, her eyes shining.

For a split second, talk of the future moved beyond the vague. Like a mirage on the horizon, the picture became clear. Their days here were numbered. A call from the NICU set everything in motion.

They cleared the table but left the dishes in the sink. They were about to walk out the door when Sally stopped.

"What about Silas?" she asked.

Olivia didn't feel bad that she wasn't the only one who hadn't thought of him.

Sally asked, looking to Olivia for guidance.

"Do you want to call him?" Olivia paused, halting her haste to get out the door and be with her babies.

Spending the last two months with Silas, Sally realized she didn't know her son. Avoidance was her answer. The not knowing was better than the knowing.

Poe, Renaye, and Barry met them at the hospital. The introductions were simple. Poe's grandmother knew Olivia's gran. Renaye was her ICU nurse, and then there was Barry. Olivia held her breath as Sally moved to shake his hand.

"I've heard your name," she said.

Barry smiled back. "I'm sure you have."

No one asked about Silas.

"There's an emergency c-section going on, so it's going to be a while," Renaye said.

"Brennon is being released today—I thought you might like to see him," Barry suggested.

Poe stepped up to assure Olivia. "We've got this until you get back."

****

Isaac was outside his father's room coordinating Brennon's release. Their plans were to return to Long Island that same day. The sale of Barry's condo had gone through as expected, but for now, Brennon wanted to return home.

"Is he still planning on retiring?" Olivia asked. It was the last update she had been given.

"Let him tell you himself." Isaac didn't sound like himself, obviously not pleased with whatever decision his father had made.

Brennon was sitting on the edge of his bed where he had spent so much recovery time. This particular room looked homey and medicinal. Brennon had been cleared of both a heart attack and a seizure. After medical clearance, he had been moved to the inpatient psychiatric unit given the profound and inexplicable events that transpired the day Olivia woke up.

To Olivia, Brennon Kaine looked alive again, the same as he did the day they met almost a decade ago.

"What happened in your room restored my faith,"

Brennon confessed.

"You believed enough to give the medals to my daughters," Olivia reminded him. "Your faith was always there. It just needed some dusting off."

"Or a miracle," Brennon said as he reached for her hand. "I spent so much time with evil that I didn't know anything else. You too know evil—in a biblical way. Both of us were shown an alternative."

Brennon released her hand, leaving behind a pristine white feather.

Olivia's thoughts raced back to the figure in her room with the snow-white wings. That same calm washed over her now as it had then.

"The angel in your room was a message. You might not be able to see all that God protects you from but He does protect you. You should have this. You've been chosen for a perilous journey, but you will not walk alone. The angel was there as your shield. This is a reminder."

Tears dripped from Olivia's eyes as she curled her fingers around the gift she had been given. "How do you know the angel didn't wake me to save you?"

"I considered that and I am fully prepared to repay the favor."

****

More tears were shed on the way home. Olivia sat in the backseat between her daughters, marveling at her creations while Barry drove. Sally gave him the keys, saying she was too excited to drive.

Finally, Olivia had the homecoming she deserved.

Chapter Twenty-Eight

The table was full. Will and Jessica, Kim and Addy. Poe and Renaye. Sally and Barry. Olivia found herself smiling more than she had in the last two months. The house was filled with love and laughter. Most of all, there was no division.

When dessert and coffee came out, Olivia exited upstairs to feed the babies and tuck them into their new beds. They each had their own crib, but Olivia put them together in one and watched as they squirmed their way to each other.

Barry stood beside her, watching them. "That's the way they came out," he whispered.

"I never thought this day would come," Olivia said, before a sob caught in her throat. Barry opened his arms to her and Olivia melded into him, much like the girls. She leaned her head on his shoulder, breathing in the scent of him. Her heart was full. Her babies were home and finally, so was she.

****

Poe entertained Father Dominic until Olivia could join them outside by the fire.

Silas was noticeably absent, but Dom made no comment. Barry trailing behind Olivia as she joined them was enough. There was unfinished business between her and the lieutenant. Dom had said as much back before he officiated her wedding to Silas. Dom had shared with her how much Gran didn't want her to be alone. In her last days, Ginny Larsin mourned what she had not given Olivia. Dom was the one who steered her toward hopes and dreams for her granddaughter. Ginny made her peace wanting nothing more than for Olivia to fall in love with a man who accepted her as she was and growing her own family. Dom knew Ginny would be happy to see Olivia had done both. But the same man did not fill both roles.

Olivia sensed they weren't the only ones gathered around a fire that had not gone out since it was lit the night she came home from the hospital. Perhaps it was a mask. Inside those flames was the ever-present sense something was watching over her. Olivia thought it best not to dwell too much on the solace she found within the embers.

The pleasantries were short and sweet. The look on Poe's face told Olivia he had pressured Dom into a confession before she arrived. Poe would have wanted to know what the man in robes wanted. She, on the other hand, liked seeing Dom back in the black frock. It suited him, just as the Church did.

"I apologize for coming with distressing news when this night should be a celebration," Dom began. He and Olivia first met when he was a young priest. Theirs was a treasured friendship, bound by tragedy. The night they faced a demon in her living room was still a vivid memory. Dom feared not only for his life that night but his very soul. Surrounded by a spiritual battle, Olivia stood her ground and retained her humanity. She was a force of nature. Dom's only fear now was for those who dared stand in her way. The battle was coming.

"It's the archbishop. Is he?" Olivia said, looking for the answer.

"Deceased," Dom said it for her. "He passed this afternoon."

"How?"

"According to the staff, he fell reaching for a book. He deteriorated from there," Dom reported. Poe had already asked these questions, but the priest had insisted on waiting for Olivia before beginning.

The rest Olivia could fill in for herself. Blood clot, pneumonia, the scenario wasn't an uncommon outcome for a frail man in his mid-seventies. Life was a fragile existence.

"But you don't believe them," she said.

"The staff went looking for him when they realized he wasn't in bed. They found him in the floor of his private library, near the ladder. They said he fell while reaching for a book."

"The rolling-ladder?" Barry specified. He had been in that room. He and the archbishop met there sometimes. The old man loved the natural light as much as he loved his books, but he also needed a cane to ambulate a flat surface. "What was a man his age doing up there?"

"I asked the same thing," Dom acknowledged.

"What book was he looking for?" Olivia asked instead.

"Something about the *deus ex machina*. Translated, it means—"

"The answer to an unsolvable problem," Poe interrupted. "It's what he used to call me."

"So, you're the demon hunter," Dom said, appraising him. He hadn't been the only one holding out on information. Rogan Poe was an interesting addition to Olivia's life. Now Dom knew why Poe neglected to share his position earlier.

"Yea, the one who defected," Poe confirmed, his eyes turning black even in the firelight.

Olivia stopped Poe with a dark look, signaling silence. When she was sure Poe got the message, she trained her attention on Dom. "Did the archbishop tell you anything else?"

With one eye on the now silent demon hunter, Dom replied. "His staff gave me an envelope he left for me. He wrote it the day before."

"You trust the message came from him?" Barry asked.

"It was sealed in wax," Dom explained. Instead of blood red, the wax was black, a sign of impending doom. "Did you really swear your alliance?" Dom asked, realizing the wax color symbolized Rogan Poe.

"I did," Poe said. He turned and faced Olivia. "To you."

Olivia nodded. She didn't need an explanation, but Poe liked saying it to the priest. Olivia turned back to Dom. "Did the room smell a particular way? Like cinnamon, perhaps?"

Poe realized too late it was a question he should have asked. Olivia was acclimating to her new normal while he was struggling.

Dom thought it was a strange request until he recalled a recent story included in his training. The significance was as obscure as the *deus ex machina*. "His breath smelled sweet and smoky all at the same time. I guess you could call that cinnamon," Dom confirmed. "He became lucid just before the end. Long enough to tell me he didn't fall. The word he used was pushed."

Sparks from the fire spewed into the air. Olivia didn't bother to acknowledge the display, but Poe did. She saw the narrowing of his eyes.

"And now he's dead," Poe finished, his eyes finding their way back to Olivia.

Dom bid his farewell with a promise to return for dessert the next evening, an invitation from Sally Branch. He would also bless the babies. A task the archbishop had promised.

Barry elected to see him out. He got the feeling Olivia and Poe needed a moment.

"He's been assigned to San Antonio. They're kicking out their other exorcist," Poe ranted after Dom disappeared out the back gate.

"That was always the plan," Olivia assured him, her tone firm.

"I guess we know why." Poe was fuming. "Any idea which demon did the deed?"

"In my meeting with the UAD, I was informed the archbishop confessed that he had lied about where Barry was the morning Amanda was killed. Do with that what you like."

Poe ran a hand over his face. His eyes were black. Olivia sensed frustration.

"I'm going back inside to say goodnight to your mother-in-law and thank her for a lovely evening," Poe said by way of a goodbye.

"I think you should tell me what's on your mind before you do that," Olivia told him. It didn't sound like a request.

Poe paused a moment to collect himself. The

blackness of his eyes paled. "I'm just tired of waiting. It feels like I'm circling the drain here," he confessed.

"The girls just came home, so that is not the reason," Olivia corrected him. She folded her arms and watched while Poe wrestled with his own words.

When he couldn't decide, Olivia did it for him. She started with something easy. "If you feel the need to leave now, to be with Mémé, I won't stop you," Olivia told him.

"She wouldn't be happy if I did," Poe confessed.

"Mémé misses you," Olivia told him. Despite her feelings, Olivia doubted Mémé used those words. "She's stronger than you think," Olivia assured him. "Things have improved at the home. Change is coming. Mistakes have been made. Whoever is behind this never considered they were implementing rules upon gifteds who have the ability to see truth before anyone else. Not only that, at this point, even the naturals know something isn't right. The fallout will be epic."

Olivia stepped closer, commanding his attention. "It's not Mémé, is it?"

Poe looked away.

"Is it because you're working without a net?" Olivia asked.

Poe froze.

"It was Mémé who told me the story of the demon hunter and the watcher," Olivia confessed. Her watcher was the last stop against her turning to the other side. As the demon hunter, Poe was supposed to be the one who caught her first. He had abandoned his post and now there was no one to get in her way.

"I see what's happening. Between you and Barry," Poe finally admitted. "He won't stop you no matter how many lines you cross."

"Mémé and I reached the realization that old stories can be woven into new ones. That's the purpose of the changeling. Maybe as the *deus ex machina* you were the turning point. The one brave enough to see a different answer to an old story."

Poe stayed silent, but Olivia knew he heard her. He just needed to wake up.

"It's okay to be afraid. Is it because of what you saw in Uncle Frank's room or what you see in those embers?" she asked.

"*It* or something like *It* is always here. Have you seen it?" Poe asked.

"Yellow eyes, yes. I'm of the belief that we all see demons differently," Olivia explained.

"Well, this one is the most terrifying thing I've ever seen. Hands like a man, teeth like a saber, ram horns, grey skin and the blackest wings. He's the full package."

"I see an ordinary man, with a ripening belly, sausage fingers and beady eyes. He performed magic tricks for kids so he could be close to his prey. I saw it at the first and last birthday party I was ever invited to. On a day when all I wanted to do was be included, I saw evil pierce the fragile veil surrounding our world. As for *Azazel*, I do not have to see him to know he's here."

Poe wavered under the sadness of her words and the weight on her shoulders. It was a reminder of why he shunned the duty of his gift to follow her.

"Stop looking at the fire and look to the light," Olivia told him.

Poe closed his eyes, hoping to wipe the memories.

When he opened them, Olivia was there. She threw her arms around him and squeezed him tight. "I can't do any of this without all of you, Mémé and Barry and all those yet to come. But you, you, have the heaviest burden to carry on this side. You have to be there for me to keep those I cherish safe."

Poe hugged her back.

"It's okay if you're afraid. So am I," Olivia whispered. "We're like siblings. We tell each other our hopes, our dreams and our fears."

"You can be the older sister," Poe agreed, sounding much more like himself.

Olivia smiled. "You didn't honestly believe we were on a journey that did not include demons."

"I just didn't think they would follow you around like the damn paparazzi," Poe admitted. "Who do you think did the archbishop?"

"If it was because of Barry, then *Azazel*," Olivia said.

"I agree, but for a different reason. The archbishop could have helped your Gran with you and he didn't," Poe told her.

"Not sure what I'm interrupting, but I agree," Barry said, joining them by the fire.

Olivia untangled herself from Poe and stretched her hand out to Barry. He took hers and they stood as one.

"I was thinking we would leave New Year's Eve," Olivia suggested.

Six more days. Barry told himself he could do it.

"Any particular reason?" Poe asked, plotting their exit strategy.

"It's simple, really. I would like to start the new year in a new place," Olivia said. "The girls have a doctor's appointment that morning that they will miss, while Sally will be next door waiting on a shipment of Rachel and Daniel's furniture which will arrive," Olivia explained. She, of course, did not tell Sally of their plans. Still, Olivia had not forgotten her promise. Sally would see her granddaughters again. The world would be a different place and the separation would not be forever.

"Most of all, Silas will be gone," Olivia revealed. "He doesn't know it yet, but they found Patrick. He was in Woodley Park. It's off the GW parkway, on his way home. Looks like a gunshot, but it's hard to tell with the decomp. Melinda called me today. She believes nothing they're telling her, but that doesn't make her husband any less dead," Olivia explained.

"Damn," Barry muttered, remembering forcing Patrick to admit past failures and misguided loyalty.

"Are we good now?" Olivia was only asking Poe.

He nodded. "I'll go say goodnight to Sally now."

Olivia nodded in return. Poe was already on his way inside when Olivia stopped him. "I understand your role change, but you need not question where my loyalty lies."

Barry felt the prick of energy rise like a heavy gulp of air and dissipate just as quickly. He saw Poe did too.

Olivia folded her arms and watched Poe's exit long after he had gone. "Too harsh?" she finally asked.

Barry didn't waiver. "No."

"I'm becoming something else," Olivia admitted.

"You became something else that night in the barn. You're doing exactly what you need to do. It is the only way forward."

Olivia turned to him. The darkness kept him from

seeing the tears standing in her eyes, but knowing him, he didn't need to see them to know they were there. "I don't frighten you?" she asked with trembling lips.

Barry shook his head, moving towards her. "Not one bit. It's glorious to watch you become what you were always meant to be."

Olivia's lip quivered and Barry went to her. He opened his arms and held her as she sobbed for the second time that night.

"You knew me before I knew myself," she whispered between the tears.

Chapter Twenty-Nine

Christmas was perfect. Silas was almost himself. Being away from the office and Dillon's influence, he seemed more relaxed than Olivia had seen since his return from Vegas. He even held the girls, but not often and not for long. He tried, but Olivia could see his heart wasn't in it.

Olivia vowed to make the most of the time they had together.

Sally, used to big holidays, busied herself in the kitchen, leaving Olivia and Silas alone with their daughters. Olivia felt sorry for her. Sally knew it was make-believe, but to her credit, she didn't let that stop her from living in the moment. Olivia did the same. She wasn't much for photos, but given the situation, she made a point to take plenty of them. Genevieve and Gwendolyn had a right to know they had a family apart from the one they had yet to build once they were free from this place.

The charm of the day faded with the sun. The festivities were over.

Sally offered to watch the girls while Olivia showered. When Olivia returned, it was Silas she found standing over the crib. She deduced Sally had planned it that way. Sally had made a valiant effort as a mother, but she could not force her son to be a father. Sally was trying to connect something that just wasn't there.

Olivia wanted to reassure her that Silas' lack of fatherhood wasn't her fault. It was no one's fault. In some ways that made it even more tragic. There was no one to blame.

Olivia thought Silas would turn as she entered the room. Instead, he remained rooted in place, mesmerized by something Olivia couldn't see. She did a quick toe-dip into the aura of the room. *Alleracsap* was hovering in the corner, but he was not intervening. If *Al* was a human and not a demon, he would have shrugged her off. He had nothing to do with what was happening in this room. That's when Olivia heard the hum of the mobile hanging over the girls. It was the moon and stars intended for Gwendolyn—her moon baby. The one in the other room, for Genevieve, was the sun and clouds. Silas painted both girls' rooms. He even stenciled their monikers as a boarder. Silas was good at going through the motions, but his execution was weak.

When Silas didn't turn at her entrance, Olivia walked towards him, stopping short of joining him in favor of observing. She peered into the crib to see Genevieve was fast asleep. As usual, Gwendolyn was awake. She had kicked free of her blanket and was staring intently at Silas. Unlike Genevieve, Gwendolyn's eyes remained a deep shade of purple. They were focused on Silas while she simultaneously kicked and waved her arms. If she was older, Olivia would have expected her to speak or at least babble. Instead, she blew a tiny spit bubble.

"Look at me, see me."

The words evaporated like soap bubbles in Olivia's mind.

Silas jumped, realizing Olivia was at his elbow.

"Whoa, are you okay?" she asked, gripping his arm.

Beneath her touch, Olivia felt him tremble. "Do you see that?" Silas asked, his voice barely above a whisper.

Only then did Olivia see the mobile moving. Music should be playing. "Surely, the batteries aren't dead already," Olivia said.

"It's not on," Silas told her.

That's when Olivia realized the music wasn't playing because the mobile wasn't turned on. The movement was all Gwendolyn's doing.

"She's doing it, isn't she? She's making it turn," Silas insisted.

"She is," Olivia said with a proud smile. "My little Luna silenced the music because she didn't want to wake her sister. She wanted you all to herself." Olivia squeezed his elbow.

Silas shook himself free. Unlike Olivia, he didn't look proud. He looked horrified.

****

It took Olivia longer than normal to get Gwendolyn to sleep. Olivia murmured how proud she was that she had not wanted to wake her sister. She indulged in multiple renditions of *Night Watch* – at least her French had improved.

Once Gwendolyn was tucked in next to Genevieve, Olivia tiptoed out the door and down the hall. The door to her former bedroom was open and the bed empty, Olivia headed out to the fire. She wondered if Silas realized that it never went out.

Olivia found him sitting in her chair, staring into the flames, clutching his tumbler. She hadn't seen much of it today, but it sparked a dark thought. If Patrick knew about Silas' previous addiction, so had Dillon. Olivia just now realized Dillon had undoubtedly used it to his advantage. The thought made her angry, but pointing it out to Silas would do no good, not in his current state of mind. One day Silas would come to his senses. It would just be too late for some.

Olivia remained standing. It was time she learned the truth. "Was it real? Any of it?" she asked.

Silas realized she was talking about them, before babies. Silas knew this was coming. He was surprised she had waited so long to ask. A couple of times he had almost made himself believe they wouldn't have to go down this road. Her meeting with Dillon told him he was a fool for ever thinking it. "Of course, it was," Silas said, without looking at her.

Olivia wasn't going to be dismissed. "Convince me," she told him. "I deserve it."

"I was assigned," Silas confessed, using air quotes, "to watch over you when you decided to come back to the bureau. They me told me what they thought they knew about you. Their info came from the agency."

Another use of air quotes told Olivia he must be talking about the CIA or maybe some other acronym no one knew.

"But you know how those guys like to embellish. At first, I thought they were full of shit," Silas admitted.

"Did you like your assignment?" Olivia asked.

A slow smile curled across Silas' lips. Used to he would have gotten a very different reaction from her.

"Of course, I did. You're beautiful and smart, an uncommon paring in our business. Most women try too hard. You were the most authentic woman I had ever met. And you were not the least bit interested in me. I got that signal pretty quick. Over time, I let it go. It was then I saw your fearlessness. And I started to believe."

"And your bosses?" Olivia inquired.

"It wasn't Dillon, if that's what you're thinking. Like you, the first time I met him was after the Good Samaritan case."

"Who, then?" Olivia wanted to know.

"For a long time, I only talked to Patrick but I knew rumbles about you went up the chain. If Patrick knew more, I didn't know. He didn't tell me. Then you came back here, to your home. Not seeing you as often had an impact. That's when the push began not to let you go."

"Jon Sharpe was sent to babysit me," Olivia filled in for him.

"I was the one to contact him, but it wasn't my idea. I wasn't opposed, however. I did like knowing what you were doing and not doing. Everything changed when Deveroux waded into something he shouldn't have. In the middle of that was our first trip to Florida."

Olivia knew the one. She had let herself slip. She wanted to blame it on the brutality of the case—two young girls gunned down and more still missing. Two cracks at the case and they still didn't find them all. Olivia wondered what she would have done if Pittman had spilled his guts during their first meeting. Would Pittman's truth have canceled the loneliness that had crept into her life? Would she have even noticed that Silas might be interested? So many questions that would never be answered.

"Those feelings were real," Silas said, as if reading

her thoughts. "All of it was. The Good Samaritan case scared the shit out of me but by then I was too deep in," Silas confessed.

"You came to this conclusion on your own?" Olivia wanted to know.

"For the most part. No one said it out loud but I think me and you being together was good."

"For them?"

"By then I was in deep. That thing in the barn was bigger than Jamie. But the more I fell for you, the more they wanted."

"When did you stop?" Olivia asked.

"I never stopped. You did. You became the thing they said you were and now, I can't get it out of my head. All I want is things to go back the way they were." Silas sounded desperate.

"And the girls?" They were all Olivia cared about.

"That was the change, the leap I can't make into a place I can't go. And now, nothing can be put back together. Rose ruined it for all of us. She's the real enemy," Silas explained.

Now he was starting to sound like Dillon. "Don't take the easy way-out Silas, and make it about someone else," Olivia told him.

"Like Barry Bartholomew doesn't have a part in this?"

"I left DC because of Gran. If it hadn't been her, I would have left because of you," Olivia confessed.

The answer shocked him. "Me?"

"You were the type of man who never looked my way and, for once, I cared. Being away from you certainly helped. Then came Jamie. And Barry. And you. You were the shiny thing I had always wanted, so when you came back and gave me everything I thought I wanted, I couldn't say no."

"But there was still Barry," Silas said for her. "I knew things changed that night in the barn but I was in too deep to get out. And I'd gotten the green light for San Antonio. No matter what anyone said, it wasn't a demotion. I had everything I wanted. But you wanted more."

"Babies." Olivia said it for him.

"Yea. I told you I would be happy with just the two of us."

"The night of the barn, you told me you wanted to marry me. All I asked was for babies," Olivia clarified.

"And Barry," Silas reminded her.

"You're right. It was always Barry," Olivia admitted. "You were just a distraction. Barry sees me for what I am. You only see the parts of me you want to see."

Olivia sighed, finally having said what she needed to say. Almost.

"Check your phone before you go to bed. I took the liberty of booking you a flight to DC tomorrow." Silas started to protest, but she silenced him with a look. "Patrick is dead and you should hear what his wife has to say. I also want you to see the life you once had and hope it brings you back to yourself, if you even know what that is. That's my gift to you."

Chapter Thirty

"Olivia, you should come see this," Sally called from the room Olivia used as her home office.

Olivia had gladly made the space available for her mother-in-law, surprised by the time she spent online. Sally liked to keep up with her friends in Maryland and was abreast of current events. Sally said she preferred to read the news rather than listen to someone read it to her.

The babies were snug in their car seats on the dining table. Genevieve was wide awake and batting at the rattles attached to the arm of her carrier. At the same time, Gwendolyn was fast asleep and Olivia was wondering what else she could stuff inside their diaper bag. Olivia was ready for the furniture delivery men to arrive so she could have the house to herself and bring down the other bags. If Sally saw the clothes and supplies, she would know they weren't going for a quick trip to the doctor. Olivia had already heard her phone go off more than once. Barry was supposed to be at the car place picking up the new SUV her mother had ordered for them. Olivia hoped it wasn't him telling her there was a delay. They had a small window of time to make their getaway appear seamless. That way, when the search for them began no one would be the wiser on when they left.

"Be right back, Sunny girl," Olivia promised

Genevieve as she made her way to Sally. Olivia noticed the wrinkles on Sally's brow and the way she bit her top lip. She clicked the paused scene on the screen and it came to life.

Jessica Tate gave the introduction. "In a shocking revelation, Deputy Director of the newly formed Urban Affairs Division of the FBI, Dillon Bradford, held a press conference regarding the on-going investigation into the former disgraced Atascosa County Sheriff Jim Tennent's murder investigation."

Jessica Tate was replaced with a view of Bradford Dillion behind a podium.

"I would like to address the media today to assure them that your pleas for information have not gone unanswered. I'm announcing today, that former sheriff Jim Tennent was murdered in a sadistic and horrifying ritual. It has been determined that he was poisoned and his body vilified before he was risen from the dead."

From the corner of her eye, Olivia saw Sally staring at her, but Olivia remained focused on the screen. Now was not the time for distractions.

"We have a brief video obtained from the alleged perpetrator. I have to warn the audience that the images you are about to see are disturbing—viewer discretion is advised."

The imagery was grainy but cleaned up enough that no one had to guess what they were watching. Olivia took a deep breath, waiting for what she had already seen. It showed the shirtless Jim Tennent rising from an unmistakable pool of blood to shuffle across his living room to the kitchen and back before collapsing to the ground. It was exactly as Olivia had imagined and Frank Tobias had described months ago.

The video was over and the camera panned back on Bradford Dillon. He looked like a man ready to deliver more bad news. "Ritualistic in nature, the murder of the former sheriff has been verified as inexplicably linked to the unfortunate murder of local psychiatrist, Dr. Amanda Santos-Greene and her unborn child. Her family has made the difficult decision to exhume her body for further investigation. If you recall, Dr. Greene was found outside the Cardinal Condominiums some months ago after sustaining a fall from the balcony of the thirteenth floor. It is now believed that she was pushed and did not willingly take her own life. Of note, the owner of that condominium at the time was the now-retired police lieutenant, Barry Bartholomew. Lieutenant Bartholomew is most remembered for the celebrated serial killer spree perpetrated by Jamie Lynne Smythe who also murdered Lieutenant Bartholomew's partner and friend, Sergeant Mark Austin."

The screen split and next to Dillon appeared a picture of Rose Corey. Olivia recognized it as the one pulled from the security footage in the hallway just outside Barry's condo.

"This woman is considered the person of interest in the death of Sheriff Tennent. She is also the likely perpetrator of murdered FBI special agent Mason Deveroux—a celebrated twenty-year agent who, before joining the Bureau, served his country as a member of the Coast Guard. Agent Deveroux will be remembered for his strong leadership after Hurricane Katrina hit his beloved New Orleans. His last assignment with the Bureau is where he most likely crossed paths with his suspected killer—Rose Corey. Agent Deveroux at the time of his death was the lead investigator into sex-trafficking of underage girls supplied to strip clubs in Las Vegas with ties to the occult.

"On this eve of the end of year celebration, the UAD is here to warn the public of the days to come. What has been uncovered here is a dark part of our history we thought was behind us in these modern times. What we thought was laid to rest in Salem, Massachusetts, never left. It only learned how to hide. Make no mistake about it – witches live among us. They seek to destroy us with their evil ways. So, you too, must be vigilant. You must take care to truly get to know those around you. At the end of this broadcast, we will supply a list of behaviors you should be aware of to know if your neighbors, or even family members, have succumbed to this affliction. Make no mistake—this darkness cannot exist without a covenant with the devil himself who sends his legion of fallen upon the very fabric of our life."

"Now I will take a few questions," Dillon offered.

"Are you saying this person of interest, Ms. Corey, will be charged with witchcraft?"

Olivia found it interesting the reporter asking the question did not appear on camera. Not to mention this had been her question. This was scripted for shock value.

"Once Ms. Corey is in custody, she will be charged with maleficium as the death of Sheriff Jim Tennent and Special Agent Mason Deveroux were determined to be *death by unnatural cause.*"

Dillon pointed from behind the podium to another unseen person.

"Do you have any leads on Ms. Corey?"

"Her last known residence was in Atascosa County." Behind him appeared a house in need of a paint job. Olivia knew it to be the home of Rose's grandmother. She and Barry had visited her. She swore she didn't know where Rose was. Olivia believed her. The holidays were coming up and Olivia held out some vague hope that Rose would get nostalgic and visit. Olivia gave the old woman her cell phone number and her mother's. Not knowing how Rose and her mother left things, Olivia assured Rose's Nana that no matter what had happened in the past, Sarah Larsin would give Rose shelter.

"We have appealed to Dr. Olivia Osborne for assistance," Dillon's voice said, slicing through Olivia's thoughts. "Through Dr. Osborne's work with the Bureau, we are very aware that she has intimate knowledge of the type of individuals capable of committing these types of offenses."

Another anonymous reporter interrupted, almost as if planned. "Is that because Dr. Osborne had an ancestor at the Salem Witch Trials?"

For his answer, Dillon stared directly into the camera. "She did indeed. Therefore, you can imagine how eager we are to work with her."

The video feed cut back to Jessica Tate.

"Those were the words of the UAD's Deputy Director, Bradford Dillon, speaking in an earlier pre-recorded press conference. Stand by for more updates to come. You can find the information Deputy Director Dillon spoke about on our website. This is Jessica Tate with the news you need to know."

Sally snapped the laptop closed. "Is he serious?"

"I'm afraid he is," Olivia said. Hearing the buzz of

her phone she took the chance to escape. Her phone was on the table next to the girls. On the screen was a text from Jessica.

— *If I had known this was happening, I would have let you know.* —

That should have been Silas' job, Olivia thought, followed quickly by the resolution that Silas hadn't known this was coming either. All Dillion had to do was wait a few more hours. Silas was probably already at the airport waiting for his flight home. What did Dillon want Silas to miss?

Olivia was still holding her phone when it buzzed again. This time it was Dom.

—*The authorities are closing the state borders tonight at midnight.*—

"This Dillon fellow is Silas' boss?" Sally abandoned her laptop to pursue Oliva. "Are you really going to work for him?"

Olivia took a deep breath, looking for an answer, when the doorbell rang. She peered past Sally and out the window. There was a big burley guy who looked like a linebacker standing at her door. Olivia's hope was answered when it turned out to be the movers. Daniel and Rachel's furniture had arrived, and Sally was needed elsewhere.

"Not today." Olivia forced a smile. "Looks like they need you next door. I'm sure Barry will be here any minute now." The furniture arriving on this day at the same time as the girls' doctor visit had been divine intervention, Olivia was sure of it.

Sally looked unsure about leaving.

"Silas will be able to explain everything when he gets home later today," Olivia promised, herding Sally towards the door.

Sally opened the door and handed the key to the man waiting for her. "I'll be over in a minute," Sally told him. She waited until he was gone to turn back to Olivia. "Are you a witch?"

"No," Olivia told her.

"But you're something, right? Rachel told me a little about what it is you do but I don't really understand it."

Kudos to Silas for not telling her. "I don't understand it myself sometimes," Olivia admitted.

Later, when Sally was asked, she would describe Olivia as looking forlorn.

Sally took Olivia's hands in hers. "That man doesn't want to work with you."

Sally saw so much more than her son. "I can help the witches," Olivia told her.

"Then you should do it," Sally said. "That man, Dillon, can't be trusted."

"He absolutely cannot," Olivia assured her.

"Those things he said about Barry, they were meant to imply some kind of guilt. I don't believe it for a second. Barry's a good man. I'm not sure who he loves more you or those babies. Probably all three of you."

Olivia couldn't speak for fear the tears would start.

Outside, they heard another vehicle. A shiny new black SUV she didn't recognize was backing into her driveway.

Chapter Thirty-One

Barry backed down the long driveway so Sally wouldn't see them packing. The backyard was empty without the dogs. They were on "loan" to Kim. She and Katie Morgan had just moved into Mark Austin's old place, a gift from Barry. The story was they wanted to help Olivia since the babies were finally home. They waited until Silas left to make the swap.

Barry knew leaving Daisy and Alvin behind was hard on Olivia. Daisy was the first dog Olivia ever owned. The greyhound had been her comfort companion after Gran died, and Alvin was an unexpected addition. He was homeless after Jamie Smythe murdered his owner. Olivia opened her home to him. Despite Daisy's reluctance, the subdued racer and the feisty rescue became best friends. Barry often thought Olivia was sadder to leave the dogs behind than Silas.

"We're running out of room," Barry cautioned her when he returned to find her holding a cooler.

"Last one, I promise. Precious cargo," Olivia smiled as she handed him the cooler.

The term translated to mean the cooler was home to all the breast milk she pumped when the girls were too young to take it. Barry was glad to see the smile. Olivia was upset when he arrived. It was understandable, given what they were about to do.

Barry couldn't help but wonder if there wasn't something else. Either way, they had a long drive ahead of them. Whatever it was could wait. Being here, now, made him feel they should make their getaway sooner rather than later.

The doorbell rang as soon as Barry disappeared out the back door.

Olivia froze. She tiptoed past the baby carriers. Genevieve was still awake, but no longer batting at her rattles. She too was listening. Olivia peeked out the window. There was no car.

Another ring of the bell came, followed by frantic knocking. "I know you're in there. I let my ride go, so please, open the door."

"Elijah!" Olivia rushed to the door and pulled him inside while checking outside for cars, no matter what he said. A quick scan down the street told her he was telling the truth.

"I told you I let my ride go," Elijah reminded her.

"What do you want?" Olivia demanded.

"Take me with you," Elijah pleaded.

"Are you reading my mind?"

"No. I can't. Believe me, I tried. Your thoughts are there." Elijah shook his head in frustration.

"What?" Olivia snapped. She didn't need a lesson from an empath, especially one she never expected to see again.

"I can read your husband's. I figured with him out of town, now would probably be a good time for you to make a get-away. He thinks so to."

"Who's this?" Barry asked, returning from the car.

"Elijah," Olivia said. "We talked about him."

Barry sized him up, saying nothing about the man

Olivia knew when he was still a boy. All Barry could focus on was as a twelve-year-old, he had killed his little brother and then lied about doing CPR.

"To be fair, there was a demon inside of him," Elijah said.

"Stop it," Olivia told him.

"Let me guess, your *Watcher*?" Elijah wanted to know.

"Yes. And even if you can read his mind,"

"I can," Elijah interrupted her.

"You won't or you'll have me to deal with," Olivia snapped. "He is off-limits."

Barry couldn't see her eyes, but he bet they were the reason Elijah raised his hands in surrender. He even took a step back. "I felt that."

Barry studied him, feeling nothing.

With some distance between them, Elijah stared back at Olivia. "Why can't I read you?" he asked. He sounded genuinely curious rather than annoyed.

"What does he want?" Barry asked Olivia rather than the boy.

"I want to go with you," Elijah answered.

"You have no idea what you're asking," Olivia told him.

"I know it would get me away from the agency. And Dillon," Elijah explained. "You don't know what it's like."

Barry didn't care what it was like. "And bring them right to our doorstep?" Barry cut him off. "Hell, no."

"I can wipe their memory," Elijah boasted.

"Before or after they find us?" Barry asked.

Olivia's eyes were closed while she strained to hear or see. She wasn't sure where the information was coming from. "Someone else is here."

Barry and Elijah both looked at her.

"I heard that," Elijah said.

"Heard what?" Barry asked.

Elijah's eyes narrowed, continuing to fixate on Olivia. "That's not coming from you." He looked over her shoulder to her daughters. "Did you know you have a *Seer*?"

Barry and Olivia both looked back at the babies.

"Sunny?" Barry asked. It was the name he had given Genevieve. Gwendolyn was Luna, Olivia's moon baby.

Olivia went to her daughter. Genevieve was still awake. As before, she was no longer playing with her rattles. She was staring at the window. Olivia blanketed her with comfort, the French words to their lullaby crossed her mind and not her lips. It wasn't long before Genevieve's eyes grew heavy.

Just in time for another ring of the bell.

Olivia looked across the room, her eyes searching for Elijah.

"He went through your office and into the kitchen," Barry said softly, explaining Elijah's disappearing act. "Oh, and he wants you to know, he's only sending, not reading."

"Dr. Osborne, it's Dillion Bradford. Your vehicle is still here so I know you're in there. I am curious, however, to know who's in the fancy black one."

"Tracker on your car," Barry whispered, the answer telegraphed from Elijah.

"Damn, I should have checked." This time it was just Barry.

Olivia shook her head and flung open the door.

"I'm sorry, did I catch you at a bad time?" Dillon asked.

"Get in here," Olivia told him.

"Not much of a greeting. I'm sure you're very busy," Dillon said, crossing the threshold.

Olivia didn't like how he wandered into her house as if it was his.

"Aw, you must be Barry Bartholomew," Dillon said. "I'm sure you've heard a lot about me."

"Nothing that bears repeating," Barry said.

"What do you want?" Olivia snapped.

"I came here to give you the opportunity to accept my job offer," Dillon said. He had been scanning the room since he entered. His eyes finally landed on the carriers on the table. "Are those your progeny? I've heard so much about them. It was disappointing when there was really nothing special about their blood, when compared to the rest. Still, I bet you will be one hell of a teacher."

"I think I'm going to pass," Olivia told him. "In case you didn't know, I severed my ties with the Bureau."

"I don't work for the Bureau," Dillon said.

"Doesn't matter. My answer is the same," Olivia told him.

"Suit yourself. Since you're not taking the job, I won't go over the benefits. I will, however, tell you the ramifications of your rejection," Dillon promised. "I'm guessing you saw my press conference?"

Barry snuck a glance at Olivia. That's what she hadn't gotten around to telling him.

"All I heard was you issuing threats," Olivia told him.

"Then let me spell it out. I firmly plan to hold Mr. Bartholomew over there with the death of Dr. Greene and her unborn baby that will turn out to be his."

"What?" Barry snapped.

Dillon looked at Olivia and smiled. "I'm guessing you didn't tell him?"

Barry was suddenly at Olivia's elbow.

"Allow me," Dillon offered. "We have the results from your urologist from several years ago. A thorough exam of the report shows you have a low sperm count. Hypothetically it could make it more difficult for you to father children, but not impossible."

Barry looked to Olivia for verification.

"It's true," she confirmed.

Pleased, Dillon turned on Olivia. "Anyway, since we have footage of Dr. Osborne entering the condo that same day, I'm sure we can connect the dots that you're the one who lured Dr. Greene there. It was a jealous spat between former friends."

"They were never friends," Barry said.

Dillon smiled. "Well, Mason Deveroux happened to record his interview with Dr. Greene a few months ago, after both you and the good doctor here dodged his requests for interviews. Dr. Greene, more than once, laments how you only wanted Dr. Osborne. The night of Dr. Greene's housewarming was a particular sore spot with her. You left that party to come here—with Dr. Osborne while her husband was away. There are FBI agents and SAPD officers who will confirm that to be true. Just like the two of you were here, together, again while poor Dr. Greene lay dead in a parking lot. Then there is Dr. Osborne's call to the archbishop, pressuring him to give you an alibi. The security

Lisa Compton

footage provided by the Archdiocese shows you were never there the morning of Dr. Greene's demise. The archbishop confessed to me, of all people, that he lied for you at the behest—his word not mine—at the urging of Dr. Osborne. In addition to that, according to my sources, the archbishop was pushed the night he fell in his library. Poor old man. I guess he was just in the way. Then, there's Agent Branch. He's wondering if those cherubs over there are even his, but I really don't want to go there—very messy. I'd rather stick to facts and not resort to personal conflict. Interesting, though, Branch isn't the last name on their birth certificates. Anyway, I would rather rely on the day at the condo. SAPD has provided photos of the witchy stuff found on your balcony that same fateful morning. I don't even have to guess that you have the skillset to concoct that," Dillon said, baiting Olivia.

"How does Rose fit in?" Olivia jumped ahead.

"Protégé of yours, after Andre Roche's death. She was also an employee of your mother's. Sarah Larsin does have many strip clubs, does she not? I have it on good authority that there are plenty of people in Vegas who know what she is and how she operates. I could also, probably, string together something from Deveroux's notes."

"What do you want?" Barry cut to the chase.

Dillon smiled at Olivia. "I want to know what kind of magic it takes to summon a demon. That is what happened in the barn and at Mr. Bartholomew's condo. Isn't that what you said in your briefing to SAPD. It was through sacrifice of not only Dr. Greene, but Andre Rosch and Ana Lutz. I want to know how you do that."

Dillon stopped and stared intently at Olivia.

"What's up with those eyes?"

"The same thing that's causing the perspiration on your upper lip," Olivia said.

Barry felt the temperature rise. Like Elijah, he couldn't see Olivia's eyes, but he knew they were glowing.

"I don't have to perform magic to summon a demon," Olivia said, sounding calmer than she should. "They show up whether I want them to or not. Would you like a demonstration?"

Dillon didn't know one was already here, but Barry did. Olivia had signaled *Alleracsap* to stay in the corner with the babies. He had shown up right after Dillion.

Before Dillon could answer, the front door opened on its own.

"Ah, so glad I got here in time for the festivities."

It was Samael Knight.

"*I thought you were gone.*"

"My dear Olivia, do you honestly think I would leave you in your time of need?" Samael answered out loud.

"I know you," Dillon interrupted. "Facial recognition doesn't work on you, but Deveroux got one good look. You're Samael Knight. What are you hiding?"

"I don't think you're ready for that conversation," Samael cautioned.

Dillon remained in place, captured by the burning orange eyes. "You're one of them, aren't you?"

Samael was about to clap his hands together in congratulations when Barry heard footsteps from behind.

Elijah dashed out of the kitchen and into the living

room.

"That's why I can't read you," he said, turning to Olivia. "While your thoughts are there, they are too disjointed to interpret," Elijah explained before turning to Samael. "You, sir, however, are a blank slate." Elijah's eyes darted between him and Olivia, obviously pleased at his answer.

His stare made Olivia feel like a science project.

"The two of you are similar but not equal," Elijah murmured.

"There's a reason for that. Do you want to know why?" Samael asked, his advance toward Dillon halted.

With Samael distracted, Dillon could focus on Elijah. "What the hell are you doing here?"

"I'm going with her," Elijah said. "She's such a badass. I can't tell you how happy I was to hear her stand up to you the other day. You really are a bully," Elijah said.

"You really think you can just quit? No one, especially the likes of you, leaves the agency," Dillon told him.

That's when Olivia saw what was in Elijah's hand.

"No, not in front of my girls," she screamed.

Elijah was too fast for her words. He raised his hand and fired at Dillon. "Consider that my resignation."

Chapter Thirty-Two

The girls were both screaming. Olivia ran and gathered them into her arms, snuggling them close as they clung to her and each other. Olivia murmured quietly, assuring them they were safe.

In full protector mode, Barry's first instinct was to run for the babies and Olivia. Seeing them tucked safely against her chest, his other skills kicked in like muscle memory. He moved in the opposite direction to disarm Elijah. The kid handed the weapon over without protest at the same time Barry wondered how he missed the gun in the kid's hand. Maybe because the priorities in his life had shifted.

"I told you I could block thoughts," Elijah told him.

"That's getting real fucking annoying," Barry snapped. "Stay out of my head."

"Where did you even get the gun?" Barry asked.

"I read the report about how Jamie Smythe came here. Dr. Osborne had a gun stashed in the kitchen."

"You used her gun? *Unfuckingbelievable*." Barry shook his head in frustration.

"It's a throwaway," Olivia told him. "Non-traceable," she assured him while her eyes strayed to Samael. He was standing over Dillon, watching. "Can't you do something?"

"He's not dead. *Yet*. Do you want me to kill him?"

Samael asked.

"He needs to bleed out somewhere else," Barry snapped.

Samael flashed him a smile. "I knew those policeman skills would come in handy. You should keep him."

Olivia didn't like how pleased Samael sounded.

"Can I go with you now?" Elijah asked.

"Absolutely not," Barry told him.

"I can save you, empath," Samael proposed.

Olivia was the one to snap this time. "No!"

The girls began to squirm again and Barry came and took them from her. "You should deal with him," Barry said with a jerk of his head toward Samael.

Olivia handed off the girls, watching him hold them close as she had done. They didn't even wake up with the hand-off. "Have I told you that I love you?" Olivia asked.

"While I like the choice of your *Watcher* better than the demon hunter, now is not the time for this," Samael interrupted. "He loves you too. You've always known it."

Samael sighed and turned back to Elijah. "I can end your torment and promise you a life where you never have to answer to a man like this again," Samael promised.

"What do I have to do?" Elijah asked.

Free of the babies, Olivia stormed toward Samael.

Samael held his hand up for her to stop, but that didn't stop her. It didn't even slow her down.

"No, not that," Olivia objected, planting herself in front of him.

"Changeling, mind your business," Samael

cautioned.

"This is still my living room," Olivia insisted.

"A room that is soon to have a non-living entity. I'll take it off your hands and your *Watcher* will clean it up."

"And me?" Elijah asked, not wanting to be forgotten. "I'll do it. Whatever it is." He turned to Olivia. "I told myself if you refused me, I was going to shoot myself. I can't stand all this chaos in my head."

"See, I'm saving lives," Samael told Olivia before turning back to Elijah. "My host body is one hundred and twenty-two years old, give or take a decade. You join with me and you'll live longer than any empath ever has."

"Never forget you're joining *him*," Olivia emphasized. "This has to be more of a partnership than whatever your current situation."

"Agreed."

Olivia looked unsure.

"We'll hammer out the finer details later, but I said I agree," Samael assured her. "This one at least comes with some valuable skills. The only thing my other one knew how to do was find the best opium and the most willing women."

"So, we're all good?" Elijah asked.

"Yes, *we* are," Samael assured him. "You really don't need her permission."

Elijah snuck a glance at Olivia.

"This is against my better judgement," she told him.

"Whatever," Elijah agreed. "What do I have to do?"

"Take the dead guy's gun and kill me."

"Not in my living room," Olivia snapped.

"Of course not," Samael assured her. "It needs to be done quickly after we're out of here.

I have a car and driver down the street."

"Tell your driver to come down the alley," Barry instructed. "Then I'll clean this up," he told Olivia.

"Put the babes down. Olivia is about to have another visitor," Samael warned.

"It's your mother-in-law," Elijah said. "She's coming up fast," he warned.

"Compel her," Samael snapped.

"What?" Olivia shook her head. "I don't—"

"Yes, you do," Samael assured her patiently, as if instructing a child. "You just did it with your daughters. Look her in the eyes and tell that very nice lady whatever story you want her to repeat. Do it now."

Olivia looked at Barry. He had soothed the girls back to sleep and tucked them back in their car seats.

"You might want to add something about how it's not bleach that she smells in here," Barry added.

"I told you he was helpful," Samael smiled.

I love you too Barry mouthed as she headed out the door.

****

Now that she knew what compelling was, it was easier.

She did it again at the border between Texas and Louisiana. While they still had hours before midnight, the line to cross the border between states was backed-up.

Barry watched the trooper up ahead. Whatever they were doing wasn't taking long. It did give Olivia time to shimmy from the backseat and into the front passenger side. Fortunately, she had just fed the babies. When she tucked them back in they were deep in the middle of their milk high and would nap for a bit. She had a blanket in the backseat where she had dozed a few hours ago between feedings. She fumbled with the blanket until it draped over the car seats. Between the tinted windows and the blanket, the girls wouldn't be so obvious. If there was a BOLO out yet it would be sure to contain *two infants* in the description.

The police scanner Herschel Gaines gave them kept them informed until they reached Houston. Earlier in the day, traffic had already started to pick up due to the holiday. Between high traffic and a raging fire in Atascosa County, there wasn't a blip about them or the missing deputy director of the UAD. That probably wouldn't come until Silas arrived home. If memory served her, Silas should already be back in San Antonio. By then, Sally would no doubt be beside herself. Worrying Sally was Olivia's only regret. She had turned her phone off for that and so many other reasons.

They kept up with Poe via text through Renaye. They were miles ahead due to frequent stops for the babies and Poe's need to arrive in time to check out Mémé from her nursing facility before it got too late. Once she was secure, they would all rendezvous just outside New Orleans and travel caravan style. GPS wouldn't get them where they were going.

As for his part, Samael didn't say and Olivia didn't want to know where they were dumping his body and Dillons. That way, if and when someone asked her or Barry about it, their surprise would be genuine.

"Between the end of year and the paper tags, they

won't be able to trace us," Barry assured Olivia. "I'm also sure your mother paid for some extra confidentiality."

Barry likened Sarah Larsin to the mob. The vehicle was paid in full. All he had to do was show up and show his ID. After verifying he was who he said he was, the clerk in the sales department made a phone call before handing it off to Barry. The voice on the other end wasn't Sarah but her 'personal' assistant. The whole transaction didn't take fifteen minutes. Barry walked out the door and into the shiny new black SUV without signing a thing. While her mother had secured their transportation, Olivia booked them on a flight to Las Vegas.

"What's up, officer?" Barry asked, uncharacteristically friendly.

"Routine stop ensuring everyone is aware there's a curfew beginning at midnight. It will be in effect for the next twenty-four hours. Where are you headed, sir?"

"Just passing through," Barry said smoothly.

"Well, just as long as you're tucked in before midnight."

The trooper leaned in with a flashlight. It was still early, but the light was fading fast.

"Looking for anything in particular?" Olivia asked, leaning across the console.

"Routine stop ensuring everyone is aware there's a curfew beginning at midnight," the trooper repeated the same greeting he gave Barry. His words sounded robotic.

Barry looked over at Olivia. Her eyes were shining.

"Where are you headed?" the trooper asked again.

"Nowhere." Olivia flashed him another smile.

The trooper nodded. It took a moment before he rapped on the side of the vehicle. "Drive safe and happy new year." The trooper stepped back and waved them through.

Before they could pass the cameras, Olivia spotted the lights that had just been triggered by twilight. A moment later they popped and exploded into sparks, followed by the cameras.

"That's a neat new trick," Barry said.

"It's a gift, not a curse."

Barry offered his hand and Olivia linked her fingers through his.

"Happy New Year."

Epilogue

The swamp was a quiet place in the winter. The plants lay brown and dormant. Below them, energy flowed. Olivia embraced her new surroundings. The amphibious life seemed like something Noah left behind. It was as if time itself had left this place alone.

It was close to midnight and Olivia was on the front porch of Mémé's house, wrapped in a blanket, staring into the night. Upstairs, she had left both her girls and Barry fast asleep. Olivia sat there listening to the creak of the porch swing and soaking up the bullfrog serenade. Occasionally, in the distance, she heard a splash. The swamp was always moving.

The light of her phone lit up the darkness. She had only turned it on after she learned what caused the raging fire in Atascosa County.

Olivia saw Silas' name. Reluctantly, she picked up.

"I need to know you're safe." Silas sounded like his old self—*almost*. If she closed her eyes she might believe it.

"And the girls."

It sounded like an afterthought, or maybe she was inflecting feelings. Olivia reminded herself the future was about letting go of the past.

"Of course, they are," she told Silas. "They are with me."

"You're obviously not in Las Vegas," Silas finally

said.

It was the reason he was calling.

"Dillon is dead and Elijah is missing," Silas told her.

Olivia remained silent.

"Things could be different now that Dillon's not in charge."

"He was never in charge. He only thought he was," Olivia replied.

"Whatever is broken can be fixed," Silas insisted.

"No, Silas, it can't. Nothing can bring Rose back."

"I agree. What happened in that field should never have happened," Silas conceded.

"Those responsible will be found and they will be brought to justice."

Now, Silas sounded like the bureaucrat he was becoming. Olivia didn't ask, but she bet he slid comfortably into Dillon's position as UAD Director. The FBI always did like seeing him on camera.

"I remember once you told me you didn't want to be the 'go to girl' for what red pepper and salt meant."

"I've learned to embrace my authentic self. Others will come whether I want them to or not. I am far from the only one."

"Are you sure that's a fight you want to pick?" Silas asked.

"We're not the ones who picked the fight. I can't stop what's coming," Olivia told him.

"You could try," Silas suggested.

"There are two kinds of evil, Silas, the ancient kind and the man-made kind. The burning of witches has returned. All of it is out of my hands. There is no going back. Those who killed Rose took that luxury away the moment they lit the fire at her feet. They turned a murderer into a martyr. If it is fire you want, I can bring it and when the time comes, I will show the same mercy granted to Rose."

With that, Olivia dropped her phone in the cup of water next to her.

It was her last goodbye to the life she used to know.

The monsters were still coming, they just looked different.

The bullfrogs grew quiet. A hush fell over the swamp.

Olivia looked into the darkness and wondered what was out there.

A word about the author...

I've been a registered nurse for more than thirty years, but my first passion has always been writing.

Growing up the youngest child of older parents I spent a lot of time entertaining myself. I discovered my love of writing through reading. I always wanted more. When I ran out of books I started writing my own. I have lived in San Antonio, Texas for almost twenty years and have adopted it as my own. I love the diversity of this city and its endless supply of ghosts which make it the perfect setting for the Olivia Osborne series. When I'm not writing I can be found with my family and any number of cats.

LisaComptonbooks.com

www.ingramcontent.com/pod-product-compliance
Lightning Source LLC
Chambersburg PA
CBHW072106020726
47501CB00003B/728